Jim Click

Jim Click
or, The Wonderful Invention

by
Fernand Fleuret

translated, annotated and introduced by
Brian Stableford

A Black Coat Press Book

Visit our website at www.blackcoatpress.com

ISBN 978-1-61227-442-3. First Printing. October 2015. Published by Black Coat Press, an imprint of Hollywood Comics.com, LLC, P.O. Box 17270, Encino, CA 91416. All rights reserved.

Introduction

Jim Click, ou La Merveilleuse invention, roman d'aventures by Fernand Fleuret, here translated as *Jim Click; or, The Wonderful Invention*, was originally published by Gallimard in 1930. It is one of the later additions to a long series of French fantasies featuring human automata, the theme having been given particular impetus in France by the examples of actual automata produced in the 1730s by Jacques Vaucanson, which caused a sensation at the time, although no one took the trouble to preserve them—a disappearance that only enhanced their subsequent legendary status.

Early stories in which Vaucansonesque automata are mistaken for human beings, such as "Mademoiselle de La Choupillière" (1832; tr. with the same title) by Jacques Boucher de Perthes, inevitably use the notion as a plotting gimmick, but—equally inevitably—dress the essentially farcical idea with a satirical commentary on the "mechanical features" of ordinary human behavior, in terms of individual psychology and social interaction.

That satirical element became sharper as the exploration of the theme advanced, becoming more scathingly critical in such works as *L'Automate, récit tiré d'un palimpseste* (1878; tr. as "The Automaton: a Story Translated for a Palimpsest") by Ralph Schropp, initially published in 1878 and reprinted as a booklet by A. Ghio in 1880, which takes up an older legend relating to the manufacture of an artificial human being, crediting the achievement to the 13th century scholar Albertus Magnus.

The scale of the manufacturing enterprise, and hence the baroque imagery, became much more lavish in *Ignis* (1883)[1] by Didier de Chousy, while the psychological analysis associated with more extensive uses of the theme even became more intense, the fundamental error taking on a hallucinatory dimension, in the most famous work in the sequence, Villiers de l'Isle-Adam's *L'Ève future* (1886; tr. as *Tomorrow's Eve*).

Jim Click, coming after all these works and several more, aspires successfully to a new level of sophistication in the relevant literary contexts, not merely in its satirical reflections and its carefully-crafted commentary on various tendencies to automatism is natural human beings, but also in its handling of the farcical aspects of the plot. The novel employs the familiar apologetic device of the "madman's manuscript," offering its central narrative as an autobiography written in a lunatic asylum by a patient who might be saner than his imaginatively-blinkered physician believes, but takes the device a step further by embedding the central madman's manuscript in another, equally uncertain, and even adding a third hypothetical interpreter in the form of the supposed translator who renders the story into French. Within that nest of deliberate complications and ambiguities, the tone of the narrative veers smoothly between the overtly comical and the poignantly tragic, and between scrupulous observation of naturalistic detail and dramatic improbability, maintaining a consistent narrative suspense as well as a heartfelt account of human folly in some of its most discomfiting aspects.

---

[1] tr. as *Ignis: The Central Fire*, Black Coat Press, ISBN 978-1-934543-88-7.

Fernand Fleuret (1883-1945) was a poet, humorist and historian of the unusual, who made a living as a journalist, frequently writing under fanciful and flippant pseudonyms. His closest associates in the Parisian literary world were the symbolist and pioneer of surrealism Guillaume Apollinaire, the militant socialist Louis Perceau, with whom he wrote a good deal in pseudonymous collaboration, Rémy de Gourmont, Max Jacob and André Salmon; he must also have been acquainted with other journalists who produced extravagant fantastic fiction, most notably André Arnyvelde—another close friend of Apollinaire—and Jules Hoche. With Apollinaire and Perceau, Fleuret wrote an account of *L'Enfer de la Bibliothèque nationale* [The Closed Section of the Bibliothèque Nationale] (1913), offering a survey of the books that the national library was obliged to keep locked away, accessible only to selected scholars, and his own ambitions as a writer were always to be contentious, challenging and controversial. He only published two novels, the other being *Histoire de la bienheureuse Raton, fille de joie* [The Story of the Blissful Raton, prostitute] (1926), which proved (unsurprisingly) much more popular, but both are as artful as they are determined in their pursuit of those ambitions.

Although it has not retained the celebrity of *L'Ève future*, mainly because Fernand Fleuret has not retained the same personal legendary status as Villiers de l'Isle-Adam, it is a better novel, more rounded as well as more pointed, if that oxymoronic combination is permissible, and also more complex. It was written at a time when androids were much in fashion throughout Europe, thanks to the widespread continuing distribution of Karel Čapek's play *R.U.R.* (1920) and Fritz Lang's film *Metropolis* (1927), and like those works, it is both a significant reflection of the spirit of its era and a work of enduring appeal and value, as readable and as effective today as it was in 1930. Like all great historical fantasies, it offers an account of history that makes more sense than the one offered by orthodox historians, precisely because it is both absurdly farcical and deeply tragic.

This translation was made from a copy of the Gallimard edition, marked "fourth edition" on the cover and the title page.

Brian Stableford

JIM CLICK
or THE WONDERFUL INVENTION

NOTICE

In 1810, an English writer, J. H. D. Robertson, issued in Edinburgh, without a named publisher, a curious work entitled *Jim Click, or the Wonderful Invention*. While passing through London I found it in the shop of a second-hand book dealer, who was unable to tell me anything about the author or the book, although he had consulted all possible catalogues and bibliographies and appealed to the critics and men of letters among his clients—for it appears that in London, such gentlemen do read books.

In addition, he assured me that he believed his copy to be unique and that the others must have been pulped, unless just Posterity, represented by grocers and housewives, had destined them for the preservation of jam, butter and mustard. So saying, my bookseller seemed to be suggesting that those destroyers were absolutely justified. I thought I could read in his thoughts that he would have done the same had his profession not obliged him to respect printed matter. I paid a modest price for the book, and the bibliopole received my money with disdain. If I did not fear offending him by what he might judge to be an impertinence, I would dedicate my translation to him.

I have not found that work entirely despicable. Without the satire that it contains, the English bookseller might perhaps have affected less intolerance, but I do not have the same reasons for disapproval as him, and I believe, on the other hand, that it is not necessary to attach overmuch importance to the ravings of a madman. I also think, with J. H. D. Robertson, that something might be gleaned from it. In any case, I shall leave the latter to speak for himself, in the prologue with which he precedes Jim Click and the rather singular epilogue that concludes it.

As for myself, I have limited myself to translating very exactly, leaving aside the identity of J. H. D. Robertson, which might not be as impenetrable as the bookseller claims, and without worrying any more about the historical accuracy of the story. I am not familiar with Admiral Gunson, and I have never heard of the Battle of Barajar, but it might, after all, be the case that both are renowned in the world under other names, as that is often the case.

F. F.

PROLOGUE

In the course of a long fatigue caused by study and toil, I was cared for last year in the house of Dr. Vilkind at Danish Camp in Norfolk.[2] It was an establishment that, by virtue of the respect for silence observed there and the solicitude with which you are surrounded, could offer a rest cure to overworked individuals, but most of the patients treated there are afflicted in their reason. To tell the truth, Dr. Vilkind had graciously urged me to stay there for a while, for it would not have occurred to any other physician to send a patient there whose faculties remained sane.

I had made the acquaintance of Dr. Vilkind at the British Library, where I was working on utopian writers of the stripe of Thomas More, Bacon, Campanella, Cyrano de Bergerac and Gabriel de Foigny, and other ancient and modern dreamers, who could fill a bookcase of huge dimensions on their own.

Dr. Vilkind, who had the seat next to mine, took an interest in my studies. In addition to being highly literate, he found that kind of philosophy particularly interesting, not because he was a utopian himself, but because he claimed that many of his patients had a bee in their bonnet of wanting to correct or regenerate the world. He classified their madness in accordance with the situation of their utopian realms.

---

[2] South of the village of Warham in north Norfolk is an earthwork hill fort now thought to have been constructed by the Iceni but long known locally as "the Danish Camp."

11

Men who imagined such realms beyond the sea, like More and Harrington, were afflicted by a particular lesion of the brain, and that lesion was distinct from the lesion of men who placed their chimeras among the stars, like Cyrano the Lunarian and Campanella the Solarian, and different again from those who established it in subterranean depths, like the novelist Ludvig Holberg in *The Voyage of Niels Klim*. Finally, he differentiated from all of the preceding those who dreamed of austral lands, like the Bishop of Exeter, Joseph Hall, who, Vilkind sustained on the basis of his experience, had been afflicted by a chilling of the marrow engendered by a rheumatism of venereal origin.[3]

I do not know exactly from what Plato was suffering to have dreamed of Atlantis, nor what multiple lesions obfuscated the brain of Jonathan Swift and provoked in him an entirely mental ambulatory mania, all the sharper because it was never satisfied.

"I would have treated Swift," he said, "firstly by making him walk five miles every morning, and I would have constrained him to dress in wool, in order that an abundant sweat would purge the acridity of his humors."

When I reached the end of my work—or, at least, nothing more remained than for me to draft it in accordance with my notes—I gave evidence of a need for rest, which, as I have said, Dr. Vilkind offered to satisfy in the best possible conditions. I think that he was counting on indoctrinating me at length and introducing his psy-

---

[3] Joseph Hall's brutal satire *Mundus alter et idem sive Terra Australis antehac semper incognita* (c.1605) was written in Latin for private circulation, and was thus a book condemned to an *Enfer* by its own author, which doubtless endeared it to Fernand Fleuret.

chiatric conclusions into my book. I therefore accepted, glad to be able to maintain with him a fire that, thanks to his care, would not consume me.

I found beautiful shade in Dr. Vilkind's establishment, in which I passed part of the mornings, usually drowsily lying on the mossy at the foot of the trees, sometimes distractedly reading a book from the communal library. That library was the doctor's pride. Not only did it contain the wherewithal to occupy the leisure hours of a cultivated man but also to fortify the meditations of a scientist like my host. What rendered it even more precious was the relatively large number of manuscripts and drawings due to the pen or pencil of inmates, which had been piling up for some thirty years.

"You cannot measure," Dr. Vilkind said to me one day, "the interest that there would have been for you in riffling through these works instead of applying yourself to reading that can be found anywhere. Some have an appearance of rationality and are not without kinship with the lucubrations of the majority of your utopians. They are also written with more disinterest and conviction—I might even say seriousness—for among professional philosophers and writers it is advisable to look for the element of mockery, paradox, rancor or the desire to do someone a bad turn. You are not unaware that the resentment of old misfortunes was resident in Swift's heart, and that it was to lay waste to the optimistic philosophy of Leibniz that Voltaire wrote *Candide*."

My host went on: "Look, here are two works of a so-called inventor. The first is a scientific paper with detailed plans and designs in a hand so masterly that one could believe in the reality of the invention. The second is a long novel that he wrote himself, which relates to an incredible adventure. He pretended, however, that it was a true story, and was bold enough to sustain that to my face. His madness consisted of wanting to identify with reality the fiction that he had conceived while straying into satire. There reigns within it, I tell you, a tone of sincerity apt to render the book dangerous if it were ever published as the brainchild of a writer. Compared with your utopians, it isn't inferior. At least he was locked up, although yours were free to be a danger to society."

I leafed through the first work that Dr. Vilkind handed me. It was indeed a collection of drawings in aquatint, of an artistry so perfect that one might have thought them engraved, and which bore, for the most part, their scale of reduction or enlargement. There were about fifteen hundred items therein, which testified to a dogged patience, and, so far as I could judge, a profound knowledge of mechanics and anatomy, because the levers, cog-wheels and crank shafts were mingled with human articulations, bones, muscles and an entire vascular system. An explanatory text, in perfectly-formed handwriting with no crossings-out, was legible at a glance. That folio treatise was dedicated to His Majesty King George III "by his very humble and very obedient servant, Doctor Click."

"Was he really a doctor?" I asked.

"Yes," my host replied, "And a doctor of almost all the sciences. It is his universal knowledge that is imposed here—but he lacked reason," Vilkind concluded, with a little snigger.

I set aside the treatise in order to take up the pseudo-novel, which interested me more, judging it more within my range and worthy of satisfying my professional curiosity.

"Well," I said, "I'll read it this evening, since I have your permission, Doctor. It appears to me to be written with very good penmanship."

"Huh!" said Vilkind. "An educated man who has forced leisure can, strictly speaking, pass for a writer, even if he has no common sense—that isn't a professional requirement…but I beg your pardon for that."

I laughed at his at his joke, and took my leave, impatient to make the acquaintance of the manuscript, which solicited reading by virtue of the nervous elegance of its calligraphy.

PART ONE

I

I was born at Danish Camp in Norfolk in 1759, the only child of my honorable father William Click, who was reputed to be an excellent clockmaker. By that entitlement, he regulated the clocks at Norwich Observatory. My mother lost her life in bringing me into the world. I was brought up by my nurse until the day I was able to do without her milk. Then my father divided his time between his watches and my little backside.

The cradle was on the left hand side of his workbench, next to a stove where things were warmed up for my usage; he dried other things on it, the odor of which cannot have been pleasant. When I cried, my father reached out his arm and imprinted me with a few cadences that threw me back into sleep. If the work was not pressing, he took me on his knees. Without taking the horn-rimmed magnifying glass out of his left eye, which was weak, he sang the Mallard song to me in a bucolic falsetto voice.[4] It doubtless seemed to him to be

---

[4] In England, "the Mallard Song" usually refers to an ancient tradition of All Souls' College, Oxford, sung at the Bursar's dinner and Gaudy Night. The words recorded by Dr. Click (in mock-English of a sort, which I have reproduced precisely) are, however, entirely different from the words sung at All Souls, and Fleuret might not have been aware of the existence of that Mallard song.

appropriate to my young age, at which no one ought to be able to understand anything:

O, I have avut, O what have I yut?
I've ayut the voot o'my mallard.
A voot voot, a toe toe nippens and all,
O, so goodum it was, my mallard.

I was less astonished by that than the sound of the watches that my father applied to my ear. He wanted, by that means, to give me a precocious taste for the mechanics that had nourished his life, and which was to be the bane of mine. I was also suspended, eyes haggard and drooling, before various pendulum clocks of his industry, which he made me admire. Among others, there was a cutter navigating in a bowl around a lighthouse with a clock-face; the hour, the quarter and the half were incessantly announced by a mariner in a white waxed cap, who glided around the lantern agitating a hand-bell and applying a loudhailer to his mouth.

That masterpiece, mounted on a mobile pedestal, was placed in the shop window. Several times a day, the scapegraces going to school or coming back pressed their noses—as ill-wiped as mine—against the window in order to admire the mysterious evolution of the little ship on veritable water and look out for the emergence of the lighthouse-keeper, whom my father had nicknamed Jack Tar.

However inconvenient the presence in the shop of an infant of my age might seem, it attracted the housewives of the neighborhood, with the result that my father received assistance and benefit from it. The natural consideration that he already had was increased thereby, and it even brought him some good opportunities for remarriage. In addition to the fact that he was no longer young, however, he preferred to spend his evenings playing the sonatas of Boyce[5] on his *viola da gamba*, or philosophizing in front of a pint of ale with a church-warden pipe in his lips, rather than get to grips with a new wife, in the ineluctable disputes that are the ransom of matrimonial pleasures, if it is true that they exist.

However, in order to display their aptitude as housekeepers, each of them did her best, as I have said, to make herself useful. One of them taught me to walk, another to talk, a third to eat without splattering the surroundings with the spoon, which I was obliged to raise to the level of my lips and not my ear or my eye. A fourth, finally, taught me to read the Bible, which is why I know so little of it and have such a mediocre grasp thereof.

I ought to add that, in truth, neither my father, who was not a handsome man, nor his situation, which was no more elevated than those of his suitors, was sufficient to earn so many precious attentions. It was known that his brother, who was devoid of marital burdens and notoriously intemperate, had accumulated a considerable fortune in India. Thus, our neighbors never failed to ask for news of his establishment and his health when the post brought some from time to time.

I shall pass over the details of my early childhood; they do not seem to me to be worthy of interest. I am, in any case, in haste to arrive at the amity that linked me,

---

[5] The composer William Boyce (1711-1779) was best known for his church music, but he also composed the tune for the naval anthem "Heart of Oak," provided with a lyric by David Garrick in 1759.

once again to my detriment, to one of the guttersnipes who watched the cutter turn in its eternal circle.

I had just completed my eighth year. I had spent them in the shop and the back room, at first doing nothing, and then applying myself to reading, writing and arithmetic with a docility and punctiliousness worthy of remark in the midst of the exemplary noise of half a dozen pendulum clocks and an incalculable number of watches. I shall not talk about the odor of Virginia tobacco and smoked fish, which I would have regretted not finding elsewhere, and which formed my domestic atmosphere. I ran errands in the neighborhood, and also helped my father, who was often gout-stricken, to prepare meals—by which I mean that I peeled vegetables, as parsimoniously as possible, and drew beer without spilling any. With regard to the latter operation my father would not have compromised, because beer, along with its brother tobacco, constituted his treasure, his pleasure and his recompense, the means by which he proved, several times a day and long before dusk, that William Click was a free man and England the foremost nation in the world.

When, while reading the paper, he said to me: "By God, lad, pull me another pint!" I was sure that the majority of the watches in the neighborhood had not been stopped by a providential magnet; that my fatherland was not in danger of displacement, that our enemies were held at the coast; and that the Whigs were holding sway over the Tories—for we were liberals. I admired, as if I had been his wife, my father's fine self-confidence, which took the place of authority, and I had no other to admire.

Another was encountered, however, in the epoch that I have just cited, in the person of a boy of my own age, or very nearly. I saw him for the first time through the window contemplating the hydraulic clock with the marks of an interest that I shall describe as intense, so much attention and desire did his features manifest. Braced against the window, his fists clenched in his armpits and his little German pigtail overflowing the collar of his dark blue coat, he did not miss a single one of the evolutions of the cutter, not a single detail of its rigging.

When the ship went around the lighthouse and its rocky jetty, he watched for its reappearance like a cat lying in wait for a mouse, frantically agitating the hat he was holding in his hand as soon as the object of his desire triumphantly doubled the obstacle that hid it from his view. He would have uttered three cheers for the emergence of Jack Tar if he had not thought that it would distract him from his contemplation.

The kind of energy he put into his desire and his mime reached me in a fluid fashion, constraining me to similar gestures and making me wish, in a intense fashion, that he might be able to acquire or steal the paternal masterpiece. Finally, he tore himself away from that examination, which had seemed to me to be interminable, although it had only lasted two minutes, and he came into the shop with a red face, in which two steely eyes were shining, which spoke for his mouth; nevertheless, the latter opened and simply said: "How much?"

"What?" said my father, who was tormenting a watch and seemed offended that anyone who come into his establishment unexpectedly.

"The boat."

"My young gentleman," my father replied, with tranquil irony, "I don't know whether I'll ever part with that clock. I constructed it under the gaze of my dear wife, Mrs. Dorothy Click, who is no more. That clock is my presage, you see, of the fatal boat of the river Acheron, which will take me to her shade. I don't know whether I'm making myself understood...and anyway, my young gentleman, the few shillings of which you perhaps dispose would not be sufficient to pay for such a whim. It is appropriate, furthermore, that you take the advice of your father, whom I do not have the honor of knowing."

"My father," said the child, with a proud impatience and a clarity of elocution that could not help but astonish, "is the Reverend Edmund Gunson, Rector of Danish Camp. My mother is the daughter of the Reverend Maurice Buckling, prebendary of Westminster. Sir Robert Walpole,[6] the minister, is my cousin..."

"My young friend," retorted my father, who plunged his horn-rimmed lens into his watch this time, "I won't ask you to bring so many persons of quality into this humble dwelling. If the Reverend Edmund Gunson cares to visit me, I shall have the honor and pleasure of seeing him."

"Well then, he'll come tomorrow. Good day, you bloody old blockhead."[7]

---

[6] This pedigree is, of course, fictitious, but it is worth noting that the maiden name of the mother of Horatio Nelson, born in Norfolk in 1858, was Suckling, and that she was the great-niece of Robert Walpole the prime minister. Nelson's father was the Reverend Edmund Nelson, and he was named after Baron Horatio Walpole, his godfather. Nelson's maternal uncle, also Maurice Suckling, was a naval captain, whose example formed his character and who patronage assisted his early naval career.

[7] The first adjective is rendered in the original as *damnée* [damned] but the author subsequently inserts a footnote ex-

An instant before, I would have liked to appease my father and retain Reverend Gunson's son, who had just expressed himself in such an irreverent manner. But the one had disappeared as he had entered, and the other, after having made as if to chase him and box his ears, had fallen back into his chair with a cry of pain. My father had forgotten his gout, but his gout had not forgotten him.

"Bloody old blockhead! Bloody old blockhead!" repeated my father. That's how the son of a rector expresses himself! Bloody old blockhead—me, the clockmaster of Norwich Observatory! By God! Let him come tomorrow, this Reverend Edmund Gunson. I shall say to him, just like his blasphemous son: 'Good day, you bloody old blockhead!' But you, Jim, standing there like a useless lump? At your age, I'd already have run after that bad lot and thumped him until the blood ran from his nostrils. However, something tells me, Master Jim, that in spite of that insult of 'bloody old blockhead,' you'd have been satisfied if I'd sold for five shillings, and perhaps less, the clock that is the honor of my life, and which I've destined for you if I don't make a gift of it one day to the great Englishman who destroys the fleet of the French dogs. Doubtless you'd run after that little guttersnipe to give it to him? Go on, you're less than a simpleton, you're a girl!"

So saying, my dear father gratified me with a clout, with which, unfortunately, his gout did not intervene,

---

plaining that the English word he is translating thus is "bloody." I have, in consequence, followed suit, and have taken the liberty of translating his "*sacré*" [sacred] as "damned," that being the nearest equivalent among English expletives with regard to the intended effect.

and I went, impelled by his imperious strength as much as chagrin, to take refuge in the back room. There I shed abundant tears.

It's true, I confessed to myself. *I would have given it to him, and I'd give it to him again!*

That my father had been called a bloody old block-head did not change my sentiment at all. However, I took the full measure of that insult, whose expression was so new to me. That measure, however, I regretted less for my father than with regard to the difficulty that Reverend Gunson's son would find on coming back the next day.

What temerity! I thought. *What spirit of decision!* Exactly what my books had made me admire most in our great men. I was still subject, with a kind of delight, but nevertheless without taking account of it, to the authority of the tone, the ascendancy of the gaze and the manners of the "bad lot," the "little guttersnipe." How glad I would have been to have him as a friend, to love and fear him! As happy as the girls whose hair young boors pull from behind and pinch their arms until they bleed. "Go on, you're a girl!" my father had said. I did not think that shameful. I was only sorry to have been divined.

That evening, I peeled the onions and carrots like a valet in a big house—which is to say that I spoiled half of them. I forgot to close the tap of the barrel, as is recommended in the *Directions to Servants* of my dear Jonathan Swift,[8] and went to bed without supper, after having received a second clout on the head. That night,

---

[8] The scathingly satirical guide-book in question, published in 1731, was one of Swift's last completed works, and presumably reflects a long and bitter disenchantment with his domestic staff.

however, I dreamed that I was a girl, that the Pastor's son beat me more forcefully than my father, and that I gave him the marvelous clock.

II

The next day, I was in the shop early, torn between hope and uncertainty. The idea that dominated those alternatives was the greeting that my father had promised to address to Reverend Gunson. Utterly oppressed, I ended up wishing that he would not come. Meanwhile, I shuddered at every passer-by who paused in front of the shop window. In order that my father should not perceive my disturbance, I pretended to recite my conjugations from the old Latin grammar on which three generations of my family had bumped my noses for the sake of elegant satisfaction on the day they educated themselves to translate the legends on sundials.

"Shut up, Jim!" said my impatient father, after a moment. "You don't know what you're saying any more than Mr. Brown the harness-maker's magpie. It would be better, for you and for me, to amuse yourself turning pieces of copper; something would remain from that. Besides which, I don't really know what to do with you. The time has come either to send you to school or to teach you the rudiments of the profession, for nothing can be properly learned on your own, even in books."

For the first time, I saw my father prey to an anxiety, but instead of being chagrined by it, I experienced contentment. *So*, I thought, *he's no longer thinking about the Pastor's visit. Perhaps he'll forget, if the latter appears, to return his son's fine compliment.*

Resolved to distract his mind from such an unfortunate memory and such a black resolution, I confided to him that I would prefer to go to class in order to be a credit to him one day, that I loved the sciences and was eager to know how to use a telescope in order to gaze at the stars. So saying, I thought that Reverend Gunson was sure to send his son to school, and that by hastening my entry, I would have a better chance of encountering him there.

"It's a fine occupation," my father replied, "that of the telescope. Those gentlemen in Norwich earn money by it. The king visits them once during his reign. And yet, they do nothing, except taking down the stars, in order to line their stomachs with them on the days when they go to the Academies. As for you, my son, you'd do better to look more closely at the ground when you close the tap on the barrel."

Heavens! I thought. *If he retraces the course of yesterday's memories, that will lead him to the exact point from which I want to keep him away.* So I began to hum a tune by Boyce that he hadn't played for a week, and had the satisfaction of seeing him pursue the tune while filing and tapping. The rather sprightly air, which might be described as the jig of the sublime, put my father into such an excellent mood that he sent me to pull a pint without recommending me to be more attentive than the previous evening. I spent some time on it, in order to avoid too great an abundance of foam and the reprimand that I would not have failed to receive in consequence.

On my return, I almost dropped the earthenware pot that I was clutching to my breast two-handed: the Reverend Gunson, his son and six other children, arranged in a semicircle in order of height, were in the shop, admiring the circular navigation of the little vessel!

My father was standing slightly to one side. Visibly, the Pastor had impressed him, to the point that he had not dared greet him in the fashion that I dreaded so much. The flattering murmurs of the entourage, too, could not have displeased him. In brief, in spite of my astonishment, I thought the affair settled. The appearance of Jack Tar was saluted by a unanimous cry.

Then the Reverend Gunson approached my father, with the intention of talking to him—but I only had eyes for the "guttersnipe" of the previous day. He was inviting his brothers and sisters to admire the six swivel-guns of the vessel, His Majesty's flag and the British flag. He named the sails and the elements of the rigging for them, pointing to tem with his finger. I heard: jib, flying jib, bowsprit, spanker, beam, horn, cathead, etc. In sum, it was as if he were aboard his own ship, in the midst of astonished landlubbers. All of them were listening to the oracle, including the younger of the two girls, who had her thumb in her mouth and was contemplating him with the eyes of a faithful dog.

From time, he cast a furtive glance in the direction of his father and mine. I feared that he might catch sight of me in the ridiculous situation in which my pot of beer put me, when my embarrassment would be multiplied tenfold. Sometimes I was standing on one foot, sometimes the other. *He'll take me for a simpleton*, I said to myself. *If he were able to read my heart, however, he'd see that I'm his best friend, the one who admires him and understands him.*

"No, Rector," whined my father. "I'd rather tell you, at the risk of disobliging you, that I don't want to, that I can't sell that clock. In sum, it serves me as a sign, you see. It attracts visitors, clients…no, no, Rector! Then again, I'm as stubborn as a *bloody old blockhead*, me..."

"Oh!" said the Rector, taking a step back and raising a reproachful hand.

"I ought to tell you," my father went on, ironically, "that the first epithet, which you judge blasphemous, was found here yesterday in the mouth of your son, as well as the second and the substantive. It was a kind of farewell that he bade me..."

"Come here, Horatio!"

Horatio! His name was Horatio! How I trembled for Horatio, with my pot of beer overflowing, spilling over my shoes.

Well, Horatio had certainly guessed everything from the tone that the Rector had just adopted. Nevertheless, he advanced like a mariner obeying an injunction of the officer of the watch.

"Beg the honorable Mr. Click's pardon for the gross insult that you hurled at him for no reason, which is unworthy of a Christian and makes you seem the son of a scoundrel. On your knees, if the honorable Mr. Click demands it!"

"No," said my father.

"Honorable Mr. Click," said Horatio, in a firm voice, "I beg your pardon."

"And now," the Reverend Edmund Gunson went on, taking an ebony ruler from the depths of his coat-tails, "Hold out your hand so that I can apply twenty-five strokes of the rod, since your host's forbearance dispenses you of kneeling down. Then your brothers and sisters will each strike you once. Are you ready, Horatio?"

"I am," said Horatio, holding out his hand and staring at my father without flinching.

At the first blows, which landed forcefully, I dropped my earthenware pot, which shattered on the floor, inundating my father's feet and my own. I would have gone to join it if I had not been recalled to life by a vigorous clout.

"Imbecile!" growled my father, without imitating the other's ceremonious tone. "Have you sworn to spoil all my ale? You deserve to be chastised like this boy. At least admire his dignity and courage!"

Meanwhile, I did not cease to shed tears. Crouching, my head hidden in the organ-pipe tails of the paternal coat, I would have liked not to hear the blows of the ruler that we falling with wooden hardness, and it seemed to me that my own fingers were breaking.

As soon as I could no longer hear anything I risked a glance in Horatio's direction. All I saw was that he was expelling the numbness from his palms by rubbing them together—one might have thought in satisfaction. He was smiling proudly. Not a single tear·obscured the limpidity of his gaze. His brothers and sisters, who had just completed the correction unceremoniously, were showing natural expressions. Satisfied with a task accomplished, they embraced the martyr as if nothing had happened.

"My young gentleman," said my father, spontaneously shaking his hand, "I can see that you're a man, and congratulate you for it. I've forgotten everything. But I wish that my son here were not a weakling. Come and see my clock as often as you wish, if it pleases you and if that is agreeable to the Rector. That way, you might perhaps become friends."

"That's not a bad idea, Mr. Click," said the Rector. "They might be able to exchange what they have of good, inasmuch as the punishment they have experienced before one another might incline them to modesty, and nothing is more valuable than having suffered together. One seems to have mildness and education, if the other has endurance and determination.

"Unfortunately, mine has listened too much to his maternal uncle, Captain Maurice Buckling, who commands the *Raisonnable*,[9] a ship of sixty-four canons. Everything that my brother-in-law says and does is, for him, something to be aped. It is not only his costume that he would like to copy. If I let him act as he wished, he'd be wearing a saber and pistols. What am I saying? He'd be smoking a pipe in the streets of Danish Camp.

"To tell the truth, the Captain is worthy of imitation. One cannot praise too highly his spirit of enterprise and his glorious deeds. But that which might be excusable, strictly speaking, in a mariner who does not search for his words and fatally maintains bad habits, is not tolerable in a child who lives in the bosom of his family and the love of the Lord. He is not required to command, to get carried away and to make himself feared in the service of His Majesty!"

Reverend Gunson's sermon went on for considerably longer. His six children, still arranged in order of stature, listened to him respectfully. As for me, I had drawn closer to Horatio, who had drawn closer to the clock, and I did my best to swallow the last hiccups of my chagrin.

"What's your name?" Horatio asked me. He looked me up and down, with more curiosity than arrogance, and even a kind of surly amiability.

"Jim."

"Well, Jim, you're pulling a funny face. One would think that it's the first time you'd received a slap."

---

[9] Although I have translated the names of the hypothetical ships cited in the narrative from French into English, I have left this one in French because the actual Captain Maurice Suckling was, indeed, in command of *H.M.S. Raisonnable*.

"Only the third."

"Is that possible? It's necessary to harden yourself, you see. Anyway, it doesn't do any harm. It's more the idea one has of it. I'd like to give you a mighty thump to get you accustomed to it and to see if you can become my friend... Yes, you're a good old blockhead, Jim. So I'll give you more of them..."

"I had received a dig in the ribs that cut off my respiration. I was experiencing the pain of it, but it was mingled with an unknown sensation, which I dare not describe as delicious, but which left me in a state bordering on wellbeing. Then Horatio held out his hand and shook mine forcefully.

Meanwhile, I held back my tears.

"Why a cutter?" said Horatio, negligently, leaning over the ship. "I'd prefer a brig—it carries more canons. It's your father who made the cannons? What about you—can you make cannons?"

"Yes, Horatio. One turns a piece of copper on that metal lathe, and then hollows it out with a borer. One makes candles the same way, but with a much thinner wick."

"You've already turned a few?"

"Yes, to amuse myself." And from a drawer, I took twenty little copper cannons, which I had mounted on cylindrical pivots in order to serve as gun-carriages. I filled his hands with them and assured him that he could take them away.

"Thanks, old blockhead!" said Horatio, sketching a jig and stuffing my gift into his pocket. "Since you can turn cannons, you really are my friend. You must know how to make lifting tackle, pulleys, tillers, belaying pins—they're diabolical, belaying pins!—anchors, all the equipment? Me, I know how to build a boat. The two of us will arrive at something good. We'll put a hundred cannons on her—a hundred! And we'll fire them all together. *Vroom! Patapataboom!* Too bad if I blow up my old gob and yours! After all, that would be more amusing than that clock behind me. Your father doesn't want to sell it—let him keep it! Tell me, Jim, do you know how to make a little mechanical man like the one on the lantern? Only, I'd like him to be the captain, and that he talks well. He'll shout, for instance, into his loudhailer: 'Furl the mizzen topgallants! First volley, fire! Launch grappling irons! Boarding divisions, charge! Hip, hip, hurray!'"

At these words, uttered in a loud and ferocious voice, I saw Horatio's six brothers and sisters arrive, their eyes staring and nostrils flaring and fists advanced. I began to tremble merely on seeing their menacing faces. My father and the Rector had gone into the back room, from which a deep and sweet chord from the viola da gamba emerged.

"Halt!" Horatio shouted. "Order arms! Stand still!" He turned to me. "That's how we often play. But there are fifteen or twenty of us and we fight for real. These are true lascars, who obey at the first gesture. I'm their Captain, Captain Horatio Gunson. Oh, old Jim, you bloody old blockhead, we'll have to get you used to receiving blows. Pooh! You strike me as a mussel—a freshwater mussel—so I'll appoint you crew-master, which is to say that you'll furnish us with pikes, axes, sabers, halberds, cutlasses and pistols, not to mention cannons. Lads, I introduce you to crew-master Jim Click. Let no one entrust their lemonade to him, because he drops his father's tankard when he's scared. Form ranks! Present...arms!"

III

No, no one, among all the children I know, and even those I don't know, no one even among the men I see, has the character, the casual manner, that indefinable quality of my dear Horatio. The dairyman's son isn't without grace on his donkey, in the midst of his churns and bottles; one might think that he's a drummer, but on foot, he's no longer anything. The baker's boy is good at ball games and has full pockets. His premature stoutness gives him the appearance of a Hercules, but a benevolent Hercules. The butcher's son has more muscles, and walks with his arms apart, making one think that he's about to seize a bull by the horns, but he has short breath and would run away from a sheep. The herbalist's is knowledgeable, placid and reserved; he's the only one I can talk to. He smells pleasantly of cinnamon, and holds you in friendship by promising to give you a handful of bonbons some day, but fundamentally, he's a miser and a prig. Mr. Brown the harness-maker's always has wax thread on him, isn't mean, and there's no one better at spinning a top. But again, none of them is comparable to my dear Horatio. He has a force like a bullet; he makes the whole world bow down to him. My father, whom he's insulted, held out his hand to him as to a man of his own age. Which son, of the dairyman, the baker, the butcher, the herbalist or the harness-maker, would have dared to say: Good day, you bloody old blockhead! I disapprove of that, though...

He also dresses like a man...like his uncle, the valiant Captain Buckling. I, who dread blows, admire him. I see him in the midst of flames and smoke, leaping with his lascars on to the deck of a French ship, a saber in one hand and a pistol in the other. 'Boarding divisions, charge! Hip, hip, hurray!' He'll receive twenty bullets, but they won't stop his surge. My father says that he's not very intelligent. But he is what he is. He's Him.[10]

I'll admit that he's only a beast...however, I'm sure that he conceals the intelligence of a leader. His is an intelligence that doesn't waste time in vain speech; its bursts forth in one unique circumstance, a circumstance foreseen by him, and even produced by him. That kind of taciturnity knocks down empires and overturns the ideas of the living and the dead. What a pride it was for a grenadier in the War of Succession to have his ear twisted by Frederick the Great! Well, I resented that pride when it struck me. At the same time, I was invaded by such a great sweetness that it seemed to me that I contained it for two. So, I'll go to his house and he'll come to mine. No, I won't talk to the others anymore! I see so little of them anyway! My father is right to say that they're not of our society—except for the herbalist's son, he adds. But herbalist or grocer, isn't it all the same?

Such were my reflections on the evening of my first contact with the person I was already calling "my dear Horatio."

"Jim," said my father, folding up his paper and snuffing out the candles, "there was a question of your going to classes. I think, in truth, that it's time for that, for you've become dreamy and distracted. Until yesterday, I've seen you abandon yourself to your books. Perhaps, lacking comrades, you're falling into melancholy?

---

[10] Author's note: "Cf Montaigne I chap. XXVI: On Friendship: 'Because that was him, because that was me.' [Translator's Note]."

That's the opinion of Reverend Edmund Gunson, to whom I was talking just now. I believe it's also mine.

"I hesitated on your behalf between study and apprenticeship, but, as the Pastor—who is decidedly a man of merit and good advice, for having raised seven children—also said, it's necessary to give everyone his chance. So I'm going to give you yours. You're going to school, Jim. You'll encounter young Horatio there, who's difficult to handle, and you can make all the racket you want together, instead of playing the fool here and breaking my windows, which is bound to happen sooner or later.

"I hope, my dear son, that you'll develop a taste for study in order to recompense me for my sacrifice. Know that one day, your uncle—to whom God grant a good life!—will doubtless push you further forward than I can. But if you don't like school after a while, you'll always find enough to occupy you here."

I was internally exultant, although I put on a very grave expression. Rationalizing and moralizing under the influence of the Rector, my father, who borrowed his loquacity, also talked to me about my mother, who was watching over me in Heaven and would rejoice at my advancement down here.

"Look at her portrait on the wall, Jim. Doesn't she seem anxious, on seeing you try your wings? You'll always be a youngster to her, Jim!"

With that, my father felt obliged to show me his tears and blow his nose vigorously. During the last blow, I heard a stifled voice through the handkerchief demanding that I pull him a pint. In my distress, I addressed myself to the viola da gamba, which was placed beside the fine varnished barrel that completed the furniture and seemed, in the image of my father, to be obese and pacific: the sovereign, the George III, of the tables, chairs, clocks, shelves, the credenza and the barometer.

"Come along, Master Jim!" sighed my father, with an indulgent smile, swallowing his final tears. "You're not thinking a pulling me a sonata into a tankard? There—gently, gently, my boy! Tilt your pot a little to avoid foam. Then draw a glass of water for yourself, so I can drink to the success of the great scientist you're going to become one day."

He went on: "Speaking of music, Reverend Gunson shares my taste for Boyce. He even rises as far as Sebastian Bach, although he finds him a trifle worldly before the severity of the Lord. The soul, it appears, doesn't dance rigadoons when it presents itself before its God. Anyway, we're going to study music together, for he plays the serpent. Since your mother's death, I don't see anyone any more. I too have fallen into melancholy."

I thought that he was glad that we had both found a friend, him in the father, me in the son, and that he was showing more indulgence to the second in order to conserve the first.

I understand now the reason for such a subjection in my sentiment then to Horatio. I had lived too much apart, occupied, in addition, with girls' tasks; I had learned, like them, to love someone who represented singularity, adventure and independence. Like them, still weak, uncertain and lymphatic, was I not bound to reserve my attachment to someone who represented my opposite? Is it necessary to set aside, in the mind of anyone who might read this, any idea of the slightest impurity, given that I think the tenderness of Nisus for Euryale equivocal, and would dread to invoke it in this regard?[11]

To get back to my meditations of that distant evening, which was, in sum, the point of departure of my sad life, I then thought about the little "mechanical man" that Horatio had mentioned to me, and which he wanted me to make for him in imitation of Jack Tar. That work surpassing my science and my skill, I questioned my father about its construction, but only obtained imprecise replies: I was too young, too inexperienced to undertake such a masterpiece. However, as the subject was dear to his heart, he confided to me that he had once dreamed of constructing, first an arithmometer, or calculating machine, and then an android of human stature; like Vaucanson's, he would have played the fife and drum at all the hours of the day.

It goes without saying that my father had not turned away from clockmaking; I even believe that he had taken up music because of its accurate rhythms and complicated mechanisms of harmony. In brief, the weakness of his resources had constrained him to renounce his dream. Nothing remained of them but the plans of the android and the arithmometer, and the little mariner with the loudhailer, which he said to be on the scale of his renown.

"So it goes," my father concluded, "with the majority of our dreams and desires! We don't produce anything much, and yet, the slight result is that of considerable effort. Rare are those who reach their goals. Humanity

---

[11] Euryale and Nisus are employed in Virgil's *Aeneid* as an emblematic example of classic Greek pederasty, the former being an adolescent in a relationship with an older man. Euryale ends up dead.

honors them because they serve, amuse or flatter, but believe me, circumstances have assisted them and the realization they have attained is very often inferior to what they conceived. So, Jim, have some grand design, some great ambition, since it's necessary to put a great deal to work in order to achieve almost nothing. It's absolutely the same as gin: you get one glass from I don't know how many measures of fruit, which represent I don't know how many Juniper bushes. Others cut down a tree for a toothpick..."

However, I was confirmed in the opinion that my father was exaggerating, out of chagrin, for the examples that he gave me of androids in history appeared to me to be more imposing in number than I would have thought. I marveled at the one made by Albertus Magnus, which opened a door when one knocked and could articulate speech. How I resented Saint Thomas, who broke it, importuned by its chatter. And what had become of the talking head cast in bronze by Pope Sylvester II?

Descartes' Francine, whom the captain had thrown into the sea, momentarily brought my enchantment to a peak.[12] I imagined that, having landed on an island, with

---

[12] René Descartes' only daughter, Francine, died of scarlet fever, aged five, in 1640. Her mother was a domestic servant, who remained with Descartes for some time thereafter until he provided her with a dowry, and he does not appear to have had any other intimate relationships thereafter. The apocryphal story somehow got around that he built a mechanical doll modeled on and named for his dead daughter, but that, while he was traveling with it, a curious ship's captain found it in his trunk and was so horrified that he threw it overboard. The fable was presumably invented as an illustration of Descartes meditations on the subject of the body being merely a machine

an untiring and graceful arm, she had been seated on the throne of the queen whose funeral had just been celebrated, and that, in the course of a two-hundred-year reign, her subjects, exempt from wars and taxes, were still congratulating themselves on their wisdom.

Among all the androids and automata, however, including the dove of Archytas of Tarentum,[13] I had a particular affection, because of its tangible reality, for a Cretan coin of which my father showed me a plaster cast. It represented a kind of winged genius, seen head on, throwing a stone with the appearance of great vigor. Beneath is written its name: ΤΑΛΩ.[14]

"It appears," my father continues, "that that android is the most ancient that is known. He defended the island of Crete and crushed enemy fleets with huge rocks which he threw from a distance. The description that remains to us does not lack a comical element in its brevity: he had only one vein, which went all the way to his ankle, where it was fixed by a nail. A vein, Jim! What need did he have of a vein? Was it not rather a cord serving to operate the catapult?"

I dare say that I had forgotten all about Jack Tar and my dear Horatio. It was partly because my father had

---

animated by a distinct soul, and the reaction of the intellectually unsophisticated to the supposed blasphemy of the notion.

[13] The original has "*la colombe d'Archylos de Tarente*"; I have retained "dove" while correcting the name of the individual cited—a Pythagorean philosopher and mathematician closely associated with Plato—although the flying machine he was reputed to have built, apparently impelled by steam while suspended from a wire, is more commonly referred to in English reportage as a "pigeon."

[14] i.e. Talo[s], or Talo[n], the bronze giant featured in the *Argonautica*.

never said so much to me. Perhaps I had never give evidence of enough curiosity on the subjects dearest to his heart. Or perhaps, too, seeing me on the threshold of my studies, he wanted to tease my mind with a nascent chimera similar to his own, his own having died for lack of nourishment.

I examined my father with a surreptitious curiosity, as someone who had long hidden something from me beneath his nonchalant humor. Then I divined, to the extent that an inexperienced child can, the disappointed hopes that had wearied his eyelids, tugged the bitter creases of his mouth toward his chin, and whitened and devastated his temples.

At that moment, he was no longer the nourishing father, but someone who had suffered, and who was offering me a chance to avoid the same disappointments. I swore to myself to take advantage of the facility that he was going me to study, not because I had found my road to Damascus, since I already loved study, but in order to continue under his gaze the path that he had reluctantly abandoned. I put my arms around him without saying anything. He understood anyway, and hugged me to his heart.

At the same moment, I thought about Jack Tar again.

"Now," said my father, unwinding our embrace, "as I'm taking you to the school early tomorrow morning, go to bed."

I took a candle. As I went up the stairs with a jaunty tread I congratulated myself on seeing Horatio again, whom my thoughts had just neglected.

Why did my candle go out at that precise moment, and why did I bump my nose on the steps?

IV

Although I had learned something in my father's back room—or, at least, put myself into a state to receive the instruction that our pedagogue, Mr. W. Spool, dispensed to us—Horatio had conserved his own intellectual terrain in a virgin condition. To tell the truth, it was an uncultivated heath, which continued to defend itself with hostile brambles and inextricable thickets. That proud and savage ignorance almost commanded respect, and it was with extreme precaution and a refined delicacy that Mr. W. Spool, so trenchant and surly with everyone else, tried to bring the sickle to it. It was obvious that he did so apologetically.

Horatio listened to him, frowning, but that expression, which denoted obstinacy rather than attention, was abandoned as soon as the master's gaze and the address of his harangue were directed elsewhere. Then, Horatio resumed working with his blade of good Sheffield steel on a large piece of pine-wood that he had sworn to rough-hew. When he had given it the form of a keel he continued the planing by means of the bottom of a bottle or various files that he had improvised. Often, in the middle of study, a sequence of little dry taps was heard, and everyone whispered furtively to his neighbor: "He's making the deck!"

Mr. W. Spool did not oppose him in making the deck; he tapped in his turn on his lectern, but as discreetly as possible, in order to recall us to our duty, and perhaps in order that we should not trouble, by an overly unanimous curiosity, the refractory stubbornness to which the power of his genius was abandoned.

"Remember, boys," our master said to us—or something analogous that could conceal his embarrassment—"that the participle relates to a noun that is neither subject nor complement but which forms a circumstantial proposition therewith, thus also putting the name into the absolute ablative: *Tarquinio Superbo regnante*. Sometimes, the participle is implicit: *Teucero duce et auspice*..."

And directing a clement eye toward the disturber of the silence, he seemed to be adding: *Imitate, imitate such patience and determination...*

For me, almost always finding an application or those examples of grammar, I saw behind Horatio's features the arrogant tyrant of Rome declaring war on the Rutules; and, also behind Horatio, the adventurous child of Telamon, Teucer, leading his twelve vessels to the siege of Troy, and building the temple of the new Salamis, in which he had human sacrifices offered. In the same way, at the hazard of reading or study, he was by turns Alexander, Caesar, Ulysses, Ajax, Achilles or Palinurus—Palinurus cleaving the sea for three days.

He tolerated me working by his side, but he sometimes nudged me with his elbow and foot, with the least possible circumspection, in order to have me admire his work or to ask me for copper nails or waxed thread, of which I always had a good provision. In order to supply his needs I continued to maintain amicable relations with the harness-maker's son, and tried to conceal from him the profound indifference into which his person and his speech had plunged me for some time.

Another subject of my dear Horatio's pride was projecting, between his legs, after having alerted me, a long jet of brown-tinted saliva, which was nothing other than tobacco juice. I admired the fact that he could chew

42

something so frightful, not only with the appearance of delectation but also without giving the slightest external sign of malaise. He also struck a flint and set fire to ribbons discarded by his older sister. His amusement was boring symmetrical holes in his books, with the exception of an atlas of geography, which he had covered with ships bearing British flags, and over which he dreamed at times when blisters forced him to put away his knife.

He dreamed, as I say, genuinely lulled by the rumor of the sea that came in through the open window, because he swayed from right to left, as if obedient to its swell. With his pursed mouth he imitated the murmur of the wake and that of the breeze in the rigging. Or, striking his thigh, he counterfeited the resounding of the surf, and sometimes that of the sails tightening in the rising wind. Or, again, affecting a great seriousness, he maneuvered an imaginary helm—and I liked to think that he was steering a ship through a difficult passage, among the coral archipelagos of the Polynesian seas.

I believe I have allowed it to be understood that such idleness, and such scorn for study, rendered Horatio the most considered student in the institution, concurrently with the "top of the class," to the extent that Mr. W. Spool would not fail to introduce them both proudly if anyone of importance paid a visit to the class. He even raised his voice to say: "And this is the bottom." He became sacred in consequence, by the same entitlement that a village mendicant, a poor and superb volunteer who lives on the margins of the law, raises his tribute from the honest man and also receives a few kind words, in which the fine self-confidence of the rich man vacillates and is humbled.

However, my dear Horatio possessed other entitlements to admiration than that of being an inveterate dunce. There is a dignity that causes smiles, and eventually unleashes persecutions if it is not relieved by the prestige of strength, which then confers upon it a character of rebellion and independence. The village mendicant has his own strength, whether he draws it from the Gospel, or appears to dispose of the resources of magic, or, finally, one simply fears the rancor of his dagger. Horatio's strength, setting his industry aside, burst forth first of all in the wild cries that he uttered as soon as our master greatened us a few minutes' recreation or liberated us until the following day. And that cry, which found an echo in our breasts, signified that Horatio, freed from constraint, was about to take charge of our games, his unchecked reign substituted for that of Mr. W. Spool.

The latter, moreover, congratulated himself for that; not only did he no longer have to rack his brains to vary our pleasures and preside over their unfurling, but he was dispensed from giving two or three shillings a month to some retired mariner who would have informed us cantankerously of the dismal principles that are inculcated into conscripts. With Horatio, and a consent devoid of any murmur, we pounced on our weapons, in the form of hazel twigs disposed against the wall of the courtyard, and marked time in several ranks, deliberately raising a cloud of dust that seemed to us to be the smoke of battle or the sandstorm that harassed columns in distant Syrtis.

On command, the front rank took up the position of prone sharpshooters, the second knelt down and the third fired over the heads of the other two. We thus formed a square against invisible cavalry, intoning the national anthem with all the firm gravity of brave men sacrificing themselves. In the center, astride one of us, Horatio raised his cap on the end of his sword. A rag hung down from a stick, the "horse" whinnied impatiently, and we felt our noses turning pale. "Fire at will!" cried our Captain, after a general discharge. And we reloaded in twelve steps, as specified by the maneuver. Some allowed themselves to fall in pathetic attitudes under the gunfire; England's eyes were upon them!

I shall not talk about all the military inventions to which my dear Horatio submitted us, from drill to the most explosive actions, which are, it seems, its logical extrapolation. I shall limit myself to saying that he commanded those pedestrian and glorious maneuvers by virtue of a kind of compensation that he thought he owed to Mr. W. Spool, who let him plant his nails in peace, and perhaps also to show him his superiority in that regard—for our master, in spite of his haughty appearance and imposing stature, had nothing martial about him. He was truly anxious to hand over to my dear Horatio, so that the class should conclude every day by delivering itself entirely to the navy.

When that time came, I was proud to be admitted to Horatio's preferred diversion—or, rather, to the exercise of his passion. We ran half a mile to the sea, and there, wading knee deep in the broad and shallow estuary of a small coastal river, we put some ship to sea, or we experimented with the one my dear Horatio was in the process of completing; sometimes it leaned to the right, sometimes to the left, or the ballast we had fused with the clay was too heavy or insufficient, or the sails left much to be desired.

"That bloody blockhead Elsie," my dear Horatio groaned, "has sewn me hemstitches again, when ratlines are needed everywhere. That's why our sails are wrinkling or differ in aplomb. Then again, sometimes she uses an inward hemstitch, and sometimes an outward one. Finally, she hasn't followed my instructions with regard to the number of ells per sail..."

And my dear Horatio, after having vituperated against the older of his sisters, gave me a lecture on the number of ells or "gathers" making up a sail. I learned in that way that on a vessel 132 feet long, 30 feet broad and thirteen and a half deep, the mainsail ought to have 22 gathers in width, sixteen and a half ells in height and contain 266 ells of canvas, and that, counting the mizzen, the artimon, the main topsail, the small topsail and the spritsail, the vessel in question carries 1404 ells. I was veritably dazzled by such precise knowledge. What, by comparison, was Mr. W. Spool, with the spondees and dactyls making up the different Latin meters?

I was even more dazzled by all the measurements that it was necessary to give exactly to a toy two feet long, in relation to a vessel of 130 feet, wondering by what miracle my dear Horatio, who was apparently ignorant of any arithmetical operation, could succeed therein. But I did not question him on that point. In any case, he did not tolerate questions; his invariable response was a cuff to the back of the neck, or a jab in the ribs, according to the measure of the impudence.

So, because I never interrogated him, I sensed his attachment increasing, in return, I mean, for the good and confident opinion that I appeared to have of him. The cannons, it is true, had a lot to do with that. Their number became so great that, in order to furnish the raw material I was obliged to steal copper in secret. My father, having noticed it, Horatio and I started unscrewing door handles, knockers and the hand-grips of bell-ropes. Sometimes, we found bronze.

In that regard, I remember a charming hand, doubtless molded from nature, which served as the knocker of the door of a rural "folly." That hand, pitted with dimples, was negligently holding a lady-apple in the tips of its slender fingers, which appears to me now to have been of a singular species, which ought to have made knowledgeable people smile. Alas, it shared the fate of the latches and hand-grips, that hand of pleasure, that hand of softness, that exquisite hand, and I extracted twenty pieces of artillery from it....

So many canons corresponded to a fleet of all models of ships that my dear Horatio was constructing relentlessly, with the design of reproducing a naval combat. Impatient, he could not wait to have more than six at his disposal, but he combined them with rafts laden with guns and a few pieces of crudely-carved wood, which he called pontoons and fireships.

It was a fine day, or promised to be. In order to devote ourselves to it we skipped school. The brothers and sisters accompanied us, unknown to the Reverend and his wife, in order to carry all of the cumbersome fleet. In my capacity as crew-master, I was responsible for the powder-keg, a reed taper of considerable length, fuses and projectiles.

After abundant preparations, Horatio lined up the ships in accordance with a preconceived plan that he had not deigned to explain to us, but, as the wind blew them toward the shore too forcefully for them to hold their positions, he undressed without modesty and played the role of Poseidon, or Neptune, the ship-breaker. We contemplated his young nudity from the shore as it labored the placid waves of the little estuary, not without producing eddies that formed a tempest on the scale of the combatants. By turns, Horatio blew into the sails with the impetuosity of Aeolus, moving the units further apart or closer together with the taper, whose tip was always smoking, shouting commands and igniting the guns. Of the latter, however, few consented to function; the anticipated thunder failed in its effect. Perhaps a tutelary divinity was this preserving us from a dose of lead fatal to the sight.

Horatio's chagrin was manifest in an outburst of anger worthy of Achilles; after vain efforts, he came ashore and bombarded the two adverse fleets—now only one in his thinking—with pebbles. Thus playing the role of coastal batteries, he commanded us to imitate him, which we did without protest, so much is the spirit of devastation in the human heart, especially that of children.

Soon, nothing any longer remained of that beautiful fleet constructed to the detriment of studies, my father's reserves of copper, the beautiful silvered bronze hand, the latches and bell-cords of Danish Camp, Mr. Brown's wax thread and nails, Elsie's late nights, Mrs. Gunson's fine linen chemises, and many other things and people, than a few fragments of wood, entangled with bits of black thread, bristling with broken stalks.

We spared it some regret, but Horatio drew us away, convinced of an immense victory and already planning new ships, of more costly workmanship and greater perfection. It was necessary to remind him that, although he was carrying his clothes under his arm and his shoes in his hand, he was nonetheless naked.

It was, above all, in the Reverend Gunson's house that Horatio showed himself in the light most favorable to his genius. No one there was occupied with anything but his person, either to reprimand him or, more often, to warn him or despair of him, to repair what he broke, soiled or ripped with an annihilating force that only he had. If he put down a glass he broke it at the foot; if he sat down, the chair did not resist his efforts, so he drank from a tin mug and sat on an unbreakable seat that he called his quarter-bench and could not tilt. Even if he had been chained to it, he would have continued to destroy the objects within arm's reach, including the spoons and forks that he would have twisted with a single thrust had they not been made of iron especially for his usage. As for knives, he had a fashion of chipping them two by two, blade against blade, that was marvelous. He did not eat, he crushed; he did not drink, he gargled; and one saw in his bearing, with his fists on his thighs, his legs parted and his arms likewise, that mastery was his, and so well disposed that he would conserve it throughout his existence, physically and morally.

If anyone was speaking, my dear Horatio could not bear so much tyranny. He raised his voice to ask for something just as the speaker was reaching the crucial point of his discourse, and he threw defensive barriers artfully into conversations calculated to arrest any train of thought. I would not say that he was a liar, but everything he put forward was incredible or temeritous: he had seen a whirlwind in fine weather and it was driving a vessel under full sail. What he said could not be other than catastrophic. Mountains were flattened by him.

When he was at rest, lost in his voyages or his strategy, his brothers and sisters did not exist. That is why I was never able to interest myself in Ralph, Arnold, Wilfred, Donald, Elsie and Dolly. As soon as he entered into movement, however, they were animated in their turn, in the exact measure that their brother seemed to desire. The severity of the parents fell upon them, and Horatio was attained by indirect reprimands, which he affected, more often than not, not to take personally.

From time to time, Mrs. Gunson or her Reverend husband protested, of course, but with so much weakness that our dear Horatio took encouragement from it, for he divined in his father, his mother and his entire entourage an admiration that inclined them to complaisance. I believe that the Reverend, who sometimes pretended to have been pushed to the limit, only took out his ebony ruler in order to astonish himself with the proud endurance of his son, and enable others to share his astonishment. Behind that, again, was the shadow of the valiant Captain Buckling, whose faults and qualities he was said to show: the valiant Captain Buckling, who called his ivory-colored brother-in-law a damned old bean, without anyone ever finding in that singular expression anything but a cordial roughness.

The granary and the barn facing it were the preferred location of our exploits. The former, baptized with the name of the *Redoubtable*, was Captain Horatio's ship; the other, called the *Amphitrite*, that of an adverse band who never succeeded in electing a definitive leader because of the incessant reverses it suffered, and which left it at the mercy of anarchy. The latter was composed of the children of functionaries and petty rentiers, none of whom went to Mr. W. Spool's institution; thus, I congratulated myself on being the only one at the school not to feel the calculated scorn of our leader—a scorn by means of which he maintained a constant prestige, a general appetency to flatter and please him.

The *Redoubtable* was pierced with four small windows—sorry, gun-ports!—facing the *Amphitrite*, for more on the opposite side, and a lattice window at one of its extremities, which passed was that of the captain's cabin, above the poop castle. Also there were the arsenal, the crew-master's powder-store, where I had fitted racks of pikes and wooden rifles, and panoplies of sabers and pistols made of the same material. In the middle, a beam stood in for the mainmast, the two other masts—not counting the bowsprit—being assumed to be found in an imaginary extrapolation. At the foot of the beam I had accumulated grenades—by which I mean bags of wax-paper filed with earth and gravel, and covered with an old canvas sack, duly renamed tarpaulin. There was also a suspended bell to announce the emotional moment of boarding, which as advertised by redoubled strokes.

The most remarkable thing, however, was our eight-piece artillery. It was composed of logs mounted on boxes in the guise of gun-carriages. Of what was lacking we formed such an exact image, in accordance with the reiterated instruction of Horatio, that, if transported into a veritable battery, our society would have been able to maneuver it without awkwardness, in imitation of the best-trained cannoneers. But what am I saying? Instruction! Corporal punishment aided that considerably; it was that known in the fleet as "running the gauntlet," or passing under the cords of the crew, with the hands tied behind the back.

To get back to the artillery, like the crew, and like myself, but including Horatio, who simultaneously filled the roles of captain and master gunner, it comprised seven individuals, the logs being estimated at eight pounders, in such a fashion as only to require seven servicemen, in accordance with naval custom. That concern for exactitude applied to everything, as much as possible, even more so to the exercise of the cannon.

"Gunners!" shouted my dear Horatio, as soon as it was agreed that we were attacking the *Amphitrite* at half pistol-range, or vice versa, and the summons to combat had already been sounded on the drum and a one-sour pipe. "Gunners, to your posts!"

In the great silence of rigor, each placed beside a piece, we waited for the sequence of orders in order to carry them out.

"Listen to the command... Remove the plugs from your guns... Unhitch the lifting-tackle... Uncover the light... Pick up the detonator... Clear the barrel... Break out the cartridge... Remove the clearer... Place the detonator... Crush the powder on the plate... Replace the detonator... Plate over the light... Pick up your pincers and spikes... Pick up the fuse...Blow on the wick to one side... Point... Put down the pincers and spikes... Remove the retreat plugs... Remove the plate... Fire!"

These commands, which are not given in action, were for the sake of the picturesque and memory. Afterwards, one fired mechanically, but always in good order and without breathing a word. The greatest pleasure was watching the powder run from the run from the horn over the light and seeing it catch fire under the taper, which one snatched from the floor, where it was embedded like an arrow. The odor of sulfur mixed with saltpeter intoxicated us, and we imitated the sound of the discharge with thunderous howls. The *Amphitrite* replied in the same fashion.

Rotten fruits, hurled by hand, crashed against the exterior walls or penetrated the lofts, sometimes reaching, to the great prejudice of his face or clothing, an unfortunate who was immediately required to play dead, but who defied the convention more often than not. That multiple cheating irritated the crews. When the resentment reached a peak, the captains judged that the moment had come for hand-to-hand combat; that was the inevitable boarding!

Dispensed from those perilous encounters by my functions, which were further increased by that of ship's surgeon, the announcement of which I had to make with strokes of the bell that always left me white and trembling, I contemplated the ups and downs of the struggle through the gun-ports if the *Redoubtable* was attacking, or timidly hid behind a crate if the *Amphitrite* had anticipated our assault. At the first strokes of the bell the assailants took hold of grenades, picked up their weapons and hurtled down the stairs uttering frantic hurrahs. "Boarding divisions charge…!"

The most terrible moment was reaching the adversary's landing, which then gave rise to a hail of projectiles filled with blinding and filthy dust. In the hand-to-hand combat that followed, one heard frightful screams mingled with the barking of the mongrel Poppy, our captain's intrepid companion. It generally happened that Horatio ran to the rescue of little Dolly, his six-year-old sister. She ran around like a little devil, and the cowardice and fury of the enemy were unleashed upon her. That cowardice and fury consisted of pulling her hair, fustigating her, and even biting her buttocks, Captain Horatio avenged such outrages with his fists. As for Elsie, she bounded like a young bacchante, her beautiful blonde hair scattering, striking with her wooden pike as if with a thyrsis.

It was not rare to see the Reverend Edmund Gunson arrive in the middle of the tumult, accompanied by his wife. They begged in the name of Heaven that so much racket and scandal should come to an end. Scratched and cut, covered with earth, unkempt, splashed with sweat, powder and rotten apples, the combatants, still poorly reconciled, trembled as they emptied glasses of lemonade and ate toast with melted butter.

I could say more for my own pleasure, but I believe that I have shown Horatio's character well enough not to put too much weight on memories of childhood, whose accumulation would only add to the overloading of my design.

In the evenings, in the back room, I went back to work, every time more penetrated with tenderness for my friend.

My father congratulated himself on my application, my cheerfulness and my good conduct. Sometimes, the Reverend Gunson came to play the serpent while my father applied himself to the viola da gamba. Their concert was mingled with the tick-tock, chimes and carillons of the pendulum clocks, watches, cuckoo-clocks and alarm clocks.

The instruments and the precision machinery formed a ridiculous harmony. It was absurd enough, already, to see the Pastor oppose his long, stiff and sickly body to my father's, majestic with fat and loose garments. The former drank water, the latter beer. I fetched both when, letting go of the discordant music, they began to dispute theology and philosophy, one basing himself on the Scriptures, the other on Hobbes and Voltaire.

My dear Horatio, whom the Reverend brought on his own in order to avoid too much turbulence, breakages of glass and perhaps petty larcenies, behaved in an exemplary fashion. It must be said that we gazed together at the herbals, the shells and a few jet weapons and stuffed animals that my uncle sent from India. We dreamed on that subject, or, leafing through some collection or other, we passed in review the different means of navigation employed by Oriental peoples: the pirogue, the junk, the canoe and various kinds of catamaran, some made of wood and others of leather or woven reeds

I still have some of their sonorous, bizarre or seductive names in my ears: sacoleva, speronara, corocora, gayou, baize, patmar, boanga, paducan, dinga, tikikirny.

My dear Horatio, however, only had a mediocre liking for books. He became more excited by the tales of pirates that his uncle, Captain Buckling, had told him. He told me delightedly about the prodigious lives of Captains Basil Ringrose, Morgan, Kidd, Stede Bonnet and many others; Edward Teach, alias Blackbeard, with his plaited beard knotted with favors, and Roberts, clad in crimson damask with golden flowers, were among the most astonishing.

I believe that he nourished a precocious passion for Mary Read and Anne Bonny, the adventuresses of the Carolinas, who handled the saber and pistol like the soldiers of fortune whose clothing they wore. "What a pity," he sighed, "that they didn't serve regularly in the British navy!" For he appeared not to comprehend, and doubtless never would, that only improvisation and indiscipline had favored their hateful genius, or, more simply, their luck.

There was scarcely an evening when Horatio did not talk to me about Jack Tar, of whom he would have liked me to make a replica in accordance with his taste. The android of the island of Crete threw him into the craziest imaginations. Everything that my father had told me, my personal ingenuity, and Horatio's persistence brought me to a kind of obsession, which I was not far from making the unique object of my life.

Then, taking a pencil, I drew, as best I could, model androids with bellies stuffed with cogwheels, in the most various military postures. My friend took possession of them to write roars in bubbles that emerged from their mouths, imagining their language. I did not know yet that circumstances, by rendering me idle, would incite me to realize a project that would have been ridiculous if I had remained devoid of fortune, but which was nevertheless to be deadly.

V

That life, during which Horatio grew in strength and idleness, lasted a little more than a year. As for me, I made such sensible progress that Mr. W. Spool, contrary to his own interests, advised my father to have me pursue my studies in North Walsham, instead of repeating every year what I would have learned the previous year. My father consented to that proudly, but my dear Horatio could not bear the idea that his provider of cannons, lifting-tackle and other trifles—his crew-master, in sum, and the person to whom he did not spare his attachment—might perhaps take his affection elsewhere and leave him with old equipment, for he always needed new items in proportions that would have attained natural dimensions.

"You can't do that, Jim! No, you can't! Aren't we going to build a dinghy that will carry all eight of us and that we're going to arm for war? And when we've constructed it, that diabolical dinghy, we're going to build another for the crew of the *Amphitrite*. That way, we're going to have real boardings instead of climbing those bloody stairs. It's there, Jim, that there'll be a great heap of damnable old mugs! Hurrah! Old red blockhead, rotten sea-cow, hurrah for the launch of the *Redoubtable*, Captain Horatio Gunson!"

I received abundant digs in the ribs, but they did not unleash the anticipated hurrahs. Then, poor Horatio put on a pensive expression and marched back and forth with his hands behind his back. I escorted him back home, after a bathing session in which I had, once more, admired his aptitudes. Swimming under water, he had imitated a whale by blowing water through a reed blow-hole.

"It's necessary, my dear Horatio," I said, finally, some distance from the door. "I can't go against my father, and I ought to think of my future, if yours is mapped out. But I won't forget you, Horatio. I'll write to you every week, and perhaps you will too. You know that you're the person I love most in all the world. I swear to you that, on my side, my friendship for you will only end with life.

Horatio spat on the ground before replying. That, it appears, is what Captain Buckling did when he was about to make a speech, in order to purge the peccant humors that might have obscured his thoughts or embarrassed his fluency. At the same time, however, as we reached the gate, a packet of rags that could be distinguished against the falling mist took human form in the person of an old gypsy woman and loomed up in front of us.

"Bloody old blockhead!" cried Horatio. "Do you take me for a damp chicken that you think you can scare me? Veer to windward and slacken your sheets, or my father's seaman will fire a broadside of twenty-fours, throw the grappling-irons on you and haul you off to Execution Dock!"

But the Bohemian had taken Horatio's hand obsequiously. She caressed the palm, very close to her face, as if she were preparing to kiss it. Horatio let her do it, certain that he had provoked that homage by his rudeness. I stood to one side, considering the old woman's multicolored rags, her aquiline nose, her ashen complexion, her short gray curly hair and the gold rings of unusual dimension that hung from her ears, glittering in the last rays of daylight. *Those are curls*, I thought, *that my father would have been curious to see...*

"My young Lord," said the gypsy, as if, in spite of the gloom and the weakness of her sight, she were able to distinguish the lines of Horatio's hand, which she seemed to be reading, "it's you that I was waiting for at the gate of this house marked by glory. I salute you, I, a poor beggar, a poor wanderer, you, a great voyager, great captain! But what do I see? What mystery? Death striking you twice, and bathing you twice in a barrel of rum. In thirty-and-six years... My young Lord, would you care to give me the other hand?"

"Damn it!" said Horatio. "She's drunk."

And, leaping over the gate with the agility of a topman, he left us both standing there and disappeared into the house.

As the witch and I remained face to face, I took a penny from my pocket in order to excuse Horatio's rep-artee. She was about to take it—she almost touched it—but uttered a loud scream and veiled her piercing eyes with her skeletal hands. I was so frightened by her ges-ture that I ran away, throwing the coin over my shoulder, not without hearing the crack of the valet's whip and the furious barking of the mongrel Poppy in the Pastor's driveway.

I told my father what had happened when I went home. He shrugged his shoulders.

"Understand, Jim, that to become a great captain it's necessary to make an early start—which is to say, to learn something when one is young. Now, your Horatio will never have the slightest idea of a cube root. He scarcely knows how to read. Do you have any suspicion, either of you, in spite of all the mariner's terms you utter at hazard, and in spite of your ripped trousers, like those of old sea-dogs, of what's involved in guiding a ship, let alone a fleet? It's more difficult, you know, than firing cannon-shots. Leave me alone with your Egyptian and your fears of another age. Perhaps it's you, my dear Jim, who'll become a great captain, if you continue to work as you have been. Yes, that old woman, with the aid of the dusk, must have mistaken the hand....

"By the way, Reverend Gunson, whom I went to inform of my decision to send you to North Walsham, also wants to send Horatio there.[15] Although he's a long way behind, his father will ask, as a favor, for him to follow the same course as you. I think that he has more in his head than all the racket of buccaneers that you make in his house, and that Horatio will consent to go away if he finds himself in your company. It's all the same to me. Pull me a pint, Jim."

I was quite content. My dear Horatio wouldn't reproach me. The idea of his dinghy would go out of his head. And I saw him, still my classmate, at North Walsham School, tranquilly nailing the deck of a frigate under the indulgent eye of our common master. Cube roots! The buccaneers of which my father spoke would take Vera Cruz without cube roots, and the pirate Blackbeard would have made spangles of them for his Assyrian beard! Cube roots! That was all right for me, who did not have genius.

At North Walsham, a few days later, I realized immediately that Horatio's good days had been counted—which is to say that the benevolence of Mr. W. Spool,

---

[15] Horatio Nelson was educated at Paston School in North Walsham from 1768-71. The school was eventually amalgamated with the North Walsham High School for Girls to form the present-day Paston College.

and the blissful admiration of our comrades in Danish Camp, were not to be rediscovered there. No one there was astonished that a pupil was the nephew of a Companion of the Garter and a hero of sixty-four cannons. There, many could have given more dazzling proofs of nobility or interest.

Horatio's attire passed for a defect of peasant taste or maternal negligence; I even heard it whispered that he had tailored the ridiculous outfit out of an old captain's uniform. I tried to laud the easygoing manner of Reverend Edmund Gunson and the liberality of his wife, who offered lemonade and bread and butter several times a week to fifteen young rascals of the best society; the naivety of those assertions did not succeed in correcting the comical impression that they took pleasure in conserving of my dear Horatio, which obscured the dignity of his birth.

I had more success with stories of our boardings, and above all with the praise I lavished on the consummate artistry that presided over the construction of our ships, but it was thought that I was exaggerating and wanted to impose. In any case, I had never had the gift of convincing people, and the modesty of my face prevented me from doing so. I understood that it was necessary for Horatio to prove his worth, with the slightest possible delay. I confess that my interest was involved, because I sensed that half of the meager opinion that they had of him was rebounding on my defenseless humility.

That opportunity presented itself the very next day. It was a matter, in accordance with the custom of our schools, of both being chosen as fags by two senior boys, in order to brush their clothes, wax their shoes, bring their breakfast and, in sum, to carry out all the orders that they cared to give us. It was impossible that I should not be my dear Horatio's fag, and yet, two older boys had designs upon us. One, placing his hand on my shoulder, was already commanding me to go and fetch the jujube that he had left on his night-stand, and exhorting me to promptitude in a cavalier tone.

"No, sir," said Horatio, marching toward m, "he won't go, for I reserve to myself alone the right to demand something from him. That's an opinion, sir, that I shall not repeat. In the same way, I shall not repeat that I do not owe anything to anyone here."

With those last words he turned toward the boy who had chosen him. The two boys did not take long to throw themselves upon my dear Horatio. In spite of their age and stature, they found themselves on their backsides in the blink of an eye, and they remained in that posture, delivered to the greatest astonishment, with the result that, looking at their paltry adversary with wide eyes, they did not even think of wiping away the blood that was running from their mouths and nostrils. Horatio waited patiently for someone to emerge from the circle that had formed, but the challenge for which he certainly hoped was not manifest. Then my dear Horatio took me by the arm, and the circle opened in front of us.

"Captain Buckling," said Horatio, "has not taught me boxing for nothing. But shut up, Jim, you bloody old blockhead! I don't want anyone thanking me—you'd look like a coward."

Thus he succeeded in making himself feared, if not respected, and I became his fag without any protest from anyone. I unpacked a mariner's trunk that must have traveled all over the world and served as its master's bed. Having found a large Captain's medallion, thrown pell-mell among the linen, I fixed it above the bed in order that my dear Horatio could contemplate the image of the hero, the only man whose fag he would have wanted to be.

I must say that the face merited contemplation—or, rather, it attracted an attention that fixed upon it for a long time, by virtue of two cheekbones where the painter had not spared the vermilion, and the imperious nose that must have been painted crimson, in accordance with its natural color, by command. I no longer accused my dear Horatio of exaggeration for having sustained that his uncle never drank anything at table but neat rum, and I would have wagered that, among the numerous decorations that ornamented his breast, the most beautiful—an effigy of George II—had been awarded to him by an intemperance society. I imagined in the same colors my own uncle, whom I had never seen, and wished the same distinction for him.

No, I had never seen anything of my uncle, whose death was to play such a large part in my life, while I knew everything about Horatio's uncle: how he walked, how he coughed, how he took snuff, how he spat, how he twirled his rattan cane with a copper ring, how…what do I know? At any rate, I only had to look at Horatio; he copied him, as Reverend Gunson had told my father, to the point that, without ever having sailed, he imprinted an agreeable rolling to his gait and could project a jet of saliva six paces with remarkable frequency and marvelous precision, without a plug of tobacco to justify the abundance or the necessity.

I don't know whether I ought to excuse myself for that digression, since I am writing for my own pleasure, at least with regard to what concerns the most insouciant period of my days. I will also add that I pinned up above the bed a marine chart on waxed cloth, printed in intaglio. He saw thereon, beneath the rose of the winds, the region of the Antilles in the middle of the division of the parallels, all accosted by thundering ships competing without frightening the dolphins. I then placed a miniature of the *Redoubtable*, made by Horatio, on a chest of drawers. I had turned sixty-four cannons for it, as well as a considerable number of pulleys.

No matter how much care I took of his room, though, where he could dream in tranquility before objects dear to his heart, or how much delicacy I showed in reminding him of our memories of Danish Camp, I never succeeded in cheering up my dear Horatio. In that room, where I brought him his shoes in one hand and his breakfast in the other, I surprised him in his nightshirt in front of the *Redoubtable*, scratching his legs, impatient with his lack of occupation, in a sort of bewilderment.

On less bad days I saw him standing on his bed before the marine chart, where pins with colored heads marked navigation routes, ports of call, enemy positions and I know not what conjectures that he did not confide to me. When he read a letter from the Reverend or Mrs. Gunson he moved a few pins and jumped down to dig me in the ribs, calling me, in his joyful voice, his damned Jim, his bloody old blockhead. I was glad to hear him proffer those words, which took me back to a heroic time and a more intimate communion—with the result that in bringing him the post, I wished on the staircase that it contained some good news of Captain Buckling, in order to savor my share of blows.

Among my schoolfellows I took on an air of importance on those days. I would have liked them to ask me questions. In truth, I would not have had anything to say to them, except that the pins had been disturbed on the chart where the honor of England was at stake, and that, given the rudeness of the blows I had received, one could be sure that it was still being maintained by the virtue of cannons and the genius of its captains. Horatio never breathed a word of his secrets.

No, it was no longer the same. His life had been changed and he was sulking. Formerly turbulent, he had become taciturn, formerly idle, he had become hard-working. Or, at least, he worked by derision, learning his lessons like a parrot and writing his impositions, which would have been judged incoherent if I had not taken care to retouch them, in the exact manner that was appropriate not to arouse suspicions—for I feared that, in spite of the Pastor's supplications, he might be sent back, war weary, to follow courses within his scope.

He was still bottom of the class, but with the decision made to remain without glory. Satisfied to have shown himself superior with his fists to the pupils whom he scorned for not having estimated his true worth immediately, he had renounced domination. He no longer commanded exercises, he no longer made war, he almost never uttered those cries that stirred my entrails. If he did utter them, moved by a juvenile force that he had been unable to vanquish entirely, he did not give them the consequences that they advertised. The other pupils, momentarily troubled, like horses waiting for the trumpet, agitated their feet, expecting something, but he left them there in their derisory expectation, hamstrings taut, mouths open, nostrils flared and eyes bulging.

I had compared him to Achilles in his anger; he was still Achilles, but in exile in Skyros; he could have been dressed as a girl. In hours of liberty, as I have said, he did not play, but, taking me by the arm, he paced back and forth like an unfortunate prince in the company of his confidant, From time to time, his hand tightened; I could have cried out in pain. Then I heard him muttering: "Unplug the cannons! Pick up your rods and spikes!" or: "Boarding divisions!" or even: "First rank, fire!" At the last command I always received a forceful shock, which shook my entire body, as if I were the planking under the sudden tension of the tiller-ropes.

Then he fell back into a melancholy mildness appropriate to benevolence. I confided to him then my ambition to construct the automaton in his image about which we had so often talked in my father's house. Then he deigned to take an interest in me and shook my hand silently to thank me for that flattering project. Sometimes, in the course of classes, I gave him drawings when the work left me time—for I was very assiduous. In order to mark the fact that we were still in communion and to keep that fire burning he slipped me sketches of ships or, when he was better disposed, flags drawn with colored pencils. He knew those of all the navies of the globe, as a well-born person knows heraldry, the genealogy of princely houses and other venerable sciences.

It was in vacations, especially, that I measured the full change in my dear Horatio. His scholarly determination, the things he had retained by dint of recounting them and hearing them recorded by our fellows had inclined his parents to greater kindness than before. He was given, among a hundred other gifts, a pony, which he refused with the worst grace in the world; he was seen with amazement to give away the vessels he had constructed. No more combats in the granaries, no more friends, except me.

His daily walk was to go to the sea shore in my company. Sitting on a dune, his knees under his chin and his hands knotted around his compressed legs, he spent entire days contemplating the expanse. From time to time, he took out a telescope and aimed it at a distant sail that his piercing eyesight had enabled him to discern. Often, I saw him pass his handkerchief over the lens, misted by a crushed tear, and immediately spit in scorn at his weakness. But how short of its aim the trajectory of that jet of saliva fell, how much tension it lacked!

I respected in that attitude a great distress, and compared him to Philoctetes on the isle of Lemnos. Timidly, I proposed to him the construction of a dinghy in accordance with the idea he had had, and for the sake of which he had not wanted me to go to school. He replied that we would not have time, and that even if we found enough to make it we would not have time to enjoy it as we wished—and that, besides, he was no longer of an age for childish games!

As for Jack Tar, who had unleashed our sympathies and nourished our dreams of exile, he scarcely spared him a glance. In the forced attention he paid to him I detected a kind of condescension. Far from being offended, however, I felt a bittersweet gratitude in which was mixed, in a low dose, the sentiment that he was drawing away from me.

What could I do or imagine to retain him? Unable to penetrate Horatio's sadness, I searched in my turn for more powerful reasons to be sad and to appear more so than him, in order that he might perceive it and testify some spontaneous mark of affection to me. Why would he not open his arms to me? We could have wept forehead to forehead.

On the contrary, jabbing me more than usual, my dear Horatio called me a bloody old blockhead. He added, in a sarcastic tone, that my subjects of affliction could not equal his, and that, in any case, I had none. He ended up ridiculing my expression and my nose, which is upturned, it seems. Personally, I was not of the grain of great men; I accepted those humiliations as well-deserved, and ornamented by brow with a more modest mourning.

My father, proud of my scholarly success, only wanted to see my gravity as a sign of reflection. Reverend Edmund Gunson, who talked to him one evening about his son's strange condition, fell in with his opinion, and the authors of ours days, for want of being able to affiance us as beings created for one another, married the serpent and the viola da gamba in a fugue that made the windows tremble: a savage concert in which each of them sought to get the upper hand in order to rise as far as our respective merits and catch up with us in the glorious future.

That evening, I pulled a lot of pints and several carafes of fresh water. Horatio, with his fists in his ears, sniffing with anger, pretended to be looking at the pirogues, baidarkas, praus, bazaras, dhows and catamarans, but, as I was soon to discover, his mind was elsewhere, aboard another ship.

VI

Since our entry to North Walsham School, it had been exactly a year and a half that my dear Horatio had been chewing on his bit. One morning, when I went into his room to fulfill my role as his fag, not finding Horatio there, I dropped the shoes and the breakfast. The bed, stripped of sheets, the wide-open window, the absence of the chart and the medallion, and an envelope addressed to me in the shrouds of the *Redoubtable* immediately let me know the truth.

Going to the window I saw the sheets cut into strips, assembled in strands like cables and attached to the sill by a mariner's knot that would have revealed its author. That kind of escape was, in any case, typical of Horatio. Anyone else would have taken less trouble and profited from a propitious moment. Among difficulties, it was always necessary for him to choose the boldest, the most difficult or the most bizarre. I shall have said all in adding that it required five brasses for his feet to touch the ground, and that it was evident from the state of the fresh earth that the body had fallen.

Horatio's letter was conceived in the following terms. I confess that I have given it a structure that it did not have.

Damned Jim,

Do you believe that it would be possible for a fellow like me to remain here any longer? No, you don't believe it. So, profiting from my father's advice that Captain Buckling is expected in Portsmouth, I am taking my leave of you in particular, but no one in general. I would have liked to set fire to this box of lice. It's not so much the fear of being hanged that stopped me as that of roasting you, Jim, in the midst of your brutish sleep. I shall, therefore, ask my uncle to take me aboard his ship. It's something he promised to do when I reached the age of thirteen. I thought I might be able to join him last vacation, but he was delayed by six months—the winds you know, heavy seas, repairs—or else some crew of drunkards had signaled him at sea at that time. That's why you saw me spend the vacation behind my telescope. If you could see me tomorrow, traveling at the compass! I shake your hand, Jim, and leave you as a souvenir the model of the *Redoubtable*. Now that I feel that I'm a man, I have no need of such frivolities. Above all, don't weep like a girl, but give three cheers for the deliverance of your joyful Horatio. Tear up this letter and swallow the pieces. You don't know which way I'm headed, do you? Goodbye, Jim, dear and bloody old blockhead.

Your very affectionate,

Horatio Gunson,
Midshipman.

It was not that I expected it, but that disappearance did not astonish me. I swallowed the letter and went to reveal my discovery, swearing to my great gods that I had no idea what my friend's plans were. In any case, from the scant insistence that they put into questioning me, I judged that they were glad to see the back of him and had no desire to see him return.

Expecting to be brutalized without his protection, and even without invoking that particularly egotistical sentiment, I cannot say how much I missed my dear Horatio. However, I had no fear for him, either of the searches that he would be able to evade, cold, hunger or hesitations in his itinerary, so ingenious and resolute was he. I imagined him on the roads, covered by the marine chart in order to be sheltered from the spring showers. Then, giving full rein to the imagination nourished by reading and illustrations, I imagined an odyssey similar to that in *The Brethren of the Coast*,[16] English and French mixed together when, on floating machines, they descended the cataracts of New Spain and reached Cape Gracias-à-Dios after sixty-eight days of adventures, having passed from the Southern Sea to the Ocean. Planted with palm trees, ebonies and mangroves, inhabited by flame-colored macaws, agoutis, monkeys and caimans, the Suffolk, Essex, Kent and Sussex that he had to traverse changed flora and fauna. The herdsmen and country folk mutated into benevolent Indians with panted faces, their noses pierced by rings of the alloy called caracoly in the stories.

In the company of lost children whom he led to fortune, my dear Horatio lived on maize, potatoes, manioc, bananas, melons, guavas, pineapples or grapes, like Robison Crusoe, but above all on *sappola*, which Raveneau de Lussan[17] describes as a kind of pear with

---

[16] There was no actual book of this title or any of its analogues in the late 18th century, in English or in French, although several have been written since; the reference is to the familiar name of a group of pirates imagined to be loosely associated in a kind of organized crime.

[17] Jacques Raveneau de Lussan (1663-1690) was an adventurer and pirate who published an account of a *Journal du voyage fait en mer du Sud, avec les flibustiers de l'Amérique en 1684 et années suivantes* (1684), which would be historically valuable if anyone thought that it were accurate (although its future setting would strongly suggest otherwise).

crimson flesh, and *avocata*, with is pale green outside and contains, beneath the skin, a kind of snow-white cream, the taste of which is delicious. My mouth started to water; in the end, I envied the lot of the traveler.

Pursuing the action of my hero I saw him in Portsmouth, in the arms of his uncle, the captain, in the midst of a crew sun-tanned by the Tropics, who adopted him enthusiastically, not as the child of the crew but rather as another master. Those rude mariners threw their waxed cloth caps into the air, danced a jig and performed the facetious rituals of Crossing the Line in his honor. The *Redoubtable* raised anchor for a perilous expedition. In the front row of crowd cheering her departure I saw Mr. and Mrs. Gunson with their six offspring, in order of height, all waving handkerchiefs soaked with tears, and the faithful Poppy hurling herself into the sea. Finally, there were the battles in which, saber in one hand and pistol in the other, Horatio led the divisions on to the enemy decks. "Boarding divisions, charge!" I varied that theme infinitely, although my dear Horatio always took the lead and the glory.

Ordinarily, I dreamed about those great deeds during leisure hours, but sometimes also during study, and a slight slackening of my work was observed. As I was believed to be affected by the disappearance on my dear Horatio, and I had conquered the benevolence of my masters, I was given time to pull myself together. Even my fellows, whose bullying I had feared, made advances to me instead of imposing a servitude that would have been painful for me. It would not, either, have been in concordance with their sentiment of deference for the place I occupied at their head, for in truth, I had become the honor of the class. They showed discretion in not enquiring about Horatio, thus informing me that he had been the cause of their coldness toward me, and that they forgave me for having given him an exclusive friendship, since the heart has its reasons. For my part, I was gratified by those homages, but without linking myself with anyone.

After a few weeks having almost recovered my usual stability, I received a parcel on which I recognized the ill-disguised handwriting of my dear Horatio. It was a small packet sent from Portugal, which contained an equinoctial compass, a proportional compass, a chart compass and a marine compass. Never having any nautical problem to resolve, I could only see that consignment as an excuse for giving me his news. Thinking that, after all, it might be found in some hidden location, I lifted up the bottom of the box and found the following letter, into which, as with the last one, I have introduced a relative coherency.

Damned Jim,

I'm aboard the *Redoubtable*, Captain Buckling. It won't be long before I go to sea, but on a ship of the India Company commanded by a friend of my uncle's. It appears that it's necessary for me to learn the business! I hope that it won't take long, and that I'll soon be in the Royal Navy. What do you expect me to become, Jim, with those bloody spice-merchants who can't fire a cannon? I must tell you that I didn't have too much trouble finding a coach after quitting your herring-box, having made friends with a postillion who was a great lover of ale, and to whom I gave the two pounds I had. He hid me under the tarpaulin among the luggage, in case the law was on my heels. Know that my father has consented to my new status. So don't worry about anything and have no fear of being inculpated in complicity. Nevertheless, as someone might open this parcel, and above all to reassure your cockroach courage, I'm hiding my letter, which you'll be astute enough to discover under the instruments, about which you can think what you like. It's all that I have to hand. But you weren't expecting a doll or treats from me. Farewell, dear old blockhead. Try to make sure that when I meet up with you again, I can make something of you—a ship's surgeon, for example, to administer the ipecac.

Your,

Horatio

At the same time, I received a letter from my father touching on the fugitive's escapade. It was, as you will guess, a fine speech calculated to warn me against a similar impulse. I read between the lines the fear that I might do the same, either out of sympathy or with the romantic design of going to join my uncle in India. My father concluded with disdainful considerations on the condition of adventurer, which was, in his mind, that of Captain Buckling, even though the latter belonged to the Royal Navy. Finally, he said a few words about Mrs. Gunson, whose affliction was so great that she never ceased to curse her brother, and he announced that her Reverend husband seemed to have renounced the delights of the serpent, etc., etc. The depiction of that tearful family was more inclined to induce laughter, but my father betrayed his own apprehensions therein, and I wept tears of my own.

It was, therefore, with the idea of reassuring him, of never awakening his alarm, that I went back to work with a new ardor, swearing to surpass myself, but nevertheless torn between two images: his, which I venerated, solitary, anxious and laborious; and that of my dear Horatio on his ship in fabulous regions. Age caused me to draw closer to the former, as if I were becoming increasingly conscious of the fact that one day, I would no longer be confronted by the model.

To abridge these overly particular memories, that came at a time when I was commencing my studies in engineering having succeeded brilliantly in the others. My uncle had preceded my father by a year, leaving him a considerable fortune, which was to revert to me, and had indicated the choice of a profession.

I was greatly affected by the death of my father, whom I would have liked to witness my success, as a tribute to him. Furthermore, I was alone in the world, without affection of any sort. Horatio, whom I had not seen again, was still traveling the seas, and my thoughts still warmed at his memory. What I knew of him I had from the Reverend or his sister Elsie, when I went to spend a few days at the elegant house that my father had built in Danish Camp.

I knew, for example, that Horatio had taken part in a polar expedition, that in his capacity as a midshipman he had spent more than a year in the Indian seas, where the climate had affected his health, and that after various adventures, he had risen to the rank of first lieutenant— which reminded me of the gypsy's oracle.

Although I felt, before the misfortune that struck me, and even more so afterwards, the necessity of choosing an affection, I was never able to resolve myself to it. It is true that I gave myself entirely to my work, and that I only sensed that necessity in the lassitude of my studious nights, but I had a kind of sloth of the heart in becoming fond of anyone, in spite of the melancholy of my isolation. In sum, my natural reserve distanced me from friendship, as certain rebarbative trees turn away birds. It would have been necessary to love me by force and impose upon my attention. An undemanding temperament did not cause me to seek out women. The opportunity to do so did not present itself, or I did not know how to seize it. For those various reasons, therefore, I was devoid of friends and, if not physically a virgin, at least a perfect stranger to amour. Thus, the sentiment that I had nourished for Horatio still inhabited me, with all its juvenile freshness. Like a brightly-colored signet, I found it in leafing through the pages of my days.

Without feeling curious as to their sequel, I lingered over their contemplation, attached by their brilliance. But it seemed that I was able to make them shine by searching for ingenious images, invoked less by my memories of Horatio than by the presence of his little ship in my student room. Placed on the mantelpiece under a dome of glass, it reminded me of him relentlessly, along with all the circumstances of my early youth. What am I saying? It also represented the future—Horatio's future. And the old woman's words sometimes sounded in my ears: "You, great voyager, you, great Captain..." Their incoherent addition seemed to me to be similar to the smoke that surrounded the pythoness, and I could not find any other reason than that ritually to obscure an overly manifest meaning.

I will add that I was complacent in my solitude, which was not without a certain elegiac charm, and that I took refuge in Poetry, for which I had always had a great predilection in spite of the nature of my studies.

Those studies I completed because I had begun them while my father was alive and in that epoch, desirous of not being a burden to him, I counted on providing for my own needs, even though I was fearful of active

life, commerce with human beings and responsibilities—
I, who, admired Horatio so much!

But I had only admired him so much, and still admired him so much, in watching him live in my stead.
There, perhaps, is the true reason for the popular wor-
ship of heroes, without which one would not read as
many books, from Homer to Daniel Defoe, that offer
them to our minds.

As an heir to a sizeable fortune, I no longer thought
about anything but enriching my knowledge, and I
promised myself that I would devote my time to medicine, without ever dreaming of practicing it. Others
might have sought a place in society and founded a family, or kept horses and mistresses, dividing their time between gambling and debauchery, or traveled, collecting
old suits of armor from the time of Arthur from Roman
ruins all over the world, or Mary Stuart wigs—what do I
know? But I repeat, I naturally followed the studious
path into which I had been pushed, and no one, no passion and no adviser, turned me away from it. I therefore
fetched up in medicine, as regular and as solitary as any
poor student.

VII

It was toward the end of my studies that I learned, from Elsie's mouth, of Horatio's return for an indeterminate time.

Twice, he had come to embrace his parents and spend short periods at home, but I had not had the opportunity to see him. This time, indisposed after the Jamaica campaign, and poisoned, it was said, by water in which the branches of the manchineel tree had bathed, he was counting on spending a few months at the waters in Bath.

I surprised in him the garden at Danish Camp, surrounded by his family. He seemed to me scarcely grown, and I would have found him almost the same as before, except that his unpowdered hair was tied in a German pigtail of extraordinary length, and his coat had tails, which he had never worn before. I was about to throw myself into his arms, prey to an inexpressible emotion, but he did not open his. He only held out a burning hand, damp with fever, while the other remained on his cane. At a sign that Elsie made to me, I understood that he could hardly stand up. I noticed then the tremor that agitated him in spasms.

He saw my tears ready to spring forth and the fear in my face.

"Bloody old blockhead," he had the strength to say to me, in a mocking tone that strove to be reassuring. "Bloody old blockhead, it seems that you're going to be a physician. That's what I expected of you?"

A wicker armchair was brought for him, for he had said too much. He let himself fall into it while gazing at me with staring eyes, and, after a long pause, he went on: "And that damned Jack Tar? Are you still thinking about it? This would be the moment, you see, Jim, to set to work. No, I'm not asking you for so much…if you could only make me move my limbs with your invention! A pulley here, a cogwheel there. Ha ha! Bloody Jim, I'd have more confidence in that than in the drugs, you know!"

I received another signal, and kept quiet. Horatio became drowsy a few moments later, abandoning his hand in mine. When a bird started chirping in the foliage, the entire family threw handfuls of gravel in that direction to make it shut up. The Reverend, who had a strange expression, designated the culpable with the stick that shored up his old age. He would have stunned the noisy Poppy with it if Heaven had not put an end to her days long before. The bird flew away to make itself heard elsewhere, and its enemies came back on tiptoe. We all stood there watching Horatio sleep. Dolly and her sister chased the flies away from the vicinity.

What! I said to myself. *In such a refuge of peace and coolness, that sleeping hero, for whom every living thing is being driven away, is still dreaming about the thunder of cannons!* From time to time, Horatio pronounced a few muffled words: the same ones that he shouted in the grain-loft, that he murmured at North Walsham, that he proffered at Fort Charles in Port Royal in Jamaica, the artillery of which had been confided to him. "Lift breeches… Take aim… First and second batteries…fire!"

I saw the eyelids of the six brothers and sisters fluttering, and Reverend Gunson's fist clench on his crow's-beak cane. As for me, informed by a few letters from Horatio to the warlike Elsie, I imagined him commanding his gunners, standing on the parapet, scorning the grapeshot, or charging barefoot under the fire of Spanish swivel-guns to take possession, in a matter of minutes, of Saint-Barthélemy island, or even before Fort San Juan, in a pestilential marsh under the soaring flight of *gallinazos*, those American vultures that tear the wounded apart.

At length, beside my dear Horatio, inanimate but articulating inconsequential words, the idea of the automaton, which he had caused to be reborn after several years of forgetfulness, hooked itself on to me like a child to his father, whom he fears losing again. I soon gave all my attention to it. My knowledge of mechanics and anatomy came together in those moments, and the waxen face of the sleeper could only maintain the reverie into which I had fallen.

I realized, therefore, in thought, an android of a new kind, in which the principal muscles, nerves, tendons and even the circulatory apparatus would be copied from nature. It happened that I had just found a substance that was still little-known, or at least devoid of usage: a kind of gum extracted from *Ficus primoides* and *Collophora utilis*,[18] which my uncle had attempted to transplant from America to India, specimens of which I had examined among the bric-à-brac of his souvenirs. I passed on to

---

[18] Both of these species are cited in the same sentence in Jules Verne's novel *Un Capitaine de quinze ans* (1878; tr. under various titles, including *Dick Sands, the Boy Captain*), but do not appear to have any existence elsewhere. Although *Ficus* is a prolific genre of plants, *Collophora* is an obscure arthropodan genre whose name was seemingly misappropriated by Verne.

other technical details, of an invention as sudden as it was complete.

I could no longer stand still, however, nor maintain my silence. I needed to walk, to reply to the questions and arguments of an imaginary listener, and, finally, to become enthusiastic with him. I therefore let go of my dear Horatio's hand, the pulse of which I could sense decreasing, and took my leave of his entourage, assuring them that I would go to see him in Bath, for which he had decided to depart the following day in spite of the seriousness of his condition.

In reality, I had no faith in the influence of the manchineel, and concluded that it was quite simply a recurrent fever of paludal origin. At the gate, I advised his parents, who were talking to me in whispers, to give him quinine.

Having reached home again, after soliloquizing along the way, ablaze with my subject, I gathered together my uncle's papers and searched for the address of an associate that he had had in Bombay, and who had notified us of his death. I wrote to him immediately asking him to procure for me, at any price, a considerable quantity of the substance on which my invention depended. Then, having sent my letter via a domestic who looked after the house during my long absences, I searched my father's writings and plans for everything dealing with his mechanical research in the time of his great project—the project whose lack of resources had ended up with Jack Tar.

To tell the truth, I only consulted those memoirs out of filial piety, and to place my enterprise under a tutelary shadow. I spent several hours in that, astonished by their development and their precision. That was sufficient for me to put them in a portfolio in order to take them away and study them at leisure, for I still required another six months to obtain my qualification as a doctor.

Invited by the calm, the distance and the silence, I made the resolution to retire to that place without keeping anyone up to date with what I was doing, and even to sack the domestic in order to have the least possible importunate society. With that aim, I revised the house from top to bottom, affecting a specific destination to each room, always with a view to my future work. One might have thought that my father had foreseen everything, including a huge wardrobe with cupboards, which I assigned for the placement of anatomical specimens, determined to copy nature to the maximum possible extent, as if to have direct recourse to it. I laughed at the idea of the maidservant coming face to face with those funereal discoveries, and all the dangerous stupidities that she might recount—which confirmed me in my resolution to be alone.

I went down into the cellar; there I found a provision of all things good to drink, of which my father had been so fond, and which had hastened the death of my uncle, some in bottles and others in casks and barrels. "Pull me a pint, Jim," I murmured, striking a full barrel. Alas, if only I had pulled pints for my father for a few more years in the back room of the village shop, I would not be where I am now!

Finally, I was a doctor. Already, my old and new books had preceded me to my house, with all the materials necessary to my work. I had also procured the most improved apparatus, in order not to have dealings with anyone; in any case, the benevolent apprenticeship that I had completed with my father at an early age, either working myself or watching him at work, and especially my studies in engineering, would have permitted me to rival, after a few weeks of practice, the best artisans in the realm. I will add that my correspondent in Bombay had replied to me by return of post, placing himself at my disposal. He also said that a variety of my *Ficus* was spread throughout continental India and that it would have been an unnecessary expense to try to be the first to transplant it.

My father's work spared me a great deal of initial exploration and irresolution, but my plan soon diverged from his. What occupied me the most was the question of the speaking machine that he had approached in accordance with his contemporaries and perhaps his predecessors.[19] The majority made use of an artificial glottis, or even a perforated copper sleeve with raised studs, like those in music boxes. My discovery was quite different. If I had had the leisure to exploit it, I would have astonished the world. I made an impression of the human voice on a cylinder of gum, which I kept provisionally in a state of consistency resembling that of wax. I hardened it thereafter by a chemical and thermal treatment. A needle passed over the impressions that the wax had received and its retained vibrations were reproduced by means of an amplifying apparatus. But the details and the plan of my speaking-machine will be found in the treatise that I shall append to this history of my life. It contains everything related to the android. You will therefore tolerate the succinctness of the explanations I give here.

I took more than a year to construct and perfect the machine, more delicate and more precise than a clock.

---

[19] Author's note: "The idea of the phonograph is encountered in Cyrano de Bergerac's *États et empires de la Lune*, *Oeuvres*, 1709, p, 109. [Translator's Note]."

As I had designed it to reproduce the voice of my dear Horatio, I thought it amusing to make use of his customary phrases such as "good day," "go to bed," "shut up, bloody old blockhead," and the commands of the battery, boarding and navigation, as well as the atmospheric or seasonal remarks that play a large part in the phlegmatic conversations of my country: "Fine weather today," "It's going to rain tomorrow," or the other way around. I made arrangements in such a way that, with the pressure of a finger, I could obtain some exclamation or opportune phrase, and I imitated Horatio's voice closely enough to be mistaken when I had to record it.

I amused myself so much with that pleasantry that I could not help allowing Horatio's family to hear his voice. I put the machine in my pocket and went to see them, under the pretext of obtaining news of the mariner, having only seen him at rare intervals and not having kept anyone informed about the nature of my research.

When Horatio's voice was heard there was a general burst of laughter instead of the amazement that I expected. No one looked for Horatio behind the doors or in the next room, but they assured me that I was an excellent ventriloquist. For the first time, in spite of my neglectful attire, Elsie and her sister testified culpable sentiments toward me, although they only expressed them hurriedly and with their gaze.

What! I had been misunderstood, or had made the mistake of not making myself known. And they suspected me of other hidden virtues, by which I might confound those who had not estimated me at my true value. Finally, I distinguished some suspicion in the interest that I had just awakened in the hearts of those young women. My self-esteem as an inventor was not very satisfied, and I had to get over it while not ceding to its impulsions; the most serious would have been to place the machine in another room and thus convince everyone that I was nor speaking by artifice. Someone would have been sure to discover the secret that I wanted to keep hidden with ridiculous obstinacy.

But I am anticipating events.

Absorbed by my invention, I had allowed some time to pass since my visit to my dear Horatio. So, after three months, while still a student, I went to Bath. I learned that, impatient to solicit an employment, he had left for London as soon as he had recovered from his illness, and that, promoted to captain of the ship that had taken him to India, he was taking soundings in the Danish sea. I was desolate, not knowing when I would see him again, and I would have liked to obtain permission from him to take exact measurements of his face and body. However, would he have had the patience to let me do it, and would he not have told me to go to the devil? A garment he had left behind in his precipitation furnished me with approximate measurements. I was assumed to be a tailor and I allowed them to believe it.

After the excursion to Reverend Gunson's house that I have related, I commenced the construction of the android with a trial of the circulatory system for which I molded the network of arteries and veins, not in its entirety, but that which is apparent at the body's surface. The heart, which was to be filled with a colored liquid of a density and viscosity analogous to that of blood, required greater application. Required to function like a living organ, it was linked to a pneumatic apparatus disposed in the thoracic cage instead of lungs. The gum that I have already mentioned furnished the material. I consumed so much, with so much wastage, that I wrote to

Bombay for a new order almost immediately after receiving the last one.

The preparation of the anatomical specimens destined for molding took up a considerable time in itself, not to mention the perpetual trips to obtain them. I dare not count the number of professions that I exercised simultaneously; I am still astonished at having succeeded in them all by myself during the five long years that I devoted to that phase of my work. But I am abridging in saying that it cost me a further eleven years, during which, except for the space of my encounters with Horatio, I lived in absolute indifference with regard to my fellow men, and also scented espionage and malevolence prowling around me, which contributed to rendering me even grimmer.

Thus, I no longer had anything human about me, in the sense that the world attaches to the term. I scarcely spoke other than by signs in the shops, pointing at the foodstuffs I desired, and I turned my back, grunting at the importunate individuals who asked me questions. Street-urchins pointed at me, laughing, and I often heard myself called a "ventriloquist." I had allowed my beard to grow, and I lived unconcerned in threadbare garments; I slept under a blanket, more often than not fully clothed. I would have been very different had the needs of amour inclined me, if not to be seductive, at least not to be repulsive, but I did not sense that anxiety, entirely given over to my work, and domestic labors, albeit reduced to a minimum.

When I was content with my work I went down to the cellar. "Pull me a pint, Jim." And I drank my ale in the fallow garden, under the arbor where my father drank. Like evil genii, stray cats came to rub their itches against my legs.

With the Cretan coin that you will perhaps recall, the *Redoubtable* under its glass bell, and Jack Tar, moving punctually of his own accord, my good days were perpetuated. By turns, memories and hopes enveloped me like an opium smoke that veiled the world from me. The viola da gamba, in its corner, sounded its profound and seductive notes for a long time beneath my fingers, but the strings broke or slackened, and I neglected to tighten or tune them.

Sometimes, in the evening, I was afraid of my work: those muscles and venous networks laid out on tables, those tibias and femurs, those macabre residues! I was apprehensive that, when it was finished, that parody of God's creation might appear sacrilegious to me, that I might be cursed by the very mouth that I had articulated. The physician got the upper hand again; I prepared myself a tisane and threw myself on to my meager bed in order to ward off those terrors, which originated from fatigue, by means of sleep.

Such was my life, with an income that made me the richest man in the region, and which I dispersed on the gum of *Ficus primoides, Cenopia peltala* and *Collophora utilis*, on old bones, instruments, metals and an incredible, repulsive and derisory bric-à-brac.[20]

---

[20] *Cenopia* is not a natural genus, but *Cecropia peltata* [snakewood, or the trumpet tree] is a fast-growing plant now renowned as a troublesome invader.

VIII

The second time I saw Horatio again it was a few months after the peace of Versailles. Without having returned to the priory, but having encountered its residents on several occasions, I knew from them the poor state of his health after a sojourn in Quebec. In spite of my desire to talk about my invisible friend I had not replied to invitations to come and receive news of him and show off my talent as a "ventriloquist."

I therefore found my dear Horatio in the same conditions of precarious health, but he was counting on making amends by returning promptly to France with a certain Captain Macnomore. His great desire was to learn to speak French fluently—for military purposes, for he never foresaw any others. He had been living all summer in London, in a small house in Salisbury Street, scarcely giving any sign of life to his family, so I was not astonished that our relative neighborhood had not incited him to write to me.

Mentally, he was still the same, although enriched by memories of war and travels, on which, however, he did not put much stress, not being loquacious. He reverted more often, with pleasure, to his intimacy with His Royal Highness Prince William, the sailor prince, and his introduction to the court, on which he based high hopes for his promotion. Everyone looked at him open-mouthed.

Finally, he deigned to ask about my work, which, his relatives had told him, caused me to live alone, and he was very enthusiastic to hear the imitations I was presumed to have made of him. I was able to take him aside to tell him about my speaking-machine and my project, asking him to keep the secret. He listened to me with amazement, and could not believe that I would one day realize those childish projects, which, he affirmed, he had never taken very seriously. I even saw that he was beginning to consider me as a madman, but I gave him so many proofs of the reality of what I was saying that he ended up believing me.

I would have liked to persuade him to come and see and put his finger on it—my most secret desire was to record his voice—but he gave the excuse of an imminent departure. In fact, I was wearying his mind, incapable of long attention to any subject other than himself. I would also have liked to make rigorous measurements of his face. Not finding the opportunity to ask him in the proximity of witnesses so indiscreet that they had spread my reputation as a ventriloquist, I contented myself with fixing the proportions in my memory.

We spent the evening together. I evoked our memories: my father's shop, Mr. W. Spool's school, the construction of the little ships, our combats in the barns, and the escape from North Walsham. He listened to me, nodding his head, but his thoughts were in the future, always in advance. Nevertheless, he and his family received as a tribute the flood that rose from my heart, in which so many melancholy wrecks were floating.

The Reverend, who missed the musical evenings, related a memory of my father, and everyone shed tears over the name of Mrs. Gunson, whom the Lord had recalled to his bosom some time ago. The valiant Captain Buckling, dead, it was said of his old wounds, but most of all of having been too fond of rum, unleashed a salvo of a hundred and one dabs of the handkerchief. In spite of the mystery that surrounded me and the curiosity of the young women whose hearts I had once stirred, there was no question of me, who had refused to make myself heard again. That was because I was not Horatio Gunson! He was taking Buckling's place. I did not take offense, though, as I was working for his glory, and already judged him to be the greatest man in the land.

Our third meeting, after an interval of four years, was of longer duration. The Captain of the *Hylactor*, he had just got married.[21] Devoured by fever, menaced by consumption, he had retired to Danish Camp. The fevers were not alone in undermining him, but also various subjects of anger, some against speculators in India, others against the Admiralty, yet others against the Americans, whom he continued to call "rebels," and even against the Treasury. I had never heard him curse and swear in that fashion, about all the bloody blockheads in the universe.

After a time however, that anger died down. It was succeeded by a rage for hunting. Gripped by that destructive fury, he fired in all directions, without bothering to shoulder his weapon or take aim, at anything that he saw moving or fleeing. That great public danger, however, only killed one mother partridge, which was trailing her wing in a furrow in order to deflect the hunter from her brood. In order to commemorate such a miracle, I was given the bird to stuff. Not only did I stuff it but I also made it flap its wings, move its head and call out in a plaintive voice.

---

[21] It was in 1787, when Nelson was in command of the *Boreas*, that he married Fanny Nisbet. In 1788, as a reservist on half pay, they settled in Norfolk for a while. He was not recalled to service until January 1793, shortly before the French declaration of war on 1 February, when he was given command of H.M.S. *Agamemnon*.

Naturally, I accompanied him in the greater number of these excursions, the fatigue of which exhausted us. He went to sleep one day under some chestnut trees. I took advantage of his slumber to take the measurements of his face so long desired and to check those furnished by the garment forgotten in Bath. While trying to make sure of the distance from the nose to the upper lip I woke him up abruptly. Doubtless mistaking me for an Indian, he gripped my neck and would have strangled me if, among the words I was stammering, he had not been struck by that of "automaton."

"It's for the automaton, Horatio, for the automaton!"

My life was saved, but Horatio's anger turned against my work.

"When will you have finished, then, bloody Jim, you old blockhead, with this thing with which you keep battering my ears? No, I don't want to see it and I won't listen to your jabbering machine. I'll go when it's all finished. Perhaps that promise will hurry you up. Then you'll abandon the imbecilic life you're leading and come work for me in the capacity of physician and secretary, since you're a scholar, You wouldn't believe, damned Jim, how difficult it is for a mariner to write letters and reports!"

During the five years of that sojourn on Horatio's part my works made a great deal of progress. He was obstinate in not wanting to visit me, sticking to the promise he had made. I took advantage of his presence to model a mask of him from memory, incessantly retouching it until the resemblance was scrupulous. His company, and sometimes that of his wife, had brought me back to a more normal existence. I no longer plunged into melancholy and no longer experienced nocturnal terrors, I had a decent exterior, I slept in a real bed, and order had returned to my house, where I hoped in spite of everything for a surprise visit. In sum, I no longer distinguished very well between amity and the sentiment that my work incarnated—the work that was my only reason for being in the world.

During the winter of 1792, my dear Horatio, no longer able to hold still, begged for any command whatsoever to be confided to him, even a dredger. He obtained the *Menelaus*, with sixty-four cannons, and was sent to the Mediterranean. Since the time that he had been gripped again by nostalgia for the sea and the somber desire for combat, I had rediscovered the Horatio of North Walsham: the one who walked around digging his fingernails into my arm and muttering between his teeth. This time it was: "Westminster Abbey or Victory!" As for me, I did not take long to fall back into the negligence of my former life, especially when Lady Gunson retired to Bath with her sisters-in-law and her father-in-law the Reverend, whom age had crippled with rheumatism.

I did not, however, remain without news of him. Lady Gunson wrote to me from time to time to make me party to his nascent glory and his lightning progress on land and sea. I shall not repeat facts consecrated by renown and which plunged me continually into the intoxication of pride; I was the friend of the great man of war who was holding in check the French, to whom he had vowed a common execration, royalists as well as republicans, and my work, instead of being a gratuitous and personal success, became collective and patriotic.

When I learned that he had lost his right arm and eye, however, I was less affected for his sake than that of my android. Should I mutilate it in the same fashion, to immortalize a glorious sacrifice? I hesitated for some time, and made the decision that I would ensure the integrity of my machine.

In 1798, I went to see the hero of the Canaries as soon as he arrived in London, covered with honors, a knight of the Order of the Bath, the victor of three cities and four naval battles. But he had suffered cruelly from a ligature of waxed thread, which could not be detached without irritation. Lady Gunson and I spent three months by his bedside, helping to change his dressings every day, and doing it ourselves. He conceived a higher opinion of me in consequence and reiterated his offer to take me aboard his ship, for, the ligature finally having been removed and the wound scarred over, he was already dreaming of leaving again. But I was nearing the end of my work, to which I assigned another two years in order to regulate it and give it his appearance.

"Well, bloody Jim," said Horatio, "in two years I'll have lost the other arm and perhaps both legs. I'll have the greatest pleasure in seeing myself as I was."

I had managed to convince him that in the meantime, I could build him an articulated arm, which orthopedics had not yet realized. Entirely given over to his passion, however, he rejoined the English fleet at the head of a squadron of three ships of the line, four frigates and a sloop. I was not to see him again until four years later, after the battle of the Nile, which almost brought his popularity to a peak. He only stayed for three months, like the last time, before going to fight in the Baltic. I did not know how to convince him to come to see me. During his perpetual expeditions, I ended up like Penelope waiting for the return of Ulysses. Without returning my android to the workshop, I took advantage of it to make incessant improvements.

When I found nothing more to revise, and my dear Horatio was sailing in the Mediterranean, where he had obtained command of the fleet, I sat the automaton down on a sofa in my drawing room. Face to face with him, I contemplated him smoking a pipe, legs crossed, his arms passed behind its back, with the most satisfied expression in the world.

"Horatio," I said to him, sometimes, "would you like Jim to pull you a pint?"

"Yes, you bloody old blockhead," Horatio replied.

And we drank. Or, as he could also eat and digest, like Vaucanson's duck, I even offered him dinner. The most difficult thing was to activate the speaking machine in such a fashion that the answers corresponded to the questions. I cannot hide the fact that Horatio often sent his interlocutor to bed or responded entirely inaptly, either by means of terrible commands or by atmospheric remarks. But how he resembled him, even in that! And how the authority of his gestures and his voice would have imposed silence on impressionable or trifling individuals!

I think that the same can be said of all great men or those who obtain an ascendancy over us. The disturbance into which their speech or presence throws us permits us not always to comprehend them. However, we have the certainty that what they are saying cannot be other than true, benevolent and profound. Let those who have not been able to have that experience place themselves in the skin of a great man by addressing themselves to their dog to say anything whatsoever, even insults; they will see the animal furrow its brow in an understanding manner and wag its tail in pleasure and gratitude. I was, therefore, not affected beyond measure by a state of affairs that I could not remedy, and which would only have passed for a defect in the judgment of superficial minds.

At other times, I went for a stroll arm in arm with Horatio, when skillfully disposed touches commanded his speech and movements. We went up the stairs together; we went down into the cellar to pull pints. There, when I had had a little to drink, intoxication amplified my illusion, and we staggered to the bower, singing the Mallard song, the only one I had ever been able to remember. What fine concerts we gave the summer moon!

I was so glad to have finished the work that had taken all my youth and led me into middle age, that I was no longer apprehensive of being cursed by his mouth or thunderstruck by a jealous God. In brief, I felt liberated, no longer waiting for anything but the veritable Horatio in order to have him admired, to exhibit him to the acclaim of the nation and perhaps offer him to some museum.

Preserved from the fatigues and skepticism of the forties by exemplary conduct, I disposed the future to my taste. For the first time, I thought about amour, about marriage, about great India, where I could go to honor the ashes of my uncle and talk about him with the children of his associate, who was also dead. But I was too enthusiastic about the liberty to which I had returned, and life, which I only glimpsed in its finest light, to pause for a moment at Horatio's proposition that I serve as his secretary and physician, on a ship where one was risking losing everything, to the wind, gunfire and the waves, humans and the sea in conspiracy.

IX

On 18 August 1805, my dear Horatio disembarked from the *Triumph* in Portsmouth, abandoning the pursuit of the French fleet, which had re-formed since the disaster of the Nile. In vain he had solicited it as far away as the mouths of the Orinoco. Then he had returned to sail along the north-west coast of Ireland, where the conjectured that the undiscoverable fleet, after a feigned destination, might rally with that of Brest in order to favor a disembarkation. When he was certain that he was mistaken, therefore, he came back to his home port, and retired to Burton Place in Suffolk, not far from Ipswich. It was there that he had acquired an estate during his last visit, in 1803.

Now, is it necessary to recall that the private life of my dear Horatio was perhaps not exempt from all criticism? In the epoch that I have just mentioned, he had installed at Burton Place a former adventuress, the famous Nelly Hackman, who, after having served as a tavern maid, had married an old lord and had shone by virtue of her beauty in a court in Italy, where she was well-known for her dissipation and misbehavior. I could not reproach my dear Horatio for having played the role of Antony, but rather for having pushed the scandal to the extent of lodging under the same roof as Lord and Lady Hackman; having cast off of his legitimate wife; and finally, for having obliged his father, by fallacious arguments to bow down before such striking disorder. But Lord Hackman had died two years before and the Reverend Gunson, aged seventy-nine, had taken the road to Heaven in his company.

I would not make allusion to these things if, from now on, my story were not partly dependent on them.

Informed by the newspapers—for, since the assurance of her misfortune, Lady Gunson maintained silence and keep her distance—I wrote to Burton, which was only twenty-five miles distant, in order to obtain a meeting with my dear Horatio and more ample news. While awaiting a response I brought elegance into what I had only put order and comfort, artfully disposing the furniture, the carpets, the engravings and the paintings that my father had accumulated, without forgetting my uncle's panoplies, where assegais, arrows and hatchets radiated around bucklers.

I burned the greater part of my materials, relegated the rest to the attic, and returned each room to its veritable destination, garnished with everything that suited it. I then supervised the tidying of my garden, shaved off what remained of my beard and bought some fine cloth from a draper. Although I had not yet engaged a numerous domestic staff, desiring to keep my secret until the day so long desired, my house was pleasant and clean, and its master becoming, able to contemplate himself in mirrors with satisfaction.

Eventually, I received a note from my dear Horatio. He announced his visit for the first week in September. I engaged a pretty hussy to serve us and ordered a dinner such as I had never eaten. The day before, I locked the fake Horatio in the drawing room, seated on a sofa, and promised myself, for the following day, the greatest pleasure of my life.

Not knowing how to spend my evening in such solemn expectation, I went to numb my impatience in the taverns where I had never been seen before. Mingled with the youthful idlers were a few of my childhood comrades, whom I scarcely saluted: the sons of the dairyman, the baker, the herbalist, the harness-maker, the scrap metal dealer, etc. I played cards and lost two hundred guineas in very little time. I could have hugged those dear fellows, although they were cheating blatantly. Was I not to have the honor of receiving at my table the victor of the Nile, the greatest Englishman in England? To each his compensation.

That was a great imprudence on my part, which might have cost me much dearer than two hundred guineas. In fact, the reality was no better...

So, I had talked so much about Horatio's arrival that, on taking the air the following morning I found the trees along the road garlanded with festoons, and groups of gawkers dressed in their best clothes, who were waiting for the admiral's arrival five hours in advance. I feared speeches by the mayor and other representatives of the authority full of their importance, as well as the obligation to invite them to my table, not to mention the imbecile crowd that would invade my garden, deafening us with music and cheers...

Nevertheless, within that disagreeable importunity shone for me the hope of showing off my masterpiece and receiving a portentous praise. The dread that they might destroy it by palpating it and carrying it in triumph immediately obscured that ray of sunlight, and I fell, behind my closed windows, with their curtains drawn, into the most painful distress. I could have wished that an axle on Horatio's carriage might break, that the horses would lose their shoes—in brief, that he would not arrive until after nightfall, or not at all. I kept my ears open regardless to every sound from outside, among which the chatter of the idlers was not calculated to appease my anguish.

Finally, those sounds decreased. The appointed hour was long past. My eyes fixed on Jack Tar, I thought that my wishes had been granted, and that Horatio was not going to arrive.

As I was about to sit down at table I heard the sound of a carriage and that of street-urchins running after it uttering shrill cries. I ran to greet my illustrious visitor and help him to get down. Already, however his faithful Allen had bounded from his seat, caressed the brats rudely with the cord of his whip, lowered the foot-step and supported his master with his vigorous arm.

While I embraced the latter, the old sailor explained that he had made a long detour to avoid the crowd, for it was necessary to spare the horses and His Honor. I therefore led His Honor toward the house, expressing to him all my gratitude and joy, while Allen, with a naval celerity and precision, was unharnessing the rig in the gloom near the small perron, already drawing water in canvas buckets and paying out cord between his legs without interrupting his conversation.

"Shut up, damn it!" his master shouted at him. "You weary me more than all Portsmouth put together. And you, dear bloody old blockhead! To table, for I have the hunger of a Carib and the thirst of Admiral Olfert Fischer, the greatest liar in Denmark, with which the devil can torture the body and the soul! The advantage of sailing, you see, Jim, is being able to cover twenty-five miles without swallowing dust."

We went in. The maidservant, rendered stupid by respect, dusted my dear Horatio down in the vestibule, dropping the brush frequently. Then I noticed all the glo-rious decorations that bedeck the breast of heroes and are reserved for official ceremonies. I touched one, enriched by diamonds. It depicted a palm-tree emerging from the waves, between a damaged ship to the right and a ruined battery to the left, the whole surmounted by a Latin motto taken from an ode by Jortin: *Palmam qui meruit ferat.*[22]

I also noticed that my dear Horatio was wearing a sword with his dress uniform. The thought occurred to me that he had only dressed in that fashion to honor me in a circumstance that I had been preparing for seventeen years—but I immediately recalled that he had always affected a vestimentary singularity and concluded that he probably thought it more becoming. So, I promised myself that I would dress my android in the same manner, procuring or having copies made of all the sparkling plaques and medallions that veritably fascinated the gaze.

The maid served us, spilling the sauces on my jacket, at which I dared not protest. But I thought I saw, in her blush and the disorder of the kerchief around her neck, that old Allen's hand had already found the route to victory.

Meanwhile, my dear Horatio ate with a hearty appetite the food cut up in advance in the parlor, and served himself generously with drink using his left hand. As for me, I kept up with him, a trifle embarrassed by his preoccupied expression. My embarrassment, I must say, further increased the great apprehension of having to show him the automaton when the meal was over, all the more so as he had not yet made any allusion to it. Ought

---

[22] "Let him who earns the palm bear it." From *Lusus Poetici* (1722) by the theologian John Jortin. Nelson adopted it for his coat of arms when he received his Barony after the Battle of the Nile.

I to say that he did not even perceive that the dishes, having waited so long, were scarcely edible?

Finally, when he was sated, he said: "Old Jim, I had to tear myself away from Lady Hackman in order to come. That's because I have to leave again in two days. Can you imagine that the fleet for which I was searching the coasts of America and Ireland is anchored off Cadiz? I need to go and beat it, so there'll be no more mention of it. But I have an evil presentiment, Jim, for my fatigue is extreme.

"In truth, I've only come in order to take you with me. You, who remove dressings so well, will be my physician, you blood-stained old blockhead, during this brief campaign. Afterwards, we'll come back to Burton Place together, where you'll live with us, what? You'll see how good and charming my dear Nelly is...

"You have nothing to say, Jim! Shut your damned mouth! Anyway, my arrangements are made; His Majesty has been informed. My officers have been informed. Your cabin is ready, next to mine, on the *Triumph*, which is at Portsmouth. Shut up, I tell you! You won't have to do anything. We're leaving again this evening, in the mist, for Burton Place. Enough! It's your Admiral who's talking to you..."

The blood was buzzing in my ears. I looked at Horatio with imploring eyes, in which he saw tears shining.

"Yes, enough, Jim!" Horatio went on. "Get rid of that imbecile expression. You imagine that I can disturb myself to contemplate your damned clock-striker? No, you can't imagine that. Come on, send for something better! Let's drink a glass, by God! And show me your good old face of old. Hurrah, bloody Jim, for the King of England! Hurrah for the *Triumph*! Hurrah for Admiral

Horatio Gunson! Hurrah for that bloody old idiot, Doctor Jim!"

I was obliged to clink glasses with him and drink as he wished, for his power of command was such that one could not resist him. He made toasts one after another so rapidly that my head spun, and I was no longer concerned about anything, feeling a wild enthusiasm for my nation and a great tenderness for my memories.

With even more abundance than at the Priory I talked about my father, the Reverend, Captain Buckling, Jack Tar, the *Redoubtable*, North Walsham—what do I know? I ended up drunk on words. However, I don't know what thought slid more powerfully into my speech, which encouraged me to play the comedy and assured me that fortuitous circumstances or some versatility on Horatio's part would free me from the constraint of departure. Nevertheless, sincere in my words and my gestures, I could have protested my sincerity without lying. I was in the same state of mind as an actor narrowly wedded to his role, laughing or shedding tears while knowing that it isn't real.

In the meantime the poorly-muffled laughter of Allen and the maid emerged from the parlor. As I thought them fully occupied and our meal was over, I proposed to my dear Horatio that I show him his double, apologizing for the simplicity of his costume. He consented. I asked him for a moment to animate my masterpiece, in order that he could see and hear himself in the animation of life. I therefore went into the locked drawing room, where I had never received a guest so desperate to satisfy his hunger, and then I called my dear Horatio joyfully, in a voice that seemed to come from my childhood, so much did it express, involuntarily, ardor and mischief.

"Good day, bloody old blockhead!" said the double, putting down his churchwarden pipe and standing up, his hand extended.

"It's perfect!" Horatio replied, simply. "And the hand is even soft and warm, by Jove! But that's no longer my case—I always have a fever. Say, damned Jim, what a good joke it would be to send this Horatio to the morose Lady Gunson, while the real one..."

"Horatio, I beg you!" I said. "You shouldn't joke about a state of affairs that the whole world deplores, perhaps even you..."

To attenuate such an audacity, having given the automaton the attitude of command, I made him reel off the cannon maneuvers, as we had practiced them in the barn of the presbytery. Horatio laughed wholeheartedly. I laughed at seeing him laugh, but the pride of my success made me shed tears at the same time. All the images of my laborious career presented themselves pell-mell to my mind with an extraordinary rapidity, and a kind of jubilant voice sang within me: *This is this moment so much desired for half a lifetime!*

Then, I was astonished that nothing more happened, and I felt myself teetering on the edge of an abyss. Was that it, then?

"Tell me, Jim," said Horatio, "before telling me about the mechanism of this fellow that resembles me more than my brothers, have you thought about teaching him to box? Perhaps you remember, Jim, that day at North Walsham..."

"Certainly," I replied. "It can do anything a man can do. Here, Horatio, parry or strike: you'll find a solid adversary at the ready..."

I recognized clearly in that my childhood friend's destructive mania. Even so, I, who had feared the roughness of the populace, made the sacrifice of my work at that moment, although poor Horatio seemed to me very debilitated.

Horatio placed a few blows. He stepped side to avoid those that his double launched at him blindly. At every touch there was a "Cursed lascar!" a "Bloody old blockhead!" a "Damned sea-cow!" or some other insult from his repertoire. Meanwhile, my automaton, steady on his feet, continued imperturbably. Tipped back on the sofa, but ready to receive the automaton in my arms, I laughed at all the trouble that Horatio was taking; his sweat was beginning to bead.

Suddenly, I saw him stagger under a resonant shock, his hand against his breast, and collapse on to the parquet like a soft mass, scarcely rendering a dull thud. I continued to laugh for some time at the discomfiture of the imprudent fellow and the countenance of his vanquisher, who continued to strike the empty air.

"Get up, Horatio," I said, finally, having approached him. "We'll drink a good glass and play a joke on old Allen!"

I could hear the latter and the maid recommencing their fun and games. The idea occurred to me to interrupt their frolics with a summons. Horatio and I would hide behind the curtains in order to appear at the right moment and fill them with confusion. Looking down at Horatio's face, however, I was frightened by his pallor, and even more so by a thin trickle of blood that was running from the corner of his mouth. On my knees, suddenly sobered up, I took his hand. The pulse was no longer beating. I opened his shirt; the heart was giving no indication. By the bruise on the skin I saw that the blow had struck him there. I raised the lid of the sound eye, and the eye did not deceive me.

Although I was confronted by the irremediable, I picked up a spoon, opened the jaws effortfully, making a gap in the teeth, and attempted tractions of the tongue, calling upon the aid of my handkerchief, which was reddened by a clot of blood contained in the mouth. That clot ended up sliding on to the parquet, after having stained the shirt.

What more could I do? Call Allen? But I had killed the national hero, my best friend—my only friend—and I would be delivered to the wrath of an entire people. I glimpsed the police, the crowd armed with stones, Allen himself squeezing my throat in his rude hands, which were caressing the maidservant...

I tried to bleed him, but only found a thick, dark, semi-coagulated blood. Why did madness not fill me with vociferations? Or, rather, why did I not kill myself? No, to begin with, I remained in a profound bewilderment, still kneeling, without a quiver, without a tear.

However, the continued movement of the automaton, the rustle of clothing, reminded me of his presence. Seized by a violent anger, as if I were dealing with a living being, I abused him verbally. Then I climbed on to the sofa in order to seize a hatchet from a panoply, in order to smash him to pieces.

As I was about to strike, I had an idea, which, in the first place, caused me to drop the weapon in order to stop the clockwork mechanism, and in the second, to go and lock the door. Precipitately, I stripped the bodies of their clothing and redressed each of them in the other's attire. Finally, I picked up the frock coat that Horatio had taken off and put it on his double, leaving the right sleeve dangling loosely.

That subterfuge was a trifle visible, but I gained time. It only remained for me to cover the face of the dead man with a table napkin, lock him in the automaton's cupboard and install the latter in an armchair, his legs crossed and his pipe in his mouth, in the nonchalant attitude that I often gave him.

Lastly, I wiped the stains from the parquet, placed the sword on a table with its shoulder-strap, opened the door wide, and sat down next to my pseudo-comrade. I was covered with so much sweat that I would not have been able to wring out the napkin that I used to mop my face, and I could hear my temples throbbing with the certainty that they were going to burst. The concern of saving my tranquility and perhaps my life drive away the very horror of the death; I was no longer giving any thought to poor Horatio.

When I had recovered somewhat from my disturbance, and I felt coolness bathing my forehead and my limbs, I thought it was time to mount the deception by making the Admiral's voice heard. I therefore chose the Mallard song in order to feign good humor. It was then that a hundred hurrahs resounded outside my windows, mingled with detonations and various cries. I thought I would die. But finally, staking everything, I drew the curtains, lowered a frame and caused the upper body of the hero to appear, his left hand raised toward the sky.

O, I have avut, O what have I yut?
I've ayut the voot o'my mallard.
A voot voot, a toe toe nippens and all,
O, so goodum it was, my mallard.

I ought to say that I was ready to blow my brains out. To my great astonishment, the crowd burst out in delirium, throwing hats into the air and renewing the hurrahs. A young woman brandished an enormous bouquet through the gate, wrapped in ribbons. I could see the moment when everyone would get over the obstacle by any means. Then I retreated into a corner and, with my nose to the wall, checked the detonator. But I had reckoned without Allen.

When I came back to dart a glance outside, while Horatio remained standing, his arm extended emphatically, the worthy mariner begged the crowd to go away without a fuss, adding that his master was very tired after a twenty-five mile journey, that he had to leave again that evening, and that he had also dined too copiously. So saying, Allen lowered his voice, in such a way that I only understood the meaning of his last words by the mime with which he accompanied them, which it is easy to imagine.

To take advantage of such a good opportunity to get away, I wanted to make the Admiral say something thankful and polite, but as I mistook the key, they heard, as he stepped backwards: "Fine weather today!" The crowd uttered further hurrahs, for there was a good deal of emphasis in that affirmation, and more than a hundred hands reached out to Allen's, whose sailor's uniform and masculine appearance made him recognizable as one of the heroes of the *Triumph*—which was, in fact, the case.

Then I had the courage to appear in my turn and repeat in noble terms what I had divined rather than heard of Allen's speech. I combined them with the thanks of the Admiral, a child of the nation, and concluded with the promise, in his name, of a sum of twenty guineas for the poor. That speech provoked a final burst of enthusiasm; in my turn I was honored.

The crowd drew away slowly, after having the young woman's bouquet handed to me. For the sake of gallantry, I kissed it.

Rid of those people, glad to have uttered their cries, all I had to fear was the faithful Allen and his indiscretions.

"My friend," I said, through the window, "you've had an excellent idea. Admiral Gunson is, indeed, very tired, and as you've told them, we've have a little to drink. He says that it's gone to his head. I'm counting on you, my friend, not to repeat this..."

"It's you, sir," Allen retorted, "who no longer knows what you're saying, with all the respect that I owe you for such a good dinner. What my glorious master sang, sir, was in every way worthy of his glorious life. And I'd like to know it by heart, sir, in order to teach it to the crewmen. Yes, sir, it's so elevated as to surpass understanding..."

Allen's bare arms, folded over his chest—his tattooed arms; his muscular arms! Allen's prognathous jaw! Allen's steely eyes!

"Well, my friend," I said to him, trembling slightly, "I believe that His Honor is going to sleep... As, before all that racket, to which he wanted to face up...before all that racket, as I say, ahem…he confided to me"—I lowered my voice—"the poor state…the deplorable state…of his health, we've decided not to leave until tomorrow, if you don't see any inconvenience in that. Or, at least, I mean, if there isn't any inconvenience of any sort. You understand, my good friend? So, stable your horses, get a bite to eat for you and the obliging maid, dine at my expense, and have a night out, if the desire takes you. Accept these two guineas, my worthy Allen, and until tomorrow, no? But don't let anyone disturb us before then."

"I'm at my master's orders," Allen replied, "and I kiss your guineas, sir. Your servant, sir!"

I had judged accurately. The enthusiastic gallant had not been thinking about anything else through all of that but making perfect love to his conquest. I was certain henceforth that the two of them would leave me in peace. It was scarcely four o'clock. I still had five hours to wait before carrying out my plan, with the doors and windows shut.

As I was harassed by fatigue and I had an atrocious headache, I threw myself down on the sofa and did not take long to fall into a heavy and dreamless sleep.

When I woke up it was almost night. I went to take account of the state of my house, and had the good fortune to find no one there. The horses had been stabled and furnished with their necessities. I stayed out breathing the fresh air, which rendered my mind more lucid and diminished my tension slightly. The effects of the wine had been dissipated by slumber, and my thoughts were beginning to apply themselves to the odious object that I wanted to avoid, in order that they might focus on another, which demanded all my composure and attention.

Surer of myself, I went back in to close my shutters, light the candles and lock my doors. Then I lifted poor Horatio out of his cupboard, put him on my back, where he weighed scarcely more than an adolescent, being short of stature and paltry in corpulence. Without having uncovered or kissed the forehead, in order not to disturb myself, I went down into the cellar and placed him on the beaten earth. There were several empty barrels there. I chose one that I could dismantle without damage.

After an hour's work I placed the cadaver inside. It took me another hour to make sure that it was perfectly sealed. Then I filled it with the aid of an earthenware jug, drawing off the rum from another barrel. That work done, I replaced the plug and picked up the candlestick, which I had already refurnished.

As I was about to draw away, some demon, no doubt, whispered the habitual phrase to me: "Pull me a pint, Jim!"

I was so frightened by that monstrous thought that I ran back upstairs, taking several steps at a time, and locked the door.

That done, it seemed to me that a thousand mouths of shadow, taking on my father's tone, where were repeating that phrase ironically, and, in my mind's eye, I saw all those winged mouths reproducing my father's mouth, fluttering in the darkness like bats. Then I took a strong dose of opium and went out again to breathe the fresh air.

Near the well, thinking that fresh water would do me good, I undressed and emptied several buckets of water over myself, which collaborated in relaxing me. As I got dressed again I felt the key to the cellar in my trouser pocket. I threw it into the well, with the sentiment that I was accomplishing a magical operation that would deliver me from the obsession.

When I went back into the house, having calmed down completely, I fought the soporific effect of the opium with a dozen cups of coffee, and drank them with a great deal of sugar, to give me strength.

What remained for me to do, in fact, demanded time and precision. It was a matter of dismembering the right arm and compensating for the disrupted equilibrium. I set to work, surrounded by tools and candles, and repeated the operation that had been carried out on Horatio two years earlier.

It was necessary for me to melt my gum in order to substitute for the ligatures of the arteries and simulated the scar. As for the bodily equilibrium, I used a corresponding counterweight of mercury, which I divided between the shoulder-blade, the seventh rib, the iliac bone and the top third of the femur. It was also necessary for me to scar those "wounds," burn the debris, with the exception of the arm, which I deposited in a drawer, and occupy myself with producing a slight leucoma in the right eye. Not being able to extract and amend the speaking machine, I reproached myself for not having made it say more, in spite of the afternoon's satisfactory experiment.

Dawn was breaking when I finished. I was astonished at having spent so few hours on a task that would ordinarily have taken me more than a day, but as I was obliged to make him heard, I was working under the empire of an inspiration that seemed to me to emanate from elsewhere and multiplied my strength tenfold without my personality intervening. No, I could not have given birth to that extravagant conception myself, or carried it through. Above all, if I had been in my natural state of mind, I would have spent my time weeping for Horatio, and without a doubt, casting aside all pusillanimous dread, I would have gone to confess the accident to the magistrate.

At any rate, I postponed for a few hours the care of reflecting on the conjectures that presented themselves to me to safeguard my liberty. Even so, the idea crossed my mind of taking my leave unceremoniously of old Allen on the road to Burton Place. Having laid out the fake Horatio on his sofa, however, I laid down on the one facing it, and fell into a deep asleep.

X

I had slept for four hours when I heard a gruff voice speaking to the horses. Without discerning Allen's voice, I spent a few moments wondering whether I might have had a nightmare.

I lit a candle, my shutters being closed. Alas, my gaze plunged into the open drawer beside me, and saw the arm excised during the night. The table, still laden with the debris of dessert, appeared with its creased tablecloth, stained with wine. The sound of clinking crockery reached me, convincing me that the maidservant had returned to restore order before my departure.

Thus, it was necessary for me to come to a decision in a matter of seconds: either to confess everything, or run the risk of overtly deceiving Allen and climbing into the carriage…or, of course, blow my brains out, as I would be obliged to do when I had plucked up the courage. But I was in the state of mind of a man due to be hanged, who waits passively for someone to come to fetch him. My thoughts, like calculations, caused my head to ache as they developed in the crannies of my brain. I waited, my head in my hands and my elbows on my knees, a sour taste in my mouth, my body painful.

Finally, Allen's tread became audible in the vestibule. Like poor Horatio, I too had a double; that double closed the drawer and marched to the door on which Allen was about to knock. I swear that it wasn't me who did that. I opened the door behind which Allen was humming, glad to be departing, like all his fellows.

"G'day, sir!" Allen said "I thought you were still asleep, sir. What news of His Honor, sir? As for me, sir, I'm ready. I'm only awaiting orders..."

"My good friend," I replied, standing in the doorway in order to relieve him of any impulse to come in, "the Admiral had a bad night. We'll leave when I've sorted a few things out, but I beg you to let him rest and not to talk to him during the journey."

"I know that, sir," Allen said. "It's not always good to irritate him. The sea will put him right, sir. Another two days...you see, sir, it's not so much the fever as the blow that the master's planning to strike against the damned French. They're already in his sights, and I wouldn't want to be in their place, sir. With all respect, sir, I'll ask you not to be too long, for it's a good time for the horses."

From having dreaded Allen's visit I passed to the other extreme, in wanting to be far away from the house where Horatio's body lay, and where I trembled to think about him. I gathered together all the liquid money I had left, wrote a note to the mayor asking him to give the guineas to the poor, and paid the maid generously, asking her to pack me a traveling bag. I confess that I ate the two breakfasts that she brought, not without contemplating one last time those rooms where I had dreamed of being happy.

I stiffened myself in front of the portrait of my mother, who gazed at me benevolently, caressed my father's viola da gamba, which was standing in a corner, with my gaze, and held back my tears at the sight of Jack Tar, who was still marking the time, and before the *Redoubtable*, the witness of my years of study. The Cretan coin reminded me dolorously of the strength of the fake

113

Horatio's catapult, and I saw it as my evil genius. Then I got up to tear it from the wall and shatter it.

Once again, I was in haste to get outside, to flee the terror and the chagrin, ready to run risks of which I dared not think, but which did not seem immediate. Finally, I took what remained on the table to the parlor myself, and stood there shuffling my feet impatiently until the maid had finished washing up and putting things away.

After that I returned to take a second pistol, which I put in my coat-tails. I animated Horatio and went with him to the perron, supporting him like an invalid. The maid, who had followed me, closed the door and bowed, more to the hero than to me. I climbed into the carriage, asking Allen, who was standing within arm's reach, to hurry. Outside the gate, the maid handed me the keys. As I was sending her to the mayor, Allen turned his head toward his master. My arm was round his shoulder. He opened his mouth, ready to proffer some remark inspired in him by such a familiar solicitude, but I had my eye on him and pressed a button.

"Prepare to depart, damned sailor!"

On these fine words, Allen put his hand to his waxed cloth cap, struck a rigid pose, and roused his foaming horses. In spite of the desire to flee my house, I looked back, weeping, thinking that I would never see it again. It was soon swallowed up in the whirlwind of trees. *Like me*, I thought, *when I'm nabbed by the law: the executioner, the eternal shame!* Meanwhile, cheers and gunshots burst forth as we passed by. Windows opened, in which I glimpsed, in a flash, individuals in shirt sleeves, waving handkerchiefs and shouting. For nearly a mile, I made Horatio salute at regular intervals.

He was still saluting when there was no longer anything but cattle to gaze at us.

When we were in open country, I let myself fall into a kind of somnolent sadness. Combined with the rocking of the suspended carriage, it numbed all reaction in me and caused me to put off until Burton Place the care of escaping punishment. In any case, it seemed impossible to me to let myself slip away, at the speed we were traveling, in any fashion that would not awaken the suspicion of Allen, who seemed to be watching my movements even from the back. I did not think it would be any easier to take advantage of a halt at an inn.

Then again, it was as if I were fascinated by what I called my crime. It appeared to me then with all its consequences—I mean the irreparable loss that my country was about to experience, and perhaps defeat when the need was so pressing. All of my dear Horatio's merits passed through my memory and before my judgment. Everything that I have written since the first line of these memoirs, I lived again in more extensive detail, which the pen could not transcribe without weighing down the story.

Sometimes, I dozed off. Woken up by a slight jolt or Allen's voice urging the horses, I was momentarily deceived by the simulacrum of my friend, or I begged pardon for the appearance that might have been his shade. At length, I took the decision to remain plunged as far as possible in a state neighboring sleep, not without having covered the Admiral's decorated breast with a mantle and hidden the hat that also identified him to the gaze. That was because Allen gave his horses a breather from time to time and took care of their necessities, usually at the entrance to a village in front of some inn or blacksmith's shop. In spite of Allen's vigilance, we were surrounded in the blink of an eye by the curiosity-seekers I never ceased to dread.

Allen was burning to ask questions himself, keeping watch on His Honor with a tenderly maternal eye. Nevertheless, I thought it prudent to ask for tea and broth several times. The Admiral drained his cup and fell back into a lethargy. I was obliged to invoke my medical knowledge of functions for Allen to cease to be astonished that His Honor's head remained exposed to the sun, while the body transpired beneath a cloak. Allen shrugged his shoulders and uttered a profound sigh, in which scorn was mingled with resignation.

At about two o'clock in the afternoon we approached Burton Place, which Allen, without turning his head, designated victoriously with his whip in the midst of poplars and pastures cut by white fences. It was necessary to draw back the cloak and replace the hat. Vagabonds ran behind the vehicle, to whom I threw pennies in order to slow them down. Villagers cheered us from the thresholds of cottages. Allen cracked his whip impatiently. A trumpet was already signaling our arrival. I was more dead than alive.

When I saw Lady Hackman, who was waiting on the steps, flanked by her domestics, while the carriage came to a halt and a valet lowered the footstep, I wanted to throw myself at her knees, embrace them and confess the catastrophe. But my legs refused me all service.

Seeing us immobile, she threw herself upon her lover, removed his hat and covered his face with kisses, passing her arms around his body. How beautiful she was like that, in her passionate anxiety, her hair undone by were impetuous gestures, her breasts half-emerged from the neckline, which was ceding to their weight, her eyes wild and drowning in tears! And her magnificent arms, which commencing maturity had scarcely thickened—the arms that Romney had made pour nectar at the table of the gods![23]

I do not know whether it was the violence of the sentiment that I experienced at the sight of her that suddenly restored my strength; naming myself, I presented my respects to her, standing in the carriage, from which she was preventing me from descending by the normal route. Without paying any further attention to me, she continued to hold Horatio in a tight embrace, lavishing the most tender and meaningless words upon him—infantile expressions of love. Unfortunately, in the course of her transports she touched one of the buttons.

"Go to bed, bloody old blockhead!"

I leapt to his other side and disputed the body with her.

"Forgive our friend, Milady," I said, "who has suffered a great deal and had very little sleep. The neuralgia that obliged us to make you wait still has him in its grip. But God be praised…"

"Oh, Doctor," Lady Hackman interrupted, "Rather excuse me! I was so anxious, even though he was with you…but forgive him what?"

And she attempted to readjust her hair, uncovering her armpit. I chose that moment, although it troubled me extremely, to get Horatio down and help him climb the steps of the peristyle between the respectful domestics.

---

[23] In her turbulent early days, long before meeting Nelson, or even Lord Hamilton, Emma Lyon, alias Emma Hart, became the "muse" of the painter George Romney (1734-1802), who painted her as Hebe, Circe, Cassandra, Ariadne, a bacchante (several times over) and in various other roles, classical and otherwise, and sometimes even as herself.

Lady Hackman accompanied us, using her foot to chase away a little spaniel that never ceased yapping at Horatio, obstinate in refusing to recognize him.

"Milady," I said, "it would be appropriate for the Admiral to rest; according to all expectation, he is due to leave tomorrow. Permit me, then, to accompany him to his room."

Already, however, the faithful Allen was preceding us. I was glad that it was him. His loquacity, I thought, would avoid many explanations, and his jealous presence other dangers. I was not mistaken, for the old factotum exercised an almost absolute empire in the house— an empire that his master had granted him, not so much in recognition of his long service as a kind of fraternity of arms, of shipboard comradeship and common exile.

I shall pass over all the ludicrous remarks that I caused my "host" to make in response to the questions that Lady Hackman heaped upon him in spite of my insistence. There were a great many "bloody old blockheads," cannons, devils in hell, and good and bad weather. Horatio was laid down on a sofa and I remained by his side. As for old Allen, he tried to deflect Lady Hackman by talking to her about my reception, the journey, his master's indisposition, about which he knew nothing but reported in good faith what he knew. He and I fell into accord to leave the invalid in peace, and I set the scene by making Horatio snore. Then I stood up on tiptoe.

Lady Hackman stayed for a few moments considering her lover through the gap in the door, with an expression of profound amour.

"How handsome he is!" she sighed, closing the door softly "And how the most martial authority never abandons him, in the worst of his ills! Let's go downstairs, Doctor, and talk about him."

First we went into the main pathway of the park, which Horatio called his "poop deck," because it was his preferred station, to which he went to deliver himself to his thoughts. I then saw the little stream that Lady Hackman had filled with fish so that he could fish with a rod and line. Doubtless she had been told that Cleopatra had provided the same pleasures to Antony, and that her delightfully mischievous sense of humor had led her to attack smoked fish to the triumvir's hook, at which they had both laughed like children. With a no less puerile and touching attention, the little stream had been baptized the Nile. Next I saw the chicken-coop, the ducks and the pigs. And all of that was closely or distantly related to the Admiral.

All my fear, my malaise and my apprehensions evaporated. I felt a sentiment born, for the memory of Horatio, that I dared not formulate as yet. Another blossomed, at the same time, at the sight of Lady Hackman. Her grace and beauty caused forgetfulness of her birth, her former condition—errors of nature—and forgiveness of the calculations that had brought her to her true rank. I was no longer astonished that she had been the friend and confidante of a queen. Thus I reasoned, under the empire of amour.

However, Lady Hackman paid hardly any attention to me, considering me as a subaltern attached to the great man, even though I was a childhood friend and received no wages. I made allusion in vain to my dwelling and my fortune, to the studies for which I had lived—all that was trivia, to which she listened with a distracted ear. Of the automaton there was no question, and perhaps she knew nothing about it.

I understood that Horatio's design, in coming to visit me, really had been nothing other than what he had revealed to me, and doubtless his mistress could only reinforce it. Maladies, remedies and treatments—that was almost the whole of the conversation; we returned to it obstinately whenever a foreign object deflected us from it.

I tried, therefore, to insinuate myself into Lady Hackman's confidence by remaining in the role of watcher and healer to which she wanted to confine me— me, the cause of Horatio's death! I talked to her about tropical fevers and secret means that I had of curing them by means of indigenous medicines subjected to the control of my science. I invented barbaric terms for them, and pushed charlatanism to the point of talking about a cure of solitude and silence, which I would be able to have respected with the aid of the faithful Allen, promising me not to let anyone near him except in cases of absolute necessity.

Naturally, we also talked about the departure, which orders rendered it impossible to elude. I thought about declaring that the Admiral was in no state to undertake a campaign, but then I would have all the medical celebrities of the land introduced to Burton Place, and what was worse, I would have his mistress installed by his bedside. The best thing, therefore, was to sustain that the violent indisposition was only temporary and that the cares of a great task would dissipate it once aboard ship.

So saying, I put myself in the hands of Fortune, which, thus far, had got me out of trouble in less complicated circumstances. But I dared not think too much about it, enjoying a day's respite and the presence of an enchanting woman.

She listened to me, leaning her elbow on the fork of a weeping willow on the edge of the stream I mentioned, and to which we returned for the third time. Her beautiful hand contained her cleavage, swollen with amour and anxiety. The position of her body caused a hip to stick out, which her full figure rendered more voluptuous, and the gauze dress, caught on a twig, allowed me to see, all the way up to a topaz-pink garter, a Junoesque leg, round and shapely, above a child-like foot. And the buckle of the garter gazed at me with the fascinating eye of an octopus. At that moment, I would have given the life that I had forbidden myself with so much harshness to be surrounded by the twin tentacles sketched by the legs. I associated the arms with them as well.

Lady Hackman could not remain distant from the object of her torment. She dared not infringe the promised she had made me, but it was necessary for her to find herself in a more intimate atmosphere. She expected that a pretext would be encountered naturally to go up to his room, and that I would not raise any obstacle to it.

The pretext in question was that of having something to eat, when we were installed in the drawing room, where the walls were garnished with portraits of Horatio and her, signed by great painters and renowned engravers. Everything, in sum, spoke of nothing but their love. The needle of hunger pricking my stomach in a very cruel fashion, I was weak enough to accept on my own behalf. I reserved my response regarding Horatio, and went upstairs to take his pulse.

In reality, I undressed him and put him to bed, as if, not feeling better, he had made that decision himself, resolved to stay in bed until the following day. In addition, I made him snore again, and in a progressive manner that ought, at length, to shake the house. Then I went back to report the results of my examination, and the pretended conversation that I had had with him, to Lady Hackman.

I added, lowering my eyes and in a confidential tone, that the repose of the evening and night should not be disturbed, and that, in order to assure myself of the decrease of the fever, it would be necessary for me to sleep in the dressing-room annexed to the bedroom, where I had observed a camp bed already made up.

That caused Lady Hackman a keen irritation, perceptible to me in the swaying of her foot. When I looked up at her, I saw her face lowered and covered by a blush that one could qualify indifferently as modest or immodest. She finally broke her silence, asking that the meal should be served. She abstained from touching it. I was very embarrassed by eating in front of her, and serving myself abundantly, although I interrupted the snack as often as possible, reverting to what I had said that afternoon and relating my memories. I saw by the expression and the sobriety of her replies, however, that Lady Hackman had conceived an implacable hatred toward me. I was an intruder who was not submissive to her law, and even had the pretention to dictate it to her.

Undoubtedly, she would build in future an entire system of challenges before which I would retreat or kiss the flag. As I had had so much difficulty in commerce with women, I did not know how to give my conversation a seductive turn, and to complete my awkwardness, I was obliged to carry the burden alone. It was, however, necessary that I drag out the tête-à-tête; I believe that I would have talked until the following day about any subject whatsoever: Prester John, squaring the circle or the bee in the bonnet of the Byzantine sophists.

The more I spoke, however, the more I felt that I was dooming myself in Lady Hackman's mind. His Honor's snoring, having become intense, enabled me to point triumphantly at the ceiling, as if that reparative sleep were due entirely to my care. Far from being satisfied, though, Lady Hackman showed herself to be increasingly impatient and disturbed, to the extent that she stood up and signaled to me that I should follow her into the park.

There, we sat down on a bench, where I had the mortification of seeing the beauty occupy herself entirely with her little dog. I did the same in order to please her, and allowed myself to be discomfited, torn, bitten and dirtied by the jealous beast. I enjoyed nevertheless the presence of her beautiful mistress, whose animal warmth I sensed by my side, in spite of the respectful distance that I maintained between us. The evening breeze, caressing her cleavage and her arms brought me her effluvia, and whenever she made a gesture I thought I might faint.

That, I said to myself, contemplating the décor in which they loved one another, *is what the love of women amounts to: an idea that they create, and which they nourish untiringly. The automaton still incarnates Horatio and I only have to make him speak, in order that she may converse with him. But what about Horatio himself? Yes, what was Horatio? The incarnation of an idea. A costume, a voice, medals. The envelope that had hidden him from me has torn today. How was I able to be duped for so long, to the point of sacrificing to him the best years of my intelligence and my life? Will it be necessary for me to kill myself for his appearance?*

But I did not despise that amorous woman, so similar to me—what am I saying?—to the entire crowd; and

I chased away those reflections, which seemed to me to be injurious to the honor of my country and human consciousness. They had sufficed, however, since their uncertain birth, in driving away from me the horror of the crime. I no longer saw it as anything but an accident, the true cause of which was Horatio's physical condition.

What? I could have taken that punch without too much trouble. The discomforts of the sea, the efforts, the fatigues of the first battle, perhaps even those of amour, could have had the same efficacy. I had a claim on the gratitude of my country for having prolonged the hero. Nonetheless, I was anxious about its judgment. And my fate depended until the following day on the passion of Lady Hackman, on the perspicacity of her beautiful azure eyes, on the very gentleness of her slender hand! That dread overturned everything that I had just built, and fear and remorse undulated like snakes in the ruins of my reverie.

We did not remain sitting there for more than an hour. Without feigning necessity, Lady Hackman moved back in the direction of the house several times. Horatio's snores worked marvelously. Lady Hackman was no longer doing anything but going back and forth, getting up and sitting down. I accompanied her like her shadow.

"Do you believe, Doctor," she said to me, eventually, "that His Honor will sleep for a long time yet in that fashion? It's absolutely incredible!"

"His Honor," I replied, with all the awkwardness of a pedant trying to please, "will sleep in that fashion until tomorrow morning, unless His Honor is woken up by the noise he is making while sleeping. It's said that it's the sleep of heroes. I shall have to reread Quintus Curtius to discover whether Alexander, whose sweat was balsamic, snored more loudly than other men, and whether, some day, his cohorts were vanquished while he slept."[24]

"It's incomprehensible that you can make jokes in these circumstances, sir!" said Lady Hackman, abandoning my title and adopting a curt tone. "But tell me, ought I to make arrangements for a meal to be made ready for him in case of need tonight? Ought I to add another for you, sir, for, having had very little rest, perhaps you'd prefer to retire than to go to table? In either case, you'll be alone; I'll have myself served in my apartment...oh, a few light dishes, for I don't have the heart to eat. I beg you to excuse me, sir..."

I blessed Lady Hackman privately for ridding herself of my presence thus, although I was torn between two sentiments: that of amour and that of my own safety. I therefore accepted the two separate meals. While protesting the honor and pleasure I would have had in keeping her company, I mentioned the fatigue that I was suffering, but that I was desperate not to let it show in surliness. After which, I bowed to Lady Hackman, who re-

---

[24] Note in the original text: "This is a singular error on the part of Dr. Click. One reads, on the contrary, not in Quintus Curtius but in the Supplements of Freinshemius to the *Life of Alexander* that the latter slept little and that, if anything of consequence happened 'He put his arm out of the bed and prevented himself from sleeping by means of the sound of a silver ball that he dropped into a bowl.'" [Note by Gaston Gallimard.]" The 17th century scholar Johann Freinsheim, who signed himself Johannes Freinhemius, added supplementary information to various works of Roman history, inevitably of dubious exactitude. One assumes that the attribution of the note to the publisher of the novel rather than the "translator" is a joke on the part of the author.

turned the salutation without offering her hand to be kissed.

In the dressing-room of Horatio's bedroom I devoured the snack of cold chicken and washed it down with an excellent wine that renewed my strength. I had bolted the bedroom door in order that Lady Hackman could not take me by surprise, and I threw myself down on the camp bed, took off my clothes and resolved to sleep before completing my restoration with Horatio's share.

I summoned sleep in vain. My neighbor's snoring kept me awake and caused my thoughts to flee. I waited for some time before reducing it in a descending progression. I was then able to obtain the repose of which I had so much need, and saw Lady Hackman in my dreams, whom I simply called Nelly. She authorized that by calling me Jim, and we found a great deal of pleasure therein.

I woke up in the middle of the night under the empire of that pleasant dream. Horatio's respiration had become normal again, but I could hear breathing from the other direction that was punctuated by moans. I stuck my ear to the partition wall, and had no doubt that Lady Hackman was having a dream analogous to mine.

The state into which that observation threw me led me spontaneously to an action of imprudence and criminal indiscretion, which I might have regretted immediately. I drew back the bolt that rendered passage between the two rooms impossible and advanced barefoot, my heart hammering, holding my breath, toward the bed of the sleeper, illuminated by a feeble nightlight.

Lady Hackman was only clad in a light lawn fabric, which would have allowed her forms to be divined if the most advantageous and the most secret had not been veiled in the movements of sleep. She was murmuring Horatio's name, her forehead and eyes covered by a folded arm. Her body was agitated by tremors; her throat and belly were heaving. I blew on the nightlight, which spread over that magnificent body a moving gilded sheen, as if precious oil from an invisible urn had coated the tender softness for combats of amour.

Now, her arm over her face, I hurled myself upon her, and was more possessed than I possessed her. In my fury, however, I was conscious that she would perceive that I was not her lover, by my stature, my hair and above all because of my right arm, which I hid behind my back. That precaution was as disadvantageous as it was unnecessary, for, in the midst of our transports, I clung to Nelly forcefully, and she continued to give me her lover's name.

The chaste life that I had always led made that enjoyment something almost new to me, and, as it had conserved all my vigor, I possessed Nelly untiringly in successive body-to-body combats, in the course of which she uttered cries loud enough to wake the household.

The forces that I had just expended permitted my mind to get the upper hand again in measuring the danger of my situation. I therefore withdrew, unsteady on my feet, from the bed of intoxication on which Nelly lay exhausted. In spite of her condition and the rapidity of my desertion, she caught hold of my hand—which was the right one.

"Horatio, my love! Why are you leaving me, Horatio? Stay, stay with me until tomorrow. We have so many things to say to one another, dear Horatio! And think that we might never see one another again! Don't abandon me, so weak, tremulous and unhappy! Oh yes, I know, your friend Jim! That imbecile, how I hate him!

But I'm not deceived, Horatio—you're thinking about the enemy squadrons. Another beautiful victory awaits you! Then you'll come back to enjoy here the happiness I reserve for you…"

Meanwhile, she had circled my hips and attached herself to me. I disengaged myself easily from a grip that the languor of amour rendered incapable, and into which Nelly put more tenderness than violence

"Shut up," I said, "you bloody old blockhead."

And I went back into Horatio's bedroom, not without hearing the little spaniel sniffing under the door to the vestibule and growling ferociously.

I waited, having shot the bolt and weighing with all my might against the door, which the tumult of my heart ought to have rendered resonant. Nelly was almost immediately behind it, begging plaintively in a low voice. I did not reply. She must have been kneeling on the floor, and recommenced her plants, which formed a kind of purr of sobs. Then I shouted, in a more boorish tone than before:

"Go to bed, you bloody old blockhead!"

I listened to her draw away, meekly, holding back her groans, and I heard her bedsprings creak. I waited a little longer before giving the fake Horatio the most eloquent tone of the satisfaction of the senses. While watching him sleep by the light of a single flame, which I veiled with my hand in order that the light would not pass through the interstices of the woodwork, I was gripped by a scornful pity for the dead man, and sniggered at his memory. Having made him snore like a conqueror for a few seconds, I devoured the second meal with the manners and the gluttony of a barbarian. Then I went to throw myself on my bed, and breathed for a long time the savage fragrances of the hair and the amour that had clung to me.

PART TWO

XI

Woken up at dawn by the song of the birds and the cries of the poultry-yard, I hastened to dress Horatio and spread water on the floor in a quantity suggestive of abundant ablutions. I could not help thinking, however, about the sensualities of the previous night, nor from evoking their beautiful object in the disorder of her bed. How many times, after completing my preparations and sitting on Horatio's bed, pensive and desperate, did I get up to draw the bolt softly and hold the door ajar in order contemplate Nelly through the gap! A final gaze upon the beauty of life, which had just been revealed to me— for I expected, during the morning of that very day, to pay dearly for my abominable deception. With the stubbornness of the weak, however, I had resolved to continue it.

So, in spite of having had it, I rejected the idea of all three of us traveling in the same carriage. Would not the memory of the night's embraces provoke in her an increase in the attention she paid to Horatio? On the other hand, would not those same embraces, evidence of his vigor, ruin all the pedantic nonsense that I have evoked with regard to her lover's health? Oh, how crazy I had been, and how could I, with such a sentiment of my imprudence, think again about amour?

The sound of Allen's voice, addressing his horses beneath my window, caused me to think about being tactful with that rude and devoted servant, who must be secretly jealous of such an entire mistress.

"His Honor," I said to him, leaning toward him and guiding my words with my hand, using it as a muffler in order to emphasize their confidential character, "is already ready. He has asked me to tell you to harness a second carriage for Lady Hackman, for His Honor, still very tired, needs to conserve his strength for the journey and to give me lengthy instructions. Have two breakfasts sent up to his room as soon as possible. Here, this is for a drink…"

I threw him a purse of several guineas. He raised his hand to his forehead in military fashion and made me understand, by means of a wink and a displacement of his tobacco-plug, that His Honor's orders would be carried out.

I ate the two breakfasts, brought by a valet, whom I sent away immediately. Seeing, through the window, that one of the carriages was ready, I went down with Horatio and made him climb into it. His slumber have been, thus far, the best safeguard, I set him to enjoy the sleep of the just, and after having signaled to the young servant who was guarding the horses to respect his master's slumber, I strolled placidly back and forth in front of the façade, in order that my comings and goings would be noticed by Lady Hackman or her chambermaid. In that way, I modeled the impatience of the early-rising master, who had brought forward the announced time and was thinking of nothing but leaving.

I had wanted to avoid Nelly's visit to the bedroom, her questions and her effusions. I was thinking, once again, about getting myself out of it, and going on as far as London; my timorous mind, however, dared not imagine the different ways appropriate to getting myself out of the embarrassment. I was waiting for a favor of fate, as I had been constantly waiting for one.

Today, now that I am sequestered by my own fault, I can see that the opportunities I desired were as good as they were numerous, but if fear lends wings to some, it fascinates and paralyzes others, and drives them, without the possibility of return, into the danger they wish to avoid. I almost took account of that, but I could do nothing about it.

From time to time I went back to the vehicle from which a sonorous and reassuring snoring was emerging. Finally, after an hour, Lady Hackman appeared, followed by domestics charged with boxes and bags. She was holding her inseparable little dog under her arm. I could see in her expression that she was annoyed by the indifference of her lover in bidding her good day, and that her wounded amour was sharpening her weapons against me. So, after having bowed to her, I anticipated her questions with the urgency of a guilty man.

"Milady," I said, "the Admiral's intention being to depart earlier in order to cover about sixty miles in relays during the day, he thought it best to come down without waking you, in order to let you sleep for a little longer. He is fatigued himself by an agitated night; he is asleep in the carriage and has asked me to beg you very respectfully not to disturb him. His intention was also to have a cabriolet harnessed for you, where you will have every comfort on your own."

I proffered these words punctuated by the furious barking of the little dog, which only stopped barking to show me her teeth. Lady Hackman's impatience was increased thereby, and my disturbance increased to the point where I felt my legs becoming unsteady beneath me. A cold sweat was running between my shoulders.

"Sir," she said, "I thank you for making me party to His Honor's 'intentions,' which appear to me to be orders, at least in the fashion in which you are transmitting them to me. In any case, sir, I understand that the emotion of such a departure might trouble the elocution of a gallant man. No, I cannot remember that His Honor, even in such grave circumstances, has ever treated me like a maidservant..."

I was very humiliated by such a haughty response, which showed me my incurable awkwardness. However, I recalled that Horatio had called her, via my mouth, a bloody old blockhead and that she had not raised any protest. I concluded therefrom that I would always be wrong and would always be inept in her eyes, since she did not love me. However, I had drunk her mouth, respired her secret odor, excited her transports, provoked her amorous words and caused her tears to flow. In a word, I had possessed her. That memory, her beauty, and the idea of a revenge, made me desire more ardently to be in London and not to profit there from the liberty to flee and hide, before having obtained the satisfaction that my heart and my desire demanded.

That is how the apprehensions that had tormented me an hour before died away—but my disorder augmented the list of my own vicissitudes.

I articulated a few inconsequential words by way of apology, holding my hat in my hand like a simpleton, walking alongside Lady Hackman, who headed with a noble tread toward Horatio's carriage. The little dog, however, never ceased growling and baring her teeth. When we reached the carriage and her mistress leaned over to admire her lover through the window, the animal nearly choked with rage and bit the gloved hand that was seeking to compress her muzzle.

Lady Hackman uttered a slight scream, and dropped the irascible beast on to the ground, where she continued her racket at liberty, bounding this way and that, her eyes exorbitant. As we sought to seize her in order to calm her down, she took flight, sat down some distance away, and howled mortally.

"That's a very sad presage," sighed Lady Hackman, wiping her eyes. "But I won't take you any more, Buonaparte.[25] You can die here!"

Hoping that such a noise might have awakened the hero, she turned back to the carriage door, but could only assure herself that he was still asleep. Nevertheless, she opened the door and touched the sleeper's arm.

"The weather's very good this morning, in truth!" he said, delightedly. Then he remained in that kind of ecstasy that my compatriots acquire when they are not thinking about anything, except that the heavens seem made for the beating of angels' wings, and the meadows for athletic games.

Lady Hackman considered him, her hands joined and drawn back against her cheek. I could not glimpse the sublime content in their words, but it seems that the assertions of great men, no matter how banal they might be, and sometimes very vulgar, conceal profound sentiment and subtle verities. "Oh, how immense he is!" cried the prince who saw the cadaver of Henry de Lorraine extended on the parquet. He was not measuring its length, as might be believed with too much simplicity. No, he meant that his death had increased his dimensions in the eyes of posterity, and that he had never been as tall.

---

[25] Buonaparte was the spelling of his surname employed by Napoléon Bonaparte's father.

Lady Hackman, who had lived in the intimacy of the great man, knew how to interpret his genius through his simplicity.

"Do you understand?" she said. "He's saying that it's the most beautiful day of his life! Yes, Horatio, the day that is shining over England is illuminated by your glory! But out there, beyond the Channel, dark clouds are accumulating. Hurrah for invincible England!"

"Hurrah for invincible England!" cried Allen, waving his boiled leather hat. As the same time as his, heated by alcohol and courage, the voices of twenty domestics were raised toward the day star.

I was bewildered by that sudden manifestation. Something stronger than me, however, made me cry in my turn: "Hurrah for invincible England!" The hat I was holding in my hand having inconvenienced me, I had replaced it on my head. I raised it again when I heard that I was no longer shouting. At the same moment, Buonaparte resumed howling, and the echoes of the boscage sent back other rustic hurrahs.

"It's time, Allen," said Lady Hackman. "Let's depart, to avoid too great a multitude. And you, Doctor"—she deigned to give me back my title—"forgive me for me impulsive impatience on such a solemn day. I am and always will be His Honor's humble servant."

Considering the Admiral, lost in his profound meditation, for a second time, she curtsied and walked backwards to the cabriolet. I bowed awkwardly; every time she lowered herself to the ground my eyes searched her uncovered cleavage and I saw her beautiful breasts rolling, free of impediment.

We each climbed into our carriages, and left, to the hurrahs of the hamlet.

"Unhitch your cannons! Pick up your rods and spikes! First and second batteries, fire!

O, I have avut, O what have I yut?
I've ayut the voot o'my mallard.
A voot voot, a toe toe nippens and all,
O, so goodum it was, my mallard."

That was all I could find to make Admiral Horatio Gunson say while the horses departed flat out. Allen, on the seat, hummed the song of my childhood, which became for him a warrior hymn, and cracked his whip, beribboned by the English colors. Meanwhile, little Buonaparte insulted the rig. Then her furious yapping became inaudible; the wheels had passed over her body.

You alone, Buonaparte, I thought, *did not recognize your master! Unlike humans, you were not deceived by the artificial formulae and sentiments that make us love one another as well as hate one another and tear each other apart for no reason. You, a dog, only had your sense of smell; it took the place of common sense. Perhaps we lost the latter in losing the former. But if one of us, recovering natural intelligence, protests spontaneously against what appears to us to be imposture or monstrosity in the world, the great blind and deaf machines of nations crush him into silence, and it is as if he never existed...*

I would have meditated further on republics and empires if the memory of Nelly had not come to interrupt my thoughts several times over, like a pretty face showing itself between curtains. In the end, I solicited it to enter entirely into my mind. Occupied with my singular mistress, I no longer saw anything but her on a devastated bed, by the shifting gleam of the nightlight.

As I have said, I was only aiming for the evening, and I plunged into the idea that, her scorn having dissipated, Nelly would belong to me forever. I therefore dreamed of a new life. When I took account of the fact that I incarnated nothing in Nelly's eyes, I abandoned that chimerical happiness, but only abandoned it to take it up again. Exhausted by such a tension of the mind and senses, I went to sleep on Horatio's shoulder, thinking bitterly that the person I had created in his entirety had become my unique support, and that I would lose everything by destroying him.

"Get out, wretch!" Lady Hackman would shout at me, if I revealed the truth to her, if, at a stroke, I ruined her passion in the past, the present and the future. And I would not get out of it so cheaply...

How many ideas and sophisms are launched into the world to which their authors do not hold, or of which they have been deprived, but which it is necessary to perpetuate, sometimes with disgust, some in order to live in the security of a lie, or in the memory and veneration of others?

However, I saw Nelly's breasts emerging from the chaos of my philosophy and my alarms. I caressed them in dream, my poor head rolling over them in delight. Those dreams of amour, in which my despair dissolved, I resumed at every relay, like a benevolent opium.

Lady Hackman never failed to come to contemplate Horatio's image, which I caused to snore open-mouthed. Then, putting a finger to my lips, I designated the hero with my gaze, still asleep. The ecstasy that was legible on her face reminded me of another, which I had provoked, and my desire was reignited by the sight. She remained thus, immobile, like a statue of Voluptuousness, animated solely by the undulations of her bosom, swollen by sighs. Then she went away, resignedly, when the team was hitched and the postillion cried: "All ready—we're going!"

"All ready, we're going, Milady!" Allen repeated. And he sent a jet of brown-tinted saliva six paces, as a sign of a decision without appeal.

When it was necessary to eat, Horatio ate, but without quitting the carriage. I offered the pretext that it not would not be convenient to expose him to curiosity and the ovations of guests; what I feared above all was that some clodhopping waiter, burdened with plates and maledictions, might knock him over while running around. He also drank when it was necessary to drink. He returned the pint that he drank in the appropriate manner, while Allen poured me a glass of ale with undissimulated scorn. In sum, when I have said that Horatio urinated through the carriage door while humming the Mallard song, in front of the maternally attentive Lady Hackman, I shall have rendered an almost full account of his actions and gestures during that interminable journey. There were also a few "Bloody old blockheads" and out of place aphorisms, but I shall not weary the reader with them.

We arrived in London in the night. I thought I was at the end of my difficulties, but some distance from Arlington Street a delirious crowd, gathered in a square, surrounded the carriage and unhitched the horses, uttering cheers addressed to Horatio Gunson.

We were surrounded by torches. Faces leaned forward in their glare to sound the depths of the carriage, where I was huddled more dead than alive, fearing that the windows might break or that the enthusiasm of the crowd might surpass its respect and cause them to carry the Admiral in triumph.

That was an ideal opportunity for me to mingle with that rabble and disappear forever, but I was too attached to Nelly to take advantage of the liberty that was offered to me, so I sacrificed it, almost certain to be imprisoned within twelve hours. The idea that I was immolating myself on the altar of Amour only reinforced my resolution; but, ready for anything, having resolved to blow my brains out rather than abandon the post to which I had so ridiculously assigned myself, I clutched the butts of my pistols in my pockets.

What I feared for my automaton I was satisfied to see realized on the person of Allen. Grabbed by twenty vigorous arms, they already-legendary mariner was hoisted on to shoulders, and the carriage, dragged by a multitude, followed the first cortege. All that was done in a trice.

Among the racket of acclamations, I made out the Mallard song, which Allen had adopted and which the crowd was braying with him, in a religious tone. I took some assurance from that and recalled that Horatio had sung it at Danish Camp in front of an excited crowd. Should I let it be heard in the carriage, or rather a few ardent words that Posterity would recognize as lapidary?

All the faces pressing around manifested sentiments bordering on fury. Such is the violence of the noblest fashions when they are raised to the sublime. Then, quitting the dread of revealing my fraud by a public demonstration for that of revealing it by an implausible silence, I lowered the glass and that Admiral cried, his head sticking out of the window: "Break out the cartridges! Load! Fire!"

As admirable a symphony as the Mallard song, those military commands were repeated from mouth to mouth. They threaded an initial theme, like a weaver's shuttle; the crowd had spontaneously given them an allegorical meaning. They meant: we who are always ready and vigilant, who maintain in our nerves the irritability of the wasp and the ant, undo the ruses of the envious; before they have lifted their little finger, let us blast them with our coastal batteries and our ships!

It was, in sum, the upheaval of the English nation.

What! I thought. *It's sufficient for a constellated manikin to stick his nose out of a window and give voice to a ludicrous formula for an entire people to reveal itself drunk on carnage, including tender women and little children!*

I remember that at the same moment, an image of my youth came back to mind: on a Carib beach, a barbaric tribe, brandishing feathered spears, was delivering itself to strange contortions to the beat of a drum. A sorcerer covered in multicolored plumes seemed to be leading the dance by himself. In the middle of the frenetic host, on a sort of altar, lay the bound body of a captive, whom they were all preparing to devour. A wild avidity was painted on the faces; young women, who seemed molded for amour, were uncovering teeth sharpened with a file, like those of sharks.

Gaudy illustration, what did you want with me at that precise moment? Was it to suggest to me that the appetite for murder in civilized human beings is closely akin to that of the savage, save that their hunger is without a defined object, by reason of which it seems less ignoble, worthy of being celebrated as a mystical appetency on the lyre of Orpheus—the lyre that tamed ferocious beasts? Yes, what did you want with me, sinister caricature of the human race?

Need I say that prudence had caused me to draw the hero back inside as soon as he had uttered his cry? We were soon in Arlington Street. I was prey to the most terrible apprehensions. The carriage stopped. I did not feel that I had enough strength to sustain myself. It was necessary to get down, though, and to help Horatio to walk Behind my window, I could see a part of the façade, illuminated and decked with flags. A double line of officers formed a redoubtable corridor in front of the door. I would have trembled less before the tribunal of Hell.

That short distance, I thought, *I will not cross; my skull will be fractured before I've taken ten steps, unless I have the sad privilege of having my throat cut.* But Allen opened the door for me and I found the courage to get out and offer my arm to the Admiral.

Such a din then burst forth that I lost almost all control over myself and became similar to my automaton. I went straight ahead, therefore, toward the door wide open to a brightly lit interior, where I distinguished the silhouette of Lady Hackman. It seemed to me, confusedly, that it was her that I had to reach, but, as in a dream, it also seemed to me that the interval separating us increased with my efforts.

Meanwhile, I was marching under a vault of swords. When they sprang from their scabbards, believing that my last hour had come, I drew my head back between my shoulders. It was no longer me that was guiding and sustaining Horatio, but him that was drawing me along and serving as my support. I almost stripped over a crease in the carpet that had been unrolled in the street for the occasion.

Finally, rigid, eyes staring and without a dry hair, I found myself in front of Lady Hackman. I had a feeling that it was necessary to make Horatio say something. In the disturbance into which I was thrown by the footfalls of the officers I could hear behind men and Nelly's presence, I pressed at hazard.

"Launch grapnels! Boarding divisions, charge!" cried Horatio, in a powerful voice, extending is hand in front of him.

Lady Hackman kissed that hand delightedly, and curtsied as if at court.

"His Honor," she told the officers, "is already in the fire of battle. Or perhaps, as Horatio is appearing helmeted before his young son, he is amusing himself by frightening me. Far from trembling, sirs, I am burning with the same enthusiasm, and if it were permissible for women..."

"Go to bed, you bloody old blockhead!" added Horatio, at which Lady Hackman caressed his arm.

"You see, sirs," she simpered, "His Honor is preoccupied with my repose. I dare admit that I am in great need of it. So, I shall have a light supper sent up to my apartment. I beg you to excuse me. In any case, I could only hinder you in a conversation as grave as the one you are about to have, concerning the plan, the preparations for the campaign and the visit that you are render, as soon as possible, to His Majesty.

"Allen will serve you, for I've ordered a modest meal in the haste of the few minutes of which I disposed before His Honor's glorious arrival. May I beg you, sirs, not to prolong your conversation too long beyond necessity? For His Honor, you know, is not wont to preserve his strength. Doctor Jim Click, who is also his friend and private secretary, will make sure that he does not abuse the pleasure that he feels in finding himself in your midst, sirs."

With a certain tone of detachment, she added: "Captain Harbinger, may I introduce Doctor Jim Click, whom you will meet again on the *Triumph*... Captain Blackstone and Captain Caldron, I introduce Doctor Jim Click..."

I shook hands with the gentlemen in question, satisfied that all those who remained outside would not be invited in as well. Lady Hackman did not take long to retire, after having escorted us to a laden table. Allen's alter ego closed the door and occupied himself with putting away the horses and carriages. The rumor of the street still reached us. From time to time it became louder. That was doubtless due to corporations and clubs uttering the regulation three cheers in front of the Admirals house.

"I drink," Captain Harbinger, sitting to his leader's right, did not fail to say, "to the Association of Apothecaries"...or the bagpipers of Edinburgh, or the cuckoo circle of North West City, or whatever. And he washed his throat, as did Captain Blackstone and Captain Caldron. I made the admiral drink; he maintained a pensive silence and emptied the bottle without being as inconvenienced as his guests, whose heads began to spin after the second dozen oysters. I had renounced nourishing Horatio on those shellfish, for an unsuccessful trial caused one to slip between his waistcoat and his shirt.

"I believe," Captain Harbinger had murmured into his plate, "that His Honor is a trifle drunk, with all due respect. We shan't take long to be, but it's better to leave him tranquil and not irritate him."

Captain Caldron deigned to address a few words to me in a low voice in order to obtain some information regarding his chief's health. I got myself out of it cleverly with the story of the machineel and a few medical considerations, which escaped him in spite of his understanding expression. He made a sign to the others, who had divined the nature of our conversation; then everyone drank, so as to prepare themselves for serious business, and no one paid any further heed to me.

The good intentions of those gentlemen completed my relaxation. I thought that my sole concern would be filling Horatio's glass until the time when he might have a plausible desire to retire. I also thought that the enthusiasm of the guests in keeping up with him might perhaps send them under the table, and that I could then, by virtue of a natural flight, install myself in Nelly's bedroom.

Meanwhile, I learned that Captain Harbinger was in command of the flagship, Captain Blackstone the *Nisus* and Caldron the *Conqueror*; and also that couriers and envoys, sent ahead of us, had signaled our arrival, which explained the gathering of the crowd and the presence of the captains.

As for the visit to His Majesty, I was counting on it taking place without me, and even that it would not happen, for I glimpsed the eventuality of my cowardly flight once I had sated my senses on Nelly's beautiful body. And I saw myself at Folkestone, seducing the owner of a boat with what remained of my money, and then touching land in a safe place, where I would be tempted to remain.

The oysters were followed by cold chicken. Headier wines, instead of plunging them into indolence, gave Captains Blackstone and Caldron ideas about strategy, to which no one had yet paid any attention. Wine has great strength in war, and I am not astonished that the god of wine was a conqueror. He was also a legislator; something of their Bacchic origin still clings to laws, which makes them appear a trifle haggard.

I thought it opportune then to make the Admiral speak. "Unplug your cannons! Release the lifting-tackle!" he cried, thumping the table with his terrible fist, which made the three captains, their glasses and their silverware jump. Allen, in the corner with the dessert, put himself on guard. His heels were heard to click, and the flat of his hands struck his thighs.

"There, sirs," said Captain Harbinger, after a moment's silent, "is the whole art of war. It's a great lesson that His Honor is giving us. We cannot thank him too much. The rest of what we learn is nothing but useless lumber, dangerous pedantry 'In war,' a great leader said, 'it's necessary not to be intelligent, but to act like idiots, without reasoning. *Unplug your cannons, release the lifting-tackle*, or *Break out the cartridges, load*—those, sirs are memorable words, which ought to be engraved in the heart of every mariner. Must I explain, sirs? The enemy is in sight, what do you do? You fire on him. But before firing, you prepare your guns, by God! Promptitude and strength, sirs!"

Captain Harbinger beckoned to Allen, still standing to attention. "Come here, fortunate imbecile. Here's the enemy—well, what have I told you? Promptitude and strength!"

And the brave captain, bounding to his feet, launched his fist at the sailor's jaw; the latter was hurled back six paces, and only stopped by the wall of the room.

"Hurrah for the King of England!" said Allen, rectifying his position.

"There's no other lesson," Captain Harbinger went on. "They can bend our ears with plans and strategies—that's good for women, drips, newspapermen and historians to stomach. So have a sentence that replaces the plan or let them suppose it, and repeat to yourselves in all circumstances, good or bad, for example: *Sink them!* That way, if you win, you double your prestige. If you lose, they'll say that Destiny was against you, and glorify your courageous presumption. As for you Allen, here's something for a drink, and continue to honor His Majesty, even when Fortune is contrary."

"The lesson is just," said Caldron. "It's only too true that they lard our heads with a heap of superfluities. It's even worse for the land army."

"Yes," said Blackstone. "Another has written: 'the whole of the art consists of crossing rivers by bridges and mountains by passes.' If there are no bridges, if the rivers are impracticable, one tries to imitate the genius of Caesar, in which the mason, the sapper and the laborer are involved."

"And to enable the laborers to work, as well as to cut one another's throats," Captain Harbinger went on, "there's nothing like a little ditty. That's what poet laureates ought to be doing, instead of sniveling at the feet of the ladies who grant them their favors and singing about gods that don't exist and are foreign to Religion..."

I wouldn't have wanted to miss such an opportunity, so I had the Admiral sing the Mallard song, which had had such a fine effect on his entourage.

O, I have avut, O what have I yut?
I've ayut the voot o'my mallard...

The three captains rose to their feet with a common accord to listen to the new hymn. Allen raised his hand in a military salute. I manifested the same marks of respect as the officers—at least, I stood up.

"Our Admiral," said Captain Harbinger, as soon as we had sat down again, "might be called the Taciturn, but when he emerges from his reserve, it's for something that gets to the point. Another strong lesson, sirs! That song...well, that song will give wings, if our enemy's gives them moustaches, as they say to one another."

"Wings!" said Caldron. "Yes, it's topgallants and royals that it will add to our masts.[26] Three cheers for Admiral Gunson, whom I nominate as the foremost able seaman in England!"

Hurrahs make one thirsty, so the gentleman did not fail to drink. Allen, in his corner, emptied the dregs from the bottles when he brought full ones. He emptied them even if they had hardly been started.

Finally, Captain Harbinger demanded punch, and toasts were drunk to very various subjects, from women to horses, passing via ships. Allen was charged with taking a bowl to Lady Hackman, who ought to have been asleep at that late hour, and whom I invoked in her bed, not without experiencing the most ardent desire to join her there. With that deign, I plunged the Admiral into a light slumber and made him snore with the delicacy of a little girl. From time to time he muttered "cannons," "spikes" or "old blockheads."

His officers were no longer paying and heed; they were occupied in searching for more to eat and drink. Caldron even attempted to go down to the cellar, to which he did not have the key. He did not come back, and nothing more was seen of Allen—but a pacific sound of breathing that resounded from below, and an-

---

[26] The wordplay in this sentence is untranslatable; the French *perroquet* [topgallant sail] also means "parrot" and *cacatois* [royal sail] is very similar to *cacatoès* [cockatoo].

other from above proved that both had made a port of call on the stairs, for want of being able to climb up or go down.

As for me, I had refrained from drinking, but it was necessary to yield to the persistence of Captain Harbinger and Captain Blackstone, who had lost a partner and were heaping me with attentions. Recalling that I was a physician, they were talking to me about scurvy, bloody dysentery, leprosy, acne, Maltese fever, elephantiasis, bubonic plague, the pox and seasickness. Captain Blackstone gave me a demonstration of the last-named inconvenience, even though he was on firm ground But it was no longer just him; Captain Harbinger could no longer support the dilation of his bladder, so that all the confidences of the wall, in the vein of Hogarth and Gillray, sealed our recent fraternity. Such is the vulgar nature of the affections that are engendered solely by our weaknesses, in which the ignoble plays the greater part, and which we call, perhaps abusively, comradeship.

I concluded that little feast with an arm round my neck. It belonged to the captain of the *Nisus*, who was fast asleep. The weight of that sleep was sensible in the arm, which I could not detach without waking its owner, whose chin was on the table. Mine was also touching it, because of that arm, oppressing me like a yoke. When I achieved my goal by means of a subtle slide and thought I would be able to join Nelly, Blackstone grabbed me by one of my coat-tails, poured me a drink and called me his dear Euryalus. He did not know how truly he was speaking, for, having fallen full length with Harbinger, in the course of a cordial demonstration that terminated in a sudden and reciprocal lethargy, he left me an open field. Like the son of Opheltes, during the games held by

Aeneas, I thus acquired the means to reach my objective—but I was scarcely thinking about Virgil!

I took my automaton away and went upstairs, holding a candlestick. I found Allen on the landing. He was snoring drunkenly alongside a candle that had been consumed in its holder,

Which room should I enter? I wondered, while I contemplated the drunkard, as if I might receive inspiration from that spectacle. A drop of hot wax fell on to his hand. He woke up. I admired his promptitude in getting to his feet and saluting militarily. Without saying a word, walking stiffly, he opened a door, and then asked, in a slurred voice, which he tried to render distinct, whether his master had need of his services. I caused him to reply by ordering him to go to bed, which was familiar and expected. He withdrew, reminded that he ought to knock first thing in the morning. We were not so far away from that. I feared that the dawn might catch me by surprise, and cursed the difficulty that had prevented me from coming up sooner.

While I examined the room I deposited the Admiral on his bed. Should I remove all appearance of life from him before my flight, or leave him in a profound sleep? I saw the physicians leaning over the false cadaver, and then the police and the magistrates. Would they succeed in discovering the real cadaver in its barrel of rum, and deducing the reasons for my action? Or would they accuse me of having murdered the mechanical being, in the case that everyone persisted in an inconceivable error? Then, I imagined the Admiral snoring forever, at least until my masterpiece wore out, watched over by generations of mariners.

I made the decision to leave him as he was, thinking that I would have more chance of not being pursued immediately.

Finally, I prepared myself to go into Nelly's room, which could only be the one adjacent to the one I was occupying. Neither the door nor the lock let any light through, but when I stuck my ear to a panel I heard rather heavy breathing. I opened the door cautiously and left it ajar in order to guide myself by means of the light of the candle I had set down on a table. That glimmer was quite insufficient, so that after a few steps, no longer seeing anything but the vague reflection of a mirror, I bumped into several objects, which began to roll, and, on colliding with my foot, rendered the sound of glass, so far as I could judge.

I stood there, nonplussed, but, still hearing the sound of Nelly's breathing, I continued to advance into the darkness in the direction of the breathing. I thus arrived next to the bed. As I extended my arm, I knocked over a bedside table and another object, which wet me slightly, and which was a bottle. A strong odor of wine and punch escaped from that corner.

I leaned over the sleeper and took her dear head in both hands, the fingers sinking into the abundant scattered hair. Then I almost recoiled in horror, for those lips exhaled the same frightful reek, multiplied tenfold.

Nelly did not budge. I let the head fall back on to the pillow. All that I provoked was a kind of groan. My beloved was dead drunk!

XII

I had raised Nelly too high for such a revelation of her penchants, and perhaps her habits, not to produce an irreparable collapse in my desire. So I no longer thought about fetching the candle to slake my eyes with the spectacle of her beautiful body. The little that I had touched of it having soiled my hands, I retreated precipitately into the bedroom in order to purify them, and I bolted the door. Romney, I thought, had only painted her as Hebe to show that if she poured out drunkenness, she took her full share of it, and perhaps he had evoked, at the same time, her first profession as a tavern maid.

Cured of my passion for Lady Hackman, I was no longer thinking about anything but quitting as rapidly as possible a roof where nothing any longer held my liberty captive. Light was passing through the curtains. I drew them; it was daylight. Already the city was becoming animated, with the grinding noise of carts, like a languid monster having difficulty resuming its movement, and creaking at every joint. I left the room.

Allen was sleeping like a gundog on the first steps of the staircase. I stepped over him cautiously, went down stealthily, went past the dining room, whose guests seemed to me to be sleeping peacefully, and guided myself through the gloom of the vestibule to the entrance door. I tried to operate the lock and the bolts, but could not open it.

Then I went back upstairs, stepping over Allen for a second time and went back into the bedroom, with the intention of jumping out of the window, which was only one floor above the ground, or of letting myself down with the aid of a sheet, or a pull-cord taken from the curtains. I opened the window, therefore, and leaned out in order to evaluate my chances.

The street was full of people. Some were sleeping against the walls, others wandering around without ever straying far from the house. At the noise I made the latter raised their heads. I threw myself back inside, fearing to awaken cheers. What could I do? Hide and wait for a favorable moment?

Not being able to think about the cellar, from which Caldron had not returned, I decided on the upper floors. Perhaps I would be able to escape over the rooftops.

"Sir," said Allen, without budging from his location, "I heard you five minutes ago, looking for something, and I saw you step over my body twice. If it's the key to the door, sir, to go in quest of something to drink, sir, I have it in my pocket, and I'll go myself, being at His Honor's service, and that of his guests, sir. There's a bar on the corner where they sell porter for the coachmen, ginger beer and ratafia, sir..."

"Yes, my worthy Allen," I said. "Something to drink is exactly what I'm looking for. Those gentlemen, too, won't be sorry to refresh themselves when they wake up. So go, my friend, and have something to drink yourself..."

I gave him a few coins, in the hope of taking advantage of the prolongation of his absence to make myself scarce. He stood up effortlessly, took my money and went downstairs. I heard him open and reclose the door. After a few seconds of reflection, however, he returned to turn the key in the lock.

Bah! I said to myself. *He won't take so many precautions when he comes back, and it won't take me long to evade his vigilance.*

"Did someone mention drink up there?" said Caldron's voice, rising from the depths.

"It's high time to disturb you, Captain Caldron!" said Blackstone's. "Captain Harbinger has been sucking his thumb since you went downstairs—or at least, on hearing mentions of various drinks, he only withdrew his thumb to allow them passage."

"Doctor Click," said Harbinger, "since you watch over us so well, would you be kind enough to see whether Captain Caldron hasn't sprained an ankle in the cellar? I'd be glad, while you're passing, to ask you for news of our dear Admiral..."

I was obliged to go down. The gentlemen were stretching and yawning, and giving one another nudges that would have stunned an ox. Caldron came back up from the cellar. The other two scarcely made fun of him. In truth, when I opened the shutters, none of them appeared to me to have suffered from such a short and uncomfortable night.

Meanwhile, bare heads came to show themselves behind the panes, and the street began to buzz, which did not seem to augur well for the facility of my departure. To the questions that were asked of me, without overmuch insistence, regarding the Admiral's health, I replied that he was still feeing an extreme fatigue and that he had gone back to sleep.

"He ought to reserve sleep for the crossing," said Harbinger, who always took the initiative of speaking first because of his rank aboard the flagship. "One never sleeps as much as in service, and it requires nothing less than the hurly-burly of battle or the Thunder of God to wake you up."

Allen came back in at a run. Warm ovations rose up as he passed by. He deposited his bottles on the table, and the gentlemen rapidly did honor to the porter, the ratafia and the ginger beer, as well as several slices of ham. As for me, refusing to take part in the refreshment, I soon expressed the desire to absent myself for a few minutes on personal business.

"You're not going to rouse the neighborhood, sir," Allen retorted. "There are five hundred fanatics out there who probably wouldn't let you back so soon, and who'd utter cries that would extract His Honor from is precious sleep. We'll be lucky if they don't force the door sir, to come and bark cheers under his nose. The landlubber is a noisy beast, sir…if you need a shave, I'm at your disposal. Similarly for these sirs the Captains."

So saying, Allen took a razor out of his jacket pocket and a brush contained in a copper cylinder, and he set about passing the blade back and forth against his callused hand.

"I'll shave His Honor next," he added, "Because we don't have any time to waste."

The officers knotted napkins around their necks.

"What time is the carriage?" asked Caldron.

"In an hour, very nearly," Allen replied. "His Majesty will receive His Honor and the Captains at ten o'clock, and we have twenty miles to cover, probably without a relay."

Shave His Honor! What a catastrophe the bumpkin was exposing me to! So I went back upstairs, giving the pretext of habitually shaving myself. In the momentary impossibility of taking flight, I started shaving myself and cursed the little detail, of which I had not thought for Horatio, but which might be sufficient to awaken the suspicions even of a dense brute. Was I, then, going to become the Admiral's factotum myself, if I did not succeed in getting away, and what scorn my entourage would heap upon me? No, my deceit could not last much longer. I was reaching its end; the best thing to do was to disappear during the morning.

At hazard, I installed Horatio in an armchair with a napkin polluted with foam under his chin, as if I had shaved him myself; then I waited for Allen to come to offer his services, in order to present him with an accomplished fact. I also had to fear Lady Hackman's embraces, although I was more reassured on that subject by my recent experiences, and because I could hear her sleeping heavily.

As for the hypothesis of the visit to the King, I could not envisage it for a single instant; it appeared to me to be of an order as burlesque and chimerical as the conversation of Lemuel Gulliver with the sovereign of Brobdingnag. I returned then to my idea of hiding under the eaves and escaping over the rooftops. Before then, however, ought I to wait for Allen, in order to put his confidence to sleep for a while?

Suddenly, there was a great tumult in the street, and I distinguished the sound of bells and the racket of carriage-wheels on the roadway. Almost immediately, Allen knocked on the door to inform His Honor that it was necessary to get dressed and let him see to his beard, the carriage being ready. I went to open the door so that he could see his mater, but I saw my plans almost annihilated by the precipitate departure, which disrupted my plans.

"I didn't know, sir," hissed Allen, on the threshold, darting a terrible steely blue gaze at me, "that you would be replacing an old servant in all respects. It's true, though, that in my youth people use to talk about surgeon-barbers. Me, I can only make splints like an orderly in the ship's infirmary, a deck-dog. In any case, sir, since His Honor is ready, we'll get aboard without delay." And, leaning over the banisters, Allen shouted into the stairwell: "Prepare to cast off, sailor! Everyone's ready!"

I shall spare my eventual reader our triumphal emergence into Arlington Street, which is easily imaginable, and which appeared to me to be so precipitate by virtue of an agreement between the two sailors on the seat. Had they not wanted to avoid the daily comedy of Lady Hackman, the mistress who took possession of their Admiral and rendered him ridiculous in their seamen's eyes? Allen's jealousy extended as far as me, and I expected to feel its effects soon. Might I to be abandoned by those two lascars, I thought, while they carried their manikin away over unknown seas?

I thought the same about the three captains. By a sudden change of tack that had no other reason than their return to their natural disposition, and perhaps the opinion they had formed of my role as pot-bearer, those gentlemen manifested a wordless scorn toward me that I accommodated very well. In any case, I returned it via the Admiral, whom I left throughout the journey to his meditations, with his hat on his knees in order not to weigh too much upon a head already heavy with thoughts. They imitated his silence, so everything was for the best. He had only produced a few nonchalant words in response to their questions regarding his health: "Fine weather today!"

In spite of that truce, which lasted a few hours, I felt that I was at the gates of death. Could my gross artifice deceive a prince in his own palace, in the midst of his ministers and officers? And great gods, what was I going to make my hero say, who only had a dozen phrases at his disposal, all as ludicrous as one another?

Of the etiquette of the court I did not have the faint-est idea. That was what tormented me the most. King George, however, whose love of agriculture caused him to be known as "Farmer George" might not demand a ceremony as complicated as I feared. Still, it was neces-sary to know him. I remembered that the prince was al-most blind and that the rumor was running around that his reason abandoned him from time to time. Far from founding any hope on his blindness or his madness, however, ought I not rather to fear them as susceptible, one of giving him a greater subtlety, and the other of going to extremes?

I was wrong. We were introduced without ostenta-tion, not into an audience room but into the shade of the terraces at Windsor. We walked there at a measured pace, in the direction of His Majesty, who would not take long to appear at the other end, the chamberlain in-formed us, before retiring without further ado. I con-cluded that the reception was private and congratulated myself on it. However, a picket of Scottish highlanders remained within gunshot range in the gardens that we were overlooking. One could see their bare legs, pink amid the foliage. In spite of the copper-clad butts of their muskets, I thought about the shepherds of Arcadia.

Arcadia! I too had lived in Arcadia, in my little re-treat at Danish Camp. Then I saw myself again in the back room of my father's shop; I saw that poor, fat, peaceful man, who had taught me to turns cannons and had borne within himself the seeds of my misfortune, with his automata, his Jack Tar and all his mechanisms! This was where the innocent chimera of his life had led me! In a few minutes, the guards with the pink legs would be summoned, and I would be taken away to a cell, culpable of lèse-majesté—unless the three captains passed their swords through my body.

They were not breathing a word. They marched as rapidly as sentries, hats in hand, sticking out their chests constellated with medals and respiring glory forcefully. As for me, I was trembling so much that I communicated my agitation to the Admiral, with the result that we resembled two ailing old men.

Finally, His Majesty appeared as we reached the extremity of the terrace. Without the *God Save the King* that the Scottish bagpipers played and in spite of his air of debonair grandeur, I would have mistaken the King for the gardener. A long pair of pruning shears and a vast straw hat, which he deigned to raise when he saw us, added to the illusion. He replaced his hat when we had bowed deeply to him. I will add that I took my time before acting as the other gentlemen did, not know what countenance to adopt, and I nearly failed to straighten up again with my automaton, so rapidly was my heart hammering.

"Are you the agronomic engineers?" asked Georgy. "The engineers who are going to propose a new graft for the pear-trees to us? I'll listen to the explanation of your system; it appears to us superior to all others, according to the report you sent. In the meantime, our pears are quite beautiful, Look at these, which we've just picked, and which we beg you to accept, as evidence of the interest that we have in your work, and agriculture in general."

So saying, His Majesty, radiant with placid pride, handed each of us a pear, which he withdrew from the depths of his coat-tails. Seeing the three captains accept, out of deference, I made the Admiral hold out his arm. Because of the King's poor sight we were obliged to bring our hands to his and to be careful that the fruit did not fall into empty space. That was, however, what happened to Horatio's, and it crashed to the ground with all the weight and softness of its maturity.

"Sire," said Harbinger, in a confidential one and taking a step forward, "Your Majesty was doubtless induced into error by a confusion of his messenger. We are three captains of the general staff accompanying His Honor Lord Horatio Gunson, our Admiral. He has come to present to Your Majesty the expression of his profound and respectful devotion before undertaking the campaign, in spite of the poor state of his health—which is to say to Your Majesty that he will consecrate his last breath to Him."

"Oh well," sighed the King, "keep our pears, even though we would have preferred to have given them to our beloved agronomists. Yes, yes, we remember now having granted you an audience. Oh, how insupportable Mr. Pitt is, with this war. War, always war! Always laying waste to Carthage! It's him, in fact, who ought to have received you. Personally, I only occupy myself with pears. My God, my God, will we never be left in tranquility?"

The mad king took out a handkerchief to wipe away the child-like tears that were flowing from his weak eyes. Then he went toward a marble bench, feeling the ground in front of him with the handle of his pruning-shears. Having sat down, he placed his handkerchief on his knees, took a sixth pear out of his coat-tails and started to peel it with the aid of a little knife. From time to time, while talking, he raised a thin sliver of fruit to his mouth. Sometimes, it remained suspended on the tip of the blade, and he considered it as if it were a sixth listener, but the most intimate one, the one closest to his own thoughts. A bird was chirping softly in the linden tree under which he was sitting, and that song was enough to spread a great bucolic serenity around the most powerful monarch in the world.

"The Kings of the Old Testament," he said, "and those of remote Antiquity, were first and foremost shepherds or agriculturalists. I cannot therefore, blush at the nickname of Farmer George, which was given to me by derision, because it attests to my peaceful tastes and the care that I can have for my flocks. Yes, Farmer George would like his infantry only to be armed with mattocks, his artillery and cavalry with harrows and plows, and that his ships, finally, should only carry grains and cereals. Mr. Pitt smiles his malevolent smile when I make him party to my ideas. He thinks that they're inapplicable, but I know full well that people will realize them one day. The name of Farmer George will have fallen into oblivion; people will have rallied without discernment to the number of other princes who see glory on the battlefield, princes that have a false idea of monarchy, just as their subjects have a false idea of honor. Let them mock Farmer George; he is with God, with God who did not create men for murder, with God who did not divide the universe into nations. Yes, Farmer George, who is also Blind George, sees the pear-tree of peace that covers the world to come, like the mother of William of Normandy, who saw an oak issuing from her loins covering the whole of Harold's kingdom.

"Yes, I see it, I see it!" he went on, emphatically, spreading his arms as if in the grip of a mystical ecstasy. "It's the Tree of Wellbeing. The Angels of the Lord are sitting in its branches, making melodious voices heard. Those who eat its fruit have rejected Gold and Silver, but they are not poor; they are rich in possessing nothing, nothing but hammers and sickles. Among them, there are no soldiers, no pastors and no priests, because the priest is a superfluous interpreter for those who have decided to live in accordance with the Gospel. There are no longer any judges, nor any policemen, for people have been obliged to perceive that the judge and the policeman stimulate crime by the ever-present image that they offer of it, unless they have disappeared with Money and the old idea of Property. And the Tree of Wellbeing, the Tree of Farmer George, has stifled beneath its shadow the Trees of Evil that poisoned men with their fruits full of ashes, and the evil plants with venomous juices. If I spoke the names of those trees and those plants, Mr. Pitt would have me locked up in my apartments. I wouldn't be able to cultivate my orchard any longer, or give fine pears to my friends. Come closer, though. I'll whisper to you…and then I'll go with you into the world, far away from Mr. Pitt, who is the devil incarnate, and we'll tell the world about Georgy's pear tree. Come closer, I say, come closer!"

We drew closer to the delirious prince, but the chamberlain, who was watching the scene from a distance, gestured with his hand, and a bagpipe started playing. Then Georgy fell silent. His features relaxed. Reason returned to his gaze. I understood that they had recourse to music to render it to him, either because it produced a great appeasement in his soul, or because a selected tune brought that reason back, by virtue of secret correspondences, to the ensemble of traditions that forms the social doctrine. And the old air of the highland clan, which the bagpiper was playing, seemed to me to be an effluvium of ancestral virtues perpetuated under the protection of the Cross and claymores, as well as a kind of Credo of Order and Power. There was then a

161

gentle sob on his part, the melancholy of old things appropriate to retain hearts resolved to abandon them.

After a few moments, the air expired in a heart-rending plaint. The King passed his hand over his forehead.

"Excuse those few words of the dreamer that we allowed ourselves to become," he said, rising to his feet, "which are the release of a great concern for affairs. Well, Lord Admiral, and you, our Captains, may God protect you and give you victory! We are fighting today for the liberty and the independence of the world. It's not only the Kingdom, but also the World that has its eyes fixed upon you. A fallacious peace has been offered to us; a trap has been extended for us into which we must be careful not to fall. Otherwise, we shall be no more than vassals, we who ought to retain supremacy over the seas and the upper hand in the direction of diplomatic affairs, for Heaven has chosen us to make peace reign over the earth, but a peace that is ours, that of the elect people who ought not to suffer, who ought to develop and extend in accordance with the numerous directions imposed by our genius. That is what Mr. Pitt thinks, whom the Nation has fully merited, and whom we protect with our assent. Go, Lord Admiral, and you, Captains; your King thanks you, and gives you his blessing..."

We bowed our heads under the King's hand, which rose above us. The bagpipes played the national anthem with the gentleness of the shepherds when they came to salute the cradle of the child of Joseph and Mary. In the distance, dull rumblings seemed to be the voice of God approving those words from the heights of Heaven, and commanding us to gird our loins for the cause of a just people.

When the hymn had finished, we raised our heads again. The King looked at us proudly, tears flowing from his eyes, which were shining through them with a bright gleam, and no longer seemed to be blind.

It was necessary to respond. The three captains turned their heads expectantly toward Horatio Gunson. Then I made him cry out the words that had enthused them so much and had stimulated the crowd:

"Unplug your canons! Lifting-tackle away! Put the light to the fuse!"

"There!" said the King, extending his hand to the Admiral, who took it and was shaken forcefully by it. "That's all we expect of you, Lord Horatio Gunson! We'd like to say soldierly words, words whose meaning isn't hidden, words of command that translate the orders of the Prince to the entire Nation, words that translate and don't betray. Farewell, then, Lord Admiral, and may the cannons on the seas respond to your voice!

"You won't lose any time," he added. "Carriages are at your disposal at the palace gates; you'll be in Portsmouth this evening."

With that, the King dismissed us with a nod of the head, and we withdrew, walking backwards for a few paces. George deigned to return our bow, but at the same time, he nearly slipped on the "pear of peace" that had escaped the Admiral's hand.

The clink of arms was heard; the Scots Guards who had advanced to the edge of the terrace presented arms to us. The officer's sword glittered at the height of his face. The bagpipers launched into *Rule Britannia* while he withdrew, and the three captains raised their hands to their temples.

Finally, when we reached the gate, the weight of rifle-butts struck the grounds, making the metal of the barrels resonate, and one might have thought that the Peace of the world was buried forever beneath a unanimous tread. The dull rumble resumed then, and gusts of displaced warm air kissed our faces avidly, as if they were the very mouths of cannons, the muzzles of wild beasts against the faces of their masters.

O King, I thought, as we traversed the antechambers and vestibules, *you are only mad when you become sage again, and you are only blind when the scales fall from your eyes. What, then, is the independence of the world and its liberty, if every nation wants, like yours, to maintain its supremacy in all things in order to obey its genius? Does it not believe itself the elect of God, which, when it crushes its rival, sings a hymn of actions and graces, as for marriages, births and assassinations? Are you not, however, all the same in the eyes of the Creator, who built, labored, trafficked and reproduced you in accordance with the common rule? The peace of others is always fallacious to whoever possesses weapons, and those who possess them always have the temptation to make use of them.*

I prefer the innocent reverie of your Pear-tree and the maledictions you gave to your own power. It was then that God illuminated you like the ancient pastors of the desert who became Prophets. But Mr. Pitt, who is, in truth, the devil incarnate, and really is "Mr. Pitt" in the world, has brought you back to the old sophisms by devious ways; now, hundreds of thousands of men are sharpening hatred and steel on what they have been told are the Tablets of the Law.

When will you come, Archangel Michael, when will you fall upon the earth to exterminate all the Pitts of the nations, the proud Pitts of the nations, from the great devils to the little impish Pitts? But I believe, O Michael, that you will emerge from the very earth, clad in a mi-nor's overalls or a peasant's smock, and it is in you alone that I hope, O sage Violence, O Fraternity!

XIII

Sitting on the bunk in the cabin, I had been sailing for several hours, prey to the profound despair that is translated by prostration. The majority of my fears had, however, dissipated, for I had acquired the certainty that nothing would cause the discovery of the fraud that had rendered me a slave. Even if I had confessed, no one would have believed me. I had, therefore, created an individual identical to the idea that had been formed of him, which fulfilled marvelously the function that was expected of him. But what would my destiny be, lost as I was on a redoubtable element, in the course of a crossing to which I could not anticipate any other conclusion, if I set aside shipwreck, than that of an encounter with the enemy fleet?

Horatio had once made me read enough accounts of naval combats for me to apprehend all their horror; the mere memory of our simulacra in the grain-lofts would have filled me with fear. Thus, rich and in the prime of life, but without ever having know anything of life except study, and the love of a kind of parody, I was about to perish in the most odious and most ridiculous fashion!

It was then that all the chances I had had to run away or liberate myself in some other manner appeared to me distinctly—which added to my affliction; and once again, I cursed my submissive and timorous character, which had caused my father to say that I was nothing but a girl.

Night had fallen completely, but it is rarely opaque over the sea. A wan clarity came in through the lattices of the poop castle, where I was lodged, and seemed to be

166

the plaintive penumbra of limbo, even more desolate than the eternal darkness. Facing me, similarly seated on a bunk, the fake Admiral was smoking a long clay pipe, of which Allen had brought several specimens, and which I had lit in front of him while he was clearing the table.

I ought to say that, for that first evening, I had refused on the Admiral's behalf to dine with the officers, not because I feared any troublesome discovery on their part, but because I aspired to solitude in order to pass through my mind all the incidents that had unfolded since our visit to Windsor and to deliver myself entirely to myself. I gave the pretext of the plan of campaign that the Admiral had to modify with the direction of the squadron as soon as we had shown ourselves at sea off the Portuguese coast.

On that matter, I had a faint idea on which I suspended the salvation of my life: to pretend to know that the French fleet had headed for the Antilles Sea, either to surprise us or in order to avoid a battle, and there, during a landing with Horatio, whose indispensable companion I was, to hide, disappear or offer the pretext of an accident to him, a sudden death from sunstroke, etc. In that, I was inspired and authorized by a recent error of Horatio's, when he went to search for the enemy in Hudson Bay and then on the north-west coast of Ireland, while the enemy was tranquilly fishing with rod and line in the Mediterranean. Furthermore, only revealing that new plan after a few days, I would demonstrate a cunning and suspicion that are always praised in great captains— because, since good old Ulysses, and even Gideon, who stopped the sun,[27] among other jests, great captains have always been exceedingly wily.

Then I applied myself to reliving the long hours of embarrassment, anguish and astonishment that I mentioned. When we emerged from the palace we climbed into our carriages, in front of a sentry that rendered the honors to Horatio and me, taking responsibility for us. Allen, who had orders to return to Arlington Street to fetch the baggage, was to meet us in Portsmouth. We arrived there at sunset, after a journey analogous to the first. I did not have to suffer the pressures of Lady Hackman, but only those of the three captains, which, moreover, were not insistent.

Portsmouth had other anxieties in store for me. First of all there was the immense crowd, which soldiers, with fitted bayonets, were trying to contain, but who were soon disarmed and trampled by them. It was necessary once again to shout: "Unplug the cannons, aim to sink!" I have no idea how many hats were thrown into the air then, which did not return to the heads of their owners, nor how many people perished, stifled.

One can evaluate glory, away from the battlefield, where it is often dubious, by the number of hats, canes, umbrellas, handkerchiefs and faded bouquets that the road-sweepers, always so placid and punctilious, collect the day after a great day, not to mention the drunkards in the gutters or the dead and the crippled in the shelters, among whom those who have fallen from trees, roofs and balconies are perhaps the most numerous.

In order to equilibrate the glory of combats and roadside glory, a list of them ought to be engraved on the

---

[27] According to the Old Testament, it was Joshua who stopped the sun, not Gideon.

gravestones of Westminster Abbey, alongside that of the cannons and standards captured from the enemy. One might read, for example: *Marlborough, a hundred thousand hats, ten thousand handkerchiefs, two and a half million bouquets of rose-hip flowers,*[28] *twenty-five thousand drunkards, twenty thousand squashed to pulp, two thousand lost children.* One could add a thousand deviations, a thousand adulteries and a thousand attempts on modesty, for military glory demands the worst catastrophes.

But what annihilated all thought within me and appeared to be, for the crowd, an immense magical incantation, which delivered it to the infernal powers that are the innumerable gods of war invoked by all peoples since the commencement of the world, was the prodigious quantity of civilian and military bands playing, without common accord, *Rule Britannia, God Save the King* and the most various and unexpected hymns, tunes and marches. Such disorder and such disharmony are necessary. They reanimate the barbaric spirit in the human heart, instead of a grave and measured music softening their courage and making appeal to the intelligence; and it is not so much to subject them to the cadence of the march that drums, fifes and trumpets are used, as to prevent them from thinking, even about their pleasures and their pains.

Escorted by troops of all weapons mustered at all the crossroads, I thus arrived, in that deafening racket,

---

[28] The author refers to "rose-hip flowers" rather than simply to roses because the term he employs for rose-hip, *gratte-cul*, also refers to the action of scratching the buttocks, thus introducing a note of contemptuous vulgarity not usually associated with the idea of a bouquet of roses.

within sight of the fleet that I, a weakling, was about to be called to command. Thirty ships were afloat on the waves, bobbing majestically at anchor, all their gun-ports open, revealing the cannons like ferocious rows of teeth. Their upper and lower yardarms and square-sails were garnished with lines of men, who raised their hand to the level of their eyes when we arrived within half a cable.

First of all, we stopped under the flag-decked mar-quee of a jetty, where Lady Hackman was waiting, with the grim Allen, numerous officers, civil functionaries and Vice-Admiral Hillockwood. The three captains fol-lowed us there, on our heels. The Vice-Admiral was ad-vancing to meet us when Lady Hackman threw herself upon Horatio, to the scorn of all protocol. She would have held him in an embrace if I had not had time to make the Admiral say: "Go to bed, you bloody old blockhead!" and imprint him with a sideways movement that brought him face to face with Hillockwood, to whom he extended his hand, saying: "Fine weather to-day!"

"It is indeed a fine day, Lord Admiral," Hillockwood replied, who heard those words both liter-ally and figuratively, as if he understood and agreed with them. And he indicated, with an angle of his tricorn hat, at the magnificent effect of the setting sun on the ships with impatient sails. A thunder of artillery saluted those words, or, rather, seemed to repeat them and magnify them. They rolled over the sea all the way to the horizon, in homage to and praise of the glorious sun.

Fine weather today, not because of the crops swol-len by nourishing sap, the harvesters, the artisans and the vine-growers of the occidental world, the lovers and spouses who were thinking of embracing one another, plucking amour like a ripe and merited fruit, but because thirty carcasses of wood stuffed with iron and powder were about to carry devastation into the distance and soil the foam of Venus! Fine weather today!

However, the spectacle of the fleet with vermilion sails, the display of power to which the destiny of my fatherland might be linked, that whole stage-set of men with precise movements, brilliant uniforms, standards, pennants and flags excited by the breeze, cannonades and fanfare, filled me in my turn with an indefinable intoxication—and it was with sincerity that I mingled my voice with the hurrahs and waved my hat when the cheers rose up in response to the artillery salvo.

At that moment, I believed that I was holding the living Horatio in my arm; my old tenderness reawoke and overflowed from my heart, and I would have thrown myself to my knees to embrace him if Lady Hackman had not done so before me, at the risk of tipping the machine over.

Then gripped again by the sentiment that it was necessary for me to avoid danger, I had the admiral cry the command to put the guns in battery, which had succeeded several times before, the next-to-last in the presence of the King himself. The audience could not hold firm before the spectacle of a hero surmounting the passion of a lover in order to render the great idea that amassed an entire people, and it burst forth once again. At the gesture that I had given the Admiral, everyone moved away, believing that it was the signal to embark in order to deliver an imminent battle.

Lady Hackman stood up, confused, her eyes moist with tears. Several functionaries replaced scrolls of paper in their pockets regretfully. A launch with oars raised had drawn up to the quay in front of us. I drew Horatio forward. The Captain of the *Triumph* followed us, and we descended the slight slope and then the stairway of the jetty, in order to reach the middle of the oarsmen, who began to ply their oars almost immediately.

I had the sentiment of passing over the River Acheron in the fatal boat, and did not expect any return to life. Casting one last glance at the shore, however, I perceived Nelly, who was waving her handkerchief. Even though that farewell was not addressed to me, I collected it in my memory in a melancholy fashion, as that of the only individual who had inspired me to amour, and for whom I had let slip the chance of liberty, the only possession that counts for anything on earth. Alas, some abandon it, others allow themselves to be captured, and it is perhaps the word that all men have in the mouth.

Are we made to bear chains?

I had reached that final reflection, leaving the rest of my recent memories aside. In front of me, Horatio was still smoking. I got up in order to turn up the lamp slightly, which I had left very low in order to be more alone with myself. I did it because fatigue and chagrin were showing me a loving Horatio. Was I going to be the dupe of my own work? At first, I was and I wasn't. Horatio was truly a machine that I had created, and yet, I spoke to him.

"Horatio," I said, "You have always been what you are now, an automaton who raises his arm and his voice, who repeats the little that has been put into his body. When young, you got it from your uncle, Captain Buckling, who got it himself from someone else. But all of you have always found people whose profession, taste or constraint was to fight and to obey. Nevertheless, when they're set in motion, they no longer listen to you, because your orders and conceptions are so incoherent, derisory and completely useless, and because your plans are thwarted by the enemy, even if you have any that are serious, and if unforeseen circumstances don't bring trouble and confusion to them.

"They no longer listen, I say, except with their own courage, which wins battles by itself—their courage and adequate supplies: which is to say, grocery, bakery and ratafia. The fact that you're there is sufficient for them, like a sign, an idol or a fetish. It's a great deal for men to have someone against whom to rage when they lose, and to whom to offer thanks when they win, because the collective soul, for lack of the ability to congratulate itself, needs someone to represent it in a tangible form in order that it can address its suffrage to him.

"Honoring and praying to a god without a face is beyond the common run of mortals, and people are very close to not believing when they can't represent God. But the faith that they accord to you, Horatio, is that which perpetuates imbecilic crimes past the time when people more civilized than their neighbors could dread being reduced to slavery or brought back to barbarism. Today, they all evaluate one another by the relative mildness of mores and the politeness of the mind, and what people could boast about enslaving forever twenty or thirty million of their fellows? That's why I'd like to put you back in your place and discredit you in public opinion, if I didn't fear for my life, so much am I still attached to that perhaps-illusory hope...

"What!" I continued, emphatically, as if I feared his response. "They dare to talk about your art and your genius? I'm not the only one to dispute it; there was already my dear Jonathan Swift. When he sent Gulliver to visit the isle of magicians,[29] the necromancer-governor showed his hero a general victorious by virtue of his cowardice and imprudence, and then an admiral who had beaten a fleet involuntarily, when he desired to allow his own to be beaten. He recognized, in addition, that historians transform stupid warriors into great captains, as well as petty geniuses into great politicians.

"Among those college pedants, some like the weak, others facile effects, and some sacrifice to the marvelous, to military mystique. It's a fine invention, appropriate to excite young people and make them desire a goal that would otherwise be repulsive to them as contrary to their natural wishes, which are to die in the bed where the majority of their fathers died.

"There was also Voltaire, whom my father disputed so bitterly with yours before they almost brought themselves into accord with the serpent and the viola da gamba. That generous philosopher, who is perhaps also the greatest modern writer, only counted among the arts eloquence, poetry, music, sculpture, painting and architecture. He deigned to add clockmaking; that was doubtless why my father worshiped him. But Voltaire hesitated to place among the arts that of war, which he qualified, as a concession, as the "heroic" art, or, if you prefer, the "abominable." *If it had beauty*, he added, addressing Frederick, *we would tell you that you were the most beautiful man in the world*…can you measure all the insolence and irony of that conclusion?

"And do you even know, you who are a great tactician and strategist, why our side lost the battle of Fontenoy? According to him, it was because bad nourishment had given them colic, and, after having fired

---

[29] Glubbdubdrib.

174

first, they no longer cared about anything but puling their trousers down.

"How much glory has been credited to the Turks? he also says. None. They have devastated three empires and twenty kingdoms, but a single city in ancient Greece will always have more reputation than all the Ottomans put together. Of Louis XIV he dared to write that his person and his reign would symbolize evil in Posterity, if all the fine arts, encouraged by his taste and munificence, had not forced Europe still to look at him with respect.

"So long as the caprice of a few men, he added elsewhere, in the manner of peroration, can make thousands of our brethren murder one another, the fraction of the human race consecrated to heroism will be the most frightful thing in the entirety of nature. And I agree with him in thinking that emulation in the arts has changed the face of the earth, from the foothills of the Pyrenees to the ice of Archangel. It is by them that civilization, physical comfort and moral elevation are imposed, not by iron and fire; and it is by virtue of them that we are superior to the beasts that battle and devour one another upon the earth, in the waves and in the air. So why debase ourselves by imitating them, since God has given us reason and has deprived us of tusks, stings, talons, claws, horns, beaks, fangs and hooves?

"Go on, Horatio," I cried, "smoke your pipe in my face with indifference or scorn—you're nothing but a brute. And as for me, I no longer have the respect for strength that you once imposed on me. That of reason will vanquish yours one day; I foresee it and I'm sure of it. But as long as historians, who only think about ordering the periods of the discourse, describe battles and design full-length portraits, so long as newspapermen, who are the domestics of regimes, continue, by means of hollow rhetoric, to represent you as models of the sublime, the image that the world still has of you cannot be weakened.

"Heroism is only linked to murder, devastation, and the loss of self-control that, if it takes way our fear of death, also makes us take the lives of others without revolt and without remorse. Let hero-worship be placed elsewhere, in disinterest and abnegation; there are civic heroisms more reflective and less ostentatious, which are left in obscurity because, until now, writers and artists have not found enough genius in them to render them picturesque, plastic or pathetic.

"Let us praise more highly the solitude and blindness of a Milton, or the poverty of a Burns in his cottage, the inventor in his loft, the miner in his mine, and even the widow burdened with children who can scarcely nourish them in her hovel. The last two have every right to be cast in bronze, and, in spite of all ridicule, I'd rather see a housewife with a broom displayed in a public square than a soldier armed with a saber in an emphatic pose, toward whom rises, from the depths of the earth, the immense moaning of shades...

"It's you, Horatio," I howled, "Who are an imbecile, a bloody old blockhead, who has no understanding of the fine arts, or any of anything!"

And I raised my hand as if to strike him, because I thought I heard a snigger—but I suddenly fell at his feet, my head in my hands, and begged his pardon for my folly.

XIV

I shall not attempt to offer a detailed depiction of life aboard; it would only elongate my memoirs unnecessarily. I will limit myself to saying that the great man lived in his cell, like a queen bee, as gross with thoughts as she with her eggs, and everyone surrounded him with a latent solicitude. Every three days or so, I transmitted his desire to be at table with his officers. There, whether he spoke or not—and you know what he could say—his presence maintained confidence and the spirit of subjection; it also reignited intrepidity.

Morning and evening, with his long pipe in his mouth, and, most often, absorbed in his charts, compass in hand, he received Captain Harbinger, and never breathed a word except for remarking on the good or bad weather, sometimes substituting one for the other without it seeming singular, and always provoking is auditor's assent. The Captain left him reports or documents to sign—which I duly signed without reading them as soon as he had gone, because I knew that all the functions of the ship and the fleet proceeded naturally, like those of a healthy organism, and that aiding them was the business of subalterns. I also knew that it would require a catastrophe to derange everything. But all of human genius could not have remedied that, God alone being the master of calm as well as the tempest.

As for an encounter with the enemy fleet, I left it to hazard, which serves or disrupts enterprises. I had no other concern than making his life and his authority manifest. I wrote three or four orders in his name to be transmitted; either he recommended that the indisposed men should be purged with ipecac, in order to take away their appetite for idleness; that the officers should be rigorously disciplined, without any whimsy; or that the decks should be washed every day—an excellent exercise against indiscipline and intelligence.

From time to time the Admiral went up on to the poop deck and scanned the horizon with a telescope. With such an observer, there was no danger of a surprise; could he not distinguish what no one else could see? Moreover, when we took a stroll together after he had put his telescope back in its case, I often heard the Mallard song—which, thanks to Allen, had become the crew's—being sung in the topmasts, denoting excellent morale.

Allen, demoted to the roles of waiter and errand boy, had been resentful of me since Arlington Street. Captain Harbinger limited himself to offering me his hand with condescension, and the officers to saluting me. The ship's doctor, Mr. Squirt, seemed more offended by my presence than anyone else. He scarcely deigned to address a nod of the head to me, after having bowed to the Admiral—not without a certain stiffness. As for Reverend Curton, the chaplain, he turned his august gaze away from us. I deduced that he could not admit without horror, even while giving signs of a reserved politeness, that the son of Reverend Gunson had left an irreproachable souse for a scandalous liaison. Personally, I felt assimilated to the individual whom I never quit by an inch.

Apart from the little strolls on the poop deck and my presence at table, I lived as a recluse, not even daring to rest my eyes on the sea that was shining beyond the portholes, for it was my enemy, the monster ready to swallow me, and also the depiction of the emptiness of my existence, with its vast unknown horizon.

All day long I was by the Admiral's side, in front of a heap of papers, my head supported on my hand, designing chimerical figures while yawning, almost devoid of dreams or definite regrets. At night, I lay down in a dressing-room annexed to the two rooms forming the Admiral's apartment. I slept lightly there, always on the alert and my stomach somewhat upset by the movements of the ship.

If any dream visited me, it was that of a distant beach, where I always landed in difficult circumstances, after complex vicissitudes, usually in shirt-sleeves or some equally ridiculous attire, like a dressing-gown, a nightcap, holding a candle that it was necessary to protect from the tempest. More often than not, I was carrying Horatio astride my back, and could not get rid of him, even when I was getting married to a colored woman of resplendent beauty whom my fate had touched, or I had to defend myself against a ferocious beast—a roaring lion or a rattlesnake.

In the former case, when I had collected my first nuptial kiss, Horatio's terrible voice commanded fire to port and starboard, and my wife fled in terror, or he called her a bloody old blackhead and I received a slap, as if I had proffered the insult myself, or she became smitten with that companion, whom she had not previously noticed, and it was him who spend my wedding night with her, while I waited, groaning, at the door of the hut, still clutching my candle in my head.

In the latter case, he excited the animal against me, or called to it when I thought I was hidden. Then I woke up abruptly, my back and loins curbed by the dampness of the sea air, utterly exhausted by the Horatio that weighed relentlessly upon my life, and was led to take my dream as an evil augury.

Finally, as we reached the latitude of Cap da Estaca de Bares, I gave the order to change direction and head for the Antilles. I also wrote to Vice-Admiral Hillockwood in order to communicate to him the reasons that were putting us on a new course, and which, until then, I had thought it necessary to keep secret, but I abstained from appearing with the Admiral in case Captain Harbinger solicited more ample details. Doubtless he would have tried if, when we encountered him on the poop castle the following day, the Admiral had not turned his back on him with the utmost ill grace. Afterwards, everyone having accepted the idea that the enemy ships would be found elsewhere than in the region where they were thought to be, according to rumor, he no longer thought about examining in depth a question that escaped him, and obeyed without question.

I shall not say anything about a crossing that did not modify our way of life and was devoid of any incident.

When we were in sight of the Lucayan Archipelago, which lies above the Greater Antilles, and brightly-plumaged birds were fluttering around our masts, sometimes perching on our yard-arms, I thought that it would not seem implausible that the Admiral might have a desire to go ashore and to see me deliver myself to the pleasures of hunting, for want of being able to devote himself to them. The topmen had captured several of the birds, which resembled green pigeons, and had found their taste delicious.

I counted on being able to add, as a better reason, that a few hours on land would have an excellent effect on the Admiral's constitution, debilitated by malady and on-board existence.

The latest information regarding the presence of a French fleet in the region, which the frigate and the cutter had obtained from navigators and the indigenes who prowled around the ships in quest of glass beads, knives and cotton cloth, was negative. Two slender Dutch sailing ships that had followed us even claimed to have it from a recent source that our enemies had not budged from the Mediterranean, where they were anchored off the southern coat of Spain. It was therefore necessary not to continue sailing where we were. Moreover, I sensed around the Admiral a silence charged with rancor and reproach. It was high time that I attempted to escape, to carry out the plan that I had nurtured since my departure from Portsmouth.

Consulting the map, I found that the nearest island that was sending us its birds was that of Gatua, which measured ten leagues across. I wrote a note to Captain Harbinger, which I had Allen deliver. I received by way of response a request for authorization for the squadron to take on fresh water, because, he said, the need would become urgent as the campaign continued. Allen also brought a double-barreled shotgun, a full powder-horn, a game-bag and a bag of lead shot.

The request for authorization, in sum, forced my hand. It signified that the squadron was expecting to quit the region and return to Europe to fight a battle that had been too long delayed. So I signed the authorization in the Admiral's name and ordered the departure for the following morning, with the Azores and Spain or objectives. Then, having filled the game-bag with a few food-supplies, not forgetting a compass and a sextant, I went up to give my order to the captain, in order to emphasize vocally the Admiral's desire for solitude and the medical reasons that I had to support it.

"It's not too soon!" Harbinger murmured, when he unfolded the note. "And since His Honor still requests solitude, we'll go ashore to fetch our water. The other captains, to whom I'll transmit this order by signals, will make their own arrangements to take on water in the Archipelago wherever seems convenient. I'll put a basket of provisions in the launch, and the men will wait for His Honor on the shore until four o'clock in the evening. It's two o'clock now. You see, Doctor, there's no medical consideration that holds; as master of my ship, I'll give His Honor two hours for his health and the pleasure of watching you miss your shots. The rest of the time is for the service. I'll use it to check the masts, the apparatus, the spare sails, etc. In sum, I'll complete the slightly hasty orders for the squadron, shall I? Your servant, sir."

I sensed more than ever how detested I was for having taken possession of the Admiral and depriving the officers of his company. When I went up on deck again with His Honor, I was able to see that another basket of provisions had been prepared for those gentlemen, in which several bottles of champagne were very ostentatiously visible. Ours only contained one, with a flask of coffee and rum and a cold meal for two. I would have liked more, because I counted on making use of it, but we were leaving the table; I was too late.

Captain Harbinger advanced to the cutting through which we were about to descend. I wanted to explain less dryly to the Admiral the reasons he had given me, whose dryness was for me alone.

"Fine weather today!" His Honor interrupted.

We went down. Admiral Gunson struck the steps forcefully to demonstrate his ill humor and his unsociability.

When I was in the launch, I saw the ship drawing away and the coast growing with satisfaction, for I was sufficiently tranquil. After all, I would have preferred to confront cannibals or live like Robinson Crusoe rather than remain aboard. For the first time, I aspired to liberty wholeheartedly, as if a kind of ether had made my head spin. It also seemed to me that the coconut palms I could see rising up at every effort of the oarsmen were coming to me from the depths of my childhood, in order to show their benevolence to someone who had contemplated them so often in engravings, and harmonious hills with thick fleeces were bounding as I approached.

I evoked the flocks of parrots, cockatoos and lyre-birds, the little monkeys swinging in the filao trees, like ugly and mocking little girls, the hinds on the grass, as gentle and gracious as Lao-Tzu's, and the bees' nests hanging from the trees, as in the Golden Age of Lucretius: everything, in sum, that surfaced from my childhood dreams, linked to the prestigious memory of my uncle.

If it is true, however, that everything one desires ardently arrives, it would be better to stop dreaming, for fear that one day, jealous Destiny will only offer us a bitter parody thereof...

We landed in a little bay where a few rocks, disposed as platforms at the level of the tranquil water, permitted us to disembark without difficulty. Six men stayed with the launch and set about searching for shellfish in the shallows. Six others accompanied us, under the command of a petty officer, all armed with rifles, in order to make sure of our direction and to be able to bring us help if anything untoward occurred.

Having discovered a beautiful valley at the foot of a hill from which a foaming cascade of blue-tinted water sprang, I signaled to the escort that we would head for a tree I designated, whose conical crown rose up in the middle of a natural meadow. The escort retreated a hundred paces, and lay down in the grass, shaded by foliage.

Birds like those that had come to visit us were fluttering in and out of the beautiful tree as if it were a pigeon-loft. Others, similar to pheasants, rose up round us to settle a little further away. There was no human vestige that could encourage the belief that the island was inhabited. In spite of my liking for Robinson Crusoe, I began to dread not being able to get off the island again.

My intention was to climb the hill from which the cascade was falling and to examine the surroundings, after having deposited the Admiral at the foot of the tree, as if he were taking a nap. I arrived there after walking for a quarter of an hour under a punishing sun, on sandy ground that gave way underfoot.

After having propped my automaton up against the trunk of the gigantic tree, I first fired shots at a few birds, with which I filled my game-bag. Then I drank half the bottle of champagne in order to give me strength for the climb. I was, in any case, very thirsty, to the extent that I could not resist drinking water from the cascade from the hollow of my hands, and then mixing it with the contents of the bottle. It was delightful in its coolness and its taste, perfumed by aromatic herbs. I also bathed my face, hand and feet in it.

Finally, I attempt the projected ascent.

When I reached the summit, I sat down, somewhat out of breath, and discovered an admirable view of the entire island, which appeared to me cut across by valleys verdant with coconut palms and various other species. Cascades similar to the one that sprang forth beneath me were the cause of that exuberant vegetation and the abundance of birds. I also discovered a few masses of dry canes that seemed to me to be huts, and then, facing me, a kind of tree trunk that had to be a canoe on the strand. I took from that a better impression than before. So, wanting to make sure of my discovery, I searched my game-bag for a telescope. Then I perceived that I had left my powder-horn and my bag of lead shot with the Admiral. I was greatly annoyed by that, and promised myself to go and recover them.

I spent a little more time looking at the huts and the canoe, and thinking about the life that the scene naturally presented to me in that land of exile. Then I tried to form a plan, in accordance with the distribution of the archipelago and the proximity of Florida, hesitating between that and Cuba, but I was incapable of doing so—all the more so because a mild torpor was invading me, with which the champagne and perhaps the quality or freshness of the water were not uninvolved.

When I woke up, I had lost track of time. I looked at my watch; it marked quarter past three. Then I remembered that I had to fetch my powder and shot, extinguish the Admiral's mechanical life, and run away and hide as quickly as possible. The extremely pure and sonorous air allowed the distant voices of the sailors collecting water on the little islands of the archipelago to reach me, and I could already see a few launches returning to the ships with their barrels of fresh water. Near the beach, the six men of the escort were sleeping peacefully. Those with the launch were also asleep in the boat, covered by a tent.

I ran down the hill as fast as I could. In spite of the heaviness of my brain, which matched the numbness of my limbs, I thought that I was no sort of adventurer, and that the least of the cooks on board would not have had my imprudence or my distraction.

When I arrived at the tree against which the Admiral was leaning I saw a young woman coming, completely naked, guided by an old man with the head of a fluvial god, who was holding her by the hand. With the other hand, the imposing old man was leaning on a staff of an extreme whiteness, which seemed to me to be the bone of a whale. I had read, perhaps in La Pérouse,[30] that a whale bone is the insignia of a chief. A bow and a quiver were suspended from his shoulder. I tried to hide in order that he would not delay my project with demonstrations or by entering into conflict with me. In the latter case I would be obliged to raise the alarm with my pistols, and the escort would come running.

Unfortunately, the man I thought of as the Savage King perceived my movement of retreat. Letting go of the young woman's hand, he ran toward me, and cried six times, while throwing away his bow and arrows: "Ouah! Ouah! Ouah! Ouah! Ouah! Ouah!"

I understood that that signified "friend," although I was not sure that it was not half of a hexameter, and I feared a longer discourse in the manner of poet laureates. I nevertheless completed the verse of welcome with another hemistich: "Ouah! Ouah! Ouah! Ouah! Ouah! Ouah!"

The old man, fill of joy, sniffed my shoulder. Although he reeked of the rancid oil in which he was coated, I did the same for the sake of politeness. Then he

---

[30] Jean-François de Galaup, Comte de La Pérouse (1741-c1788) was commissioned in 1785 to undertake a scientific expedition involving a voyage around the world. The written documents he sent back to France en route were published posthumously in Paris following his disappearance in the Pacific.

drew me forward, after having picked up his weapons, and forced me to sit down before an extraordinary spectacle whose commencement had escaped me during the brief interval of our courtesies: the spectacle of the young woman giving the Admiral all the testimonies of an active tenderness.

Ought I to recall, in spite of decency, that I had copied nature very exactly, and must I say that I had pushed scrupulousness to the point of favoring my copy with the permanent advantages of Hercules—those that rendered the fifty daughters of Thespius mothers in a single night?

I admired, with surprise, the beautiful forms of the nymph, of whom I could only see the back, which appeared to be made of bronze, animated by the most lively, but also the most gracious, movements. Her long black hair, shiny with palm oil, undulated with the rhythm of the body, and the flowers with which it was dotted escaped. As the variously colored flowers fell, one by one, at the strongest embraces, they seemed to represent the soul that quit her when the pleasure reached its peak.

That child had several souls, unless her unique soul had the faculty of rebirth in new desires of different colors, which appeared to me to be in conformity with the diversity of amour and the thoughts that it suggested, even though I was poorly acquainted with them.

Meanwhile, the speaking machine, activated involuntarily by her own hands, delivered all the phrases I had inscribed within it at full blast. The beauty responded with violent sighs and words that must have been words of love. Alas, would it be necessary for me to rediscover Lady Hackman in another latitude?

At those words and sighs, the Savage King clapped his hands, and then slapped me on the thigh, continually repeating the same thing, with an accent of pride: "*Eloa miti tanina manou!*"—which I interpreted as: "My daughter is the greatest slut in the land!"

I confess that, in my confusion, I had some desire to have my share of such a generous feast. I made the Savage King understand that by pointing at his daughter and then at myself, but he looked at me with as much pity as astonishment. Then he shook his head with an expression that signified that I had no idea of local custom. After a meditative pause, he took my arm and showed me that my sleeve lacked the golden marks that are signs of virility and command. To establish an honorable parallel, he showed me with pride the bird-bone that he wore in his nasal septum, and invited me to appreciate a girdle of herbs that, without hiding his sexual parts, conferred a peerless dignity upon him. Finally, he counted on his fingers an incalculable number, which I deduced to be that of his wives.

I was about to deliver myself to philosophical reflections on the "virtuous savage," who, from Christopher Columbus to Diderot, has personified the most enviable candor combined with a spirit of justice and equity, and I was thinking, at the same time, of going in quest of my powder-horn and bag of lead shot, when I saw Captain Harbinger surge forth, with Allen and the six men of the escort.

"Doctor Click," said Harbinger, marching toward me, "your conduct, in the circumstances, is neither that of a man of his word nor a self-consistent physician. What! You're more than half an hour late, and you're allowing His Honor, who is not yet on his feet, to catch the pox! His Honor, whom you've cloistered like a monk in his cell! And look at these lascars, who were sleeping like logs! You're setting them a fine example now. Do

188

you know, Mr. Physician-Secretary, that it's forbidden to the men of the Royal Navy to fornicate with this filth? Are you the one who's going to cure them? And you over there, Allen, what are you waiting for to snatch that slattern from the arms of your honored master?"

I was far less distressed by those reproaches devoid of amenity than the sentiment of the lost opportunity that would not come again. I thought, too, that the sailors of the Royal Navy had been the first to import for export—like Captain Cook's crews, who had left pigs and cereal grains on islands scantly favored by nature—in order to find ample provisions on their return and to be able to re-embark fresh flesh.

Meanwhile, Allen did not have to be asked twice. He threw himself on the poor child, grabbed her by her beautiful hair, still streaming with flowers, threw her to the ground and took possession of his inanimate master, whom he lifted on to his back. But the Savage King did not intend to allow his innocent daughter to be maltreated. He drew his bow and let fly an arrow at the escort. It pierced the ear of a sailor, where it remained embedded to the fletchings.

The irritated father was immediately seized, and was tied up in the blink of an eye, in spite of his strength, which was more apparent than real. Then Captain Harbinger gave the order to march. The Mallard song emerged cheerfully from Horatio's mouth, and it was to that tune that we returned to our boats.

Not knowing how to dissimulate the dishonest spectacle that the Admiral still offered, I hung his hat on the natural peg, and tremulously followed the interment of my liberty. The Savage King also followed the interment of his own, stripped of his bow and quiver, his girdle and his whalebone staff, but as he put up resistance, two men drunk on anger struck him with rifle-butts and pricked his poor buttocks, tattooed with glorious suns, with the tips of their bayonets

On turning round to dart one last glance at the land where I had almost been the most fortunate guest, I perceived the young woman fleeing in bewilderment, her arms raised to the heavens to take them as a witness to her disgrace, and I thought that, by virtue of her running and her skin the color of bark, she was reminiscent of the figure of Danaë, running away from the divine rival of Leucippus.

Scarcely had we left the shore than we heard a dull and continuous sound that appeared to us to be that of tom-toms, and which was mingled with piercing cries. The Savage King seemed to be taking a great interest in that growing rumor. In spite of the blows raining down on him, he could not be prevented from turning his head toward the shore, from which, perhaps, he expected salvation.

Captain Harbinger doubtless had the same presentiment, for he had the guns reloaded and ordered six men of the escort to remain facing the shore and to be ready for anything. The others leaned more vigorously on the oars, with the result that we were half a rifle-shot away when we saw a horde of warriors, women and children, erupt from the dunes, who were uttering war-cries or insults addressed to us. In front of them ran the daughter of the Savage King, her hear streaming, brandishing a spear. Arrows, but most of all pebbles, launched by hands as forcefully as by a sling, fell into the water a few feet behind us. The canoe that I had distinguished with the telescope was already cleaving through the waves, impelled by a great turbulence of paddles.

I thought that the Admiral ought to distinguish himself in such a beautiful opportunity to renew the luster of his authority, so I pressed a button.

"Take aim!" he cried.

"Fire!" Captain Harbinger added, almost immediately, watching the beach from the prow, his back turned to the marine horizon.

I took advantage of that to correct the aforementioned disorder in the hero's attire, and made him replace his hat on his head.

The musket shots had all struck home in the multitude. The black Amazon was lying face down in the sand, agitated by spasms. Her nonplussed companions ceased shouting and took flight. However, the canoe was gaining on us.

Our men reloaded their weapons without any further command. They were already getting into position to fire when a little cloud rose up from the flank of the *Triumph* and the light vessel flying over the sea disappeared in a splash of foam. Nothing more remained of it than a few paddles and pieces of splintered wood. Five or six black balls, which could only be seen at intervals, reached the shore with prodigious rapidity. They were completed by arms, torsos and legs, those very animated.

"A quart to the rangefinder!" said Harbinger

"Hurrah for old England!" replied the Admiral.

I have no idea what the Savage King shouted, but he tried howling in such a way that those who had their hands free were obliged to plug their ears. It reminded me of a dog howling at the moon, for I never heard Jeremiah. He lamented while shaking his head, his great fluvial beard sweeping his chest. Tears were streaming from his closed eyelids. I took account of the fact that he was weeping for himself and that he would have thrown himself at the Admiral's feet to beg for mercy if his bonds had not prevented him from doing so. The sailors were still striking and pricking him.

Meanwhile, the Admiral remained calm and dignified, and I read in Captain Harbinger's eyes, slightly veiled by fear and confusion, that he repented of having misjudged his chief, whose composure and presence of mind had not abandoned him in such perilous circumstances, and perhaps still under the influence of champagne and amour. Take aim! How great that Gunson seemed, at the head of his six marine fusiliers!

The crew of the *Triumph* was proud of their exploit. We were no less so of ours. Captain Harbinger sent for the gunner, shook him by the hand and shoved him by the shoulders toward the Admiral, who gave him the same sign of gratitude. There was a kind of little fête, to which the others ships responded with signals when they were informed, in like manner, that the Admiral was safe, thanks to the presence of mind of a skillful rangefinder.

"And now," said Captain Harbinger, "We're going to expedite this rogue! He had drawn Your Honor into a trap, Lord Admiral."

As the Savage King was no longer shouting and was showing a great submission, uttering profound sighs, his bonds had been removed. He understood that his life was at stake and that they were not about to encumber themselves with his person. So, when he was untied, he threw himself at the Admiral's feet and addressed a long speech to him, in which the sempiternal phrase "*Eloa miti tanina manou*" recurred.

Had he not done his best to honor the chief of the floating huts with cannons and rifles, to wish him welcome with his weapons and his staff of command, and spontaneously expressing hospitality by a gift that was only offered after the other presents, as the dearest and the most worthy? *Eloa miti tanina manou!* Why had that rare pearl, the black pearl of the isle of Gatua, been spurned?

But the Admiral remained icy.

He took the hands and kissed them.

"Go to bed, you bloody of blockhead!"

With those words the Savage King was seized, trussed up like a sausage, and thrust into a sack whose bottom was furnished with a cannonball. The sack was tied around his neck, and a noose was placed under the chin. He was lifted from the deck by a block-and-tackle at the end of a yard-arm, and, when it was judged that he was dead, he was dropped to a depth of three hundred feet, to the great amusement of the crew.

I took Admiral Gunson to the poop castle, and surrendered to the violence of despair.

After an hour, Allen came to bring me a quantity of orders to be signed and reports to read concerning the condition of the *Triumph*, the fleet and its crews, among which several cases of scurvy had been identified. In addition, Vice-Admiral Hillockwood announced his visit. I sent him an invitation to dinner, along with Captain Blackstone and Caldron.

To begin with, that dinner presented all the character of an official reception on the eve of a great event. Everyone fell silent in expectation of the words that the Admiral was about to pronounce, but his silence, populated by grave meditations, was admired even more, especially when Hillockwood congratulated him on having escaped assassination. Neither the sentiment of death, nor the dread of the pox, nor the memory of pleasure affected that heart of iron!

A small, mildly thankful gesture of the hand, which seemed to make it understood that they should let him alone with such frivolities, was all that they could get out of His Honor, who would only make the orders known when everyone was at his post, to receive and carry them out. And they thought that, in sum, he was showing a great deal of comradeship and delicacy in not raising questions of service while receiving at his table officers who had proved themselves already and were ready to continue.

The following morning we went up on deck to watch the preparations for departure. It was not without a constriction of the heart that I heard the capstans and pulleys groaning over my lost liberty. I was giving one last glance to the island as it began to shrink, and which, an hour later, was sinking into the waves like a memory sinking into the utmost depths of the mind, when the lookout signaled something following us in the wake. As we were with Harbinger and a few officers on the poop deck, leaning on the rampart, we only had to turn our heads.

We saw the Savage King, emerging up to the waist, his face turned toward us, gazing at us with wide open eyes, which allowed nothing to appear but the cornea. Shrieking albatrosses were wheeling around him. He was following us, as I say, swaying backwards and forwards and sideways, with his beard and his long hair streaming, and his frightful face, of the Genius of Tempests. For me, it was Remorse, which would accompany us forever.

The officers could not retain a cry of amazement. But I soon explained, timidly that intestinal ballooning had caused him to rise back to the surface, where he was floating, the cannonball not being heavy enough for his tall body. The officers started to laugh heartily, to prove to one another that they had not been afraid, and Captain Harbinger, taking a pistol from his belt, began testing his skill on that moving target. The others followed his example, and cried out when a bullet hit the target. I withdrew with the Admiral, as if he were dragging me away to mark his disapproval, and the game ceased immediately—but I saw in the glance that Harbinger darted at me that he put that attitude down to my account, and that he despised me without redemption.

Farewell, I said, internally, still contemplating Gatua with its green palms and its azure cascades, *farewell, enchanted abode of innocence, fresh boscage, placid retreat of happiness that we have troubled! May my soul soon inhabit your foliage, and flutter there like your birds!*

I surprised myself with that philosophical rhetoric, and plunged into the cabin, without yielding to any further eloquence, my mouth bitter with chagrin.

XV

I would have contemplated the island drawing away forever under the last blaze of the sunset if, in raising my gaze blurred with tears toward it, I had not distinguished the Savage King, still half-emerged and following us with his cortege of storm-birds. I hope that a shark would end up delivering us from him. At dawn, however, he was still following us. With their scissor-like beaks the birds had devoured his nose, eyes and mouth, with his moustache. He had become the mask of Death, but a hairy and bearded Death, even more horrible than the other.

I had scarcely looked at him when a blunderbuss, opening his belly with a dozen pellets, provoked an explosion of the gas by which he was monstrously ballooned. The head floated for a few ends, as if to curse us with the mute eloquence of its four red wounds. Even when he had disappeared, I could not look behind us. The memory forbade me to do so, for the floating king surged forth in my memory whenever it represented the marine region that we had quit.

The same life as before resumed on board, in its monotony. As we drew nearer to the Azores, the ships whose paths we crossed gave us more precise information. I sensed that we could not avoid the encounter and that the circle of my days was shrinking further and further. I could have broken it myself, but as I was sure that the blow would fall anyway, I was resigned to waiting another week.

Finally, we were in sight of the coasts of Spain and Africa. In the fine weather, they stood out above the waves like a light mist.

On the twentieth of October, in the morning, the frigates fell back toward us to announce that the enemy fleet had quit the haven of Gibraltar in order to come to met us, and that it counted thirty-three ships of the line, fifteen of them Spanish. The frigate fired thirty-three cannon shots to confirm that number, already transmitted by signals, and a few artillery volleys from time to time to indicate the positions.

I was then in the poop cabin writing the log in accordance with the reports transmitted to me every hour since the previous day. They dealt with the movements of the adversary, the famous plan of genius, apparently, that it was necessary to modify when they had an exact knowledge of our forces. I don't know what idea went through my head to order the fleet to form up in two lines, one of which would plunge upon the enemy under full sail while the other, commanded by Hillockwood, would be reserved cut off the route to the port of attachment and attack from the rear. It might succeed as well as anything else. But like all plans, it could not be executed. It was important, above all, to inspire confidence in the officers and the crews, either by making them believe that a powerful brain was organizing and multiplying their valor a hundredfold, by proposing a definite goal to them.

I was so certain of losing my life that I did not feel any disturbance, for it is in calculating the chances of escaping death that courage softens. I even found my destiny so absurd that I had a desire to laugh, all the more so because I imagined my machine surviving me and, I dare say, throwing the world into astonishment and incoherence.

The carpenters soon penetrated into my cabin and liberated the glass from the windows, which they sealed with four pieces on bronze, as lovingly polished as a housewife's best copper saucepans. Above and below me there were precipitate footsteps, hammer blows, dull thuds and whistles, an indescribable hubbub announcing that everything was being put in place or in condition. The instructions relative to that bustle Horatio had once had us copy and learn by heart, and all that tyranny had been exercised all the way to little Dolly, who repeated the words emphatically, most of which she did not understand.

Mechanically, I recited those instructions to myself. They emerged from the dusty arsenal of memory, where they had been so long awaited. I saw, through the mind's eye, the boats of each ship being lined up, the false suspensions mounted, the grappling irons hoisted at the end of the yard-arms, the topmasts being armed with heir blunderbusses, the fire hoses being unrolled from the forecastle and the poop, the spare tiller-ropes being arranged near the helm, the ensigns and colors being struck, ready to be hoisted on the halyards of each mast and the flag being carried in its sheath on to the poop.

I saw the packages of cartridges and grenades being distributed, the musketeers and top men climbing up from the foot of each mast, the sabers and pistols of the men operating the maneuvers and all those weapons covered with tarpaulins Then, heaped up next to the launch, ropes, lifting gear, spikes, tallow and hatchets. A number of pallets protected the shrouds from the flames of the cannonades.

Every gun had its provision of sixty shots. Unlit firepots were fixed to the foot of the mainmast, with a sack of detonators, adjustment screws, screwdrivers, drills and barrel-clearers. The rifles of the men in the battery were placed in buckets, those of the men in the castles on the deck, between the masts and the bollards. Racks of pikes surrounded the mitan and mizzen masts. Finally, mattresses were laid out in the middle of the false deck.

In the hold, operating beds had been set up, surrounded by buckets of water and sand, and the barrels of each battery filled with a mixture of water and wine. That attention reminded me of Mrs. Gunson, preparing us lemonade, ginger beer and bread and butter while we were battling in the grain-lofts.

All that, and all the labor of my sad life, to end at the moment when I was no longer anything in the midst of the extermination of men and things. It was truly derisory. I drank a glass of salty water corrected with whisky, and the pacific voice of my father sounded in my ears: "Pull me a pint, Jim!" But I made an effort not to be thrown back into the past, and prepared to perish stoically.

The winds, which had varied from north-east to south-east, veered to the west, and finally to the southwest, with the result that we were running large with studding-sails, at a speed of three knots. The enemy had to sail into the wind. We thus arrived off Cape Barajar.

The arid shores of the Straits of Gibraltar appeared at daybreak, beaten by seething water. I hung all the Admiral's decorations on his breast in order to impress the crew. I would have added more if I could. Then I traced the memorable phrase on a piece of paper, which I had Allen take to Captain Harbinger, with an order to transmit it: *England expects every man to do his duty.*

Allen, crimson with rum, had passed a cutlass and a pistol through his belt. Ferocity was shining in his gaze. He only came down when he looked at his master with the eyes of a good dog, and put his hand to his forehead to salute him. For me he had nothing but ironic scorn. *We'll soon see*, he was thinking, *how the landlubber can comport himself.* The cold steel of his gaze would have chilled me more than anything else if I had not been, in sum, mithridated by every day's despair.

The sails of the combined fleet were soon announced. Then I went up on to the poop with the Admiral, and made him proffer, by way of a salutation to his united officers, the "Fine weather today" that had already served so well, and to which the cheers of the crew responded, and those of our rearguard vessel which was following us closely. Then I made the Admiral raise his telescope, with which he scanned the expanse for a good twenty minutes.

Meanwhile, the drums and fifes, after having made a circuit of the deck three times, took up a position under the gangways, and every man went to his battle station. As we were expecting a boarding, when the French were softened up, grenades were distributed in barrels at the mainmast and the mizzen mast, on the poop and the forecastle. Cannonballs and wooden stands were brought on to the deck, and then spare wheels for the guns, lifting-tackle, spikes and mooring-ropes, which were divided up between the batteries. The charges of powder in their bags were arranged by caliber in coffers in the middle of the "lions'-den", and I saw once again the lighted tapers that had once amused us so much, fixed in the water-buckets beside each gun.

After which a great silence reigned, in order that everyone could hear and act.

I could no longer perceive anything but the sound of the wind in the rigging. It reminded me of the wind of Danish Camp in the trees of the Priory. For a second time, I saw us in the lofts, and once again had to chase away the idea that had assailed me of the end of a human life commenced under the same auspices. I contemplated the crew; everyone was devoid of anxiety but devoured by impatience, their eyes ardently fixed on the ships, whose rigging we were beginning to distinguish.

The enemy, it seemed, having counted our twenty vessels instead of their own thirty-three, had provisionally formed a second fleet of reinforcement, numbering twelve vessels. As soon as they recognized the reality of our forces, judging the rearguard too weak, they developed their battle-line in the form of a crescent, in order to surround and destroy us. The wind, which was not favorable to them, and the consequent mediocre execution of the maneuver, left wide gaps breaking the regularity.

The *Bucéphale*, the French flagship presented herself to us. It goes without saying that the *Triumph* had to measure herself against that worthy adversary. Her commander recognized our flag and steered toward us as we were steering for her. But the commandant of the *Formidable*, a French 74-gunner, seeing the perilous situation the *Bucéphale* was in by virtue of the distance of its rearguard vessel and the impossibility of the latter taking up her position, came to place herself on our flank by forcing her sails. That maneuver ought to have had the result of spoiling our plan—or, rather, my plan—although the enemy's had been compromised solely by the fault of the elements. It also happened that we were about to come under fire from three ships of the line.

We arrived within five hundred meters of the *Bucéphale* without either vessel opening fire, but a cannon shot from the French vessel *Impétueux* dispensed me from making Admiral Gunson speak—which no one aboard cared about, including Captain Harbinger, who was on the poop deck but occupied with nothing but the maneuver.

That cannon shot was the signal for a continuous fire that threw all the crewmen I could distinguish flat on the decks. Ours, which held to the honor of not flinching, had eight men scythed down by a branched cannonball that reached them on the poop deck, and five others were put out of action by fire from the three ships of the line I mentioned.

Our mizzen mast was snapped clean through beneath the topgallant, and the helm shattered. We passed behind the *Bucéphale* regardless, to which a carronade sent a round ball and five hundred rifle bullets through her poop windows, while fifty guns loaded with double and triple projectiles shattered her castle and put more than twenty cannons out of action.

Then Admiral Gunson launched into his repertoire, but no one could hear in the midst of the racket of five thousand fire-mouths, not to mention the musketry.

The screams, howls and oaths of hundreds of men wounded at the same instant were scarcely perceptible. The hail of projectiles was so dense that missiles could be seen colliding with one another in mid-air.

Almost immediately, the *Formidable* accosted us along her full length. Locked together, the two vessels launched their broadsides at such close range that I could see the gunners' barrel-cleaners passing from one gun-port to the next in their furious desire to reach us by any means.

From that moment on I lost sight of the general melee, all the more so because the ships were surrounded by whirlwinds of smoke and licked by monstrous tongues of flame. I saw nothing but the spectacle of two decks littered with corpses, wounded men and scattered limbs. Busy men were slipping in pools of blood or brains, tripping over intestines spilled from opened bellies, and falling.

In spite of their orders, most of the servicemen were obliged to take off their jackets, so copiously were they sweating, and splash their torsos with water from the combat buckets. Half-naked, their heads wrapped in colored kerchiefs, they were acting mechanically, without being commanded by anyone, with gestures of incredible rapidity and precision.

Splinters of wood, shards a foot long, more redoubtable than cannonballs and grapeshot, were flying innumerably, like arrows, often piercing the beautiful muscular torsos, the smooth and shiny backs of young men, made to be enlaced by the arms of passion.

Stop, furious madmen! I said, internally. *Out there, in lands of green pastures and fleecy skies, there are women with soft breasts who are waiting for you in cool dwellings, orderly and clean. Is the rage to kill so intoxicating that you will scorn amours and innocent stains, and do you not believe that in an hour, a minute or a second you will have an account to render to God?*

My noble and futile indignation, which many would find ridiculous, odious or out of place, was cut off by the devil Allen, who, three-quarters drunk, started singing the Mallard song, a smoking rifle in his fist. I could only see him, without being able to hear him, but I knew what he was singing because of the chorus of five hundred voices that did make themselves heard.

Another song rose up from the *Formidable* in response, which must have been their Mallard song, and the carnage continued, more furiously. Perhaps Allen had judged that the determination was faltering, or perhaps he was manifesting his own enthusiasm for some blow or exploit that I could not appreciate.

From the yard-arms and rigging of the *Formidable* musket-fire departed at that moment directed by the soldiers that the French call "Tyrolean sharpshooters," because they are armed with long rifled carbines of great precision, which are fitted with a hammer and used in Austria to hunt wild goats. That fusillade strewed the gangways with dead and wounded, and a few bullets whistled past my ears. I took account of the fact that those were departing from the yard-arm of the mizzen mast, where an infantry sergeant was firing repeatedly at his ease.

I thought that the swine would end up hitting me, although he was doubtless aiming at Admiral Gunson, who was recognizable by his decorations. However, I wanted a bullet in the head to put an end to a life that no longer knew anything but constraint and horror, and which might perhaps suffer a more frightful conclusion. I waited, therefore, for the shot that was to follow, which the man was lining up carefully.

Almost at the same time as the smoke appeared, I heard a noise of hectic wheels; it indicated that the Admiral had been hit. Then a delightful peace invaded me entirely; I breathed deeply of an air laden with sulfur, smoke, tar and the exhalations of butchery, but which appeared to me to be as pure as that of Gatua, and I let my automaton fall backwards. In my fit of gaiety, however, I glimpsed, in the memory of Gatua, the floating figure of the Savage King.

Pulling myself together, I bent over the automaton and observed that it was out of service. Its pseudo-blood was flowing from two holes, one near the clavicle beneath the left shoulder, the other above the sacrum. The bellows of the right lung was still respiring weakly, with a whistling noise. The bullet, fired from fifty meters and almost perpendicularly, had re-emerged after traversing the body diagonally.

I do not know what madness gripped me, having been so resolved to die a few seconds before. I waved my hat and sketched the steps of a little jig that Horatio had taught me. In spite of his great modesty, he was not indifferent to the attention of Captain Harbinger, who launched himself to the rescue of the great man.

"Sir," he shouted to me though his loudhailer, directly against my ear, "you must have lost your head, or that I'm looking at a monster of indecency, to dance a jig at such a moment! Our Admiral is wounded, perhaps dead…will you not sustain him?"

"He's dead, and quite dead," I said, tranquilly, "and doubtless smiling at the angels."

"Sailor!" howled the captain, kneeling down beside the Admiral, "run and fetch Mr. Squirt. As for you, Mr. Physician-Secretary, I've been thinking of disagreeable things to say to you for a long time, which I'll confide to you in other circumstances, when they'll afflict you more, if we're still alive…" Harbinger took his Admiral's hand. "Milord," he said, "Milord, can you hear me?"

But Mr. Squirt arrived in great haste, followed by Reverend Curton, the chaplain. An infantryman and two helmsmen, who were already surrounding the body, stepped aside in order to let the surgeon through. The latter put a hand on the heart and took the pulse. At that touch, the speaking machine emitted feeble sounds, at the end of which one could scarcely here the word "blockhead," and then, in response to another pressure, "Fire!"

The pulse is extinct," said Mr. Squirt. "The heart is no longer beating."

"We collected his last words," said Reverend Curton then, "but since he's dead, it was his soul speaking through his lips. The first word was for the enemy, the second to command you to exterminate them."

"That's what we'll do—be sure of it!" replied the Captain, firmly. "Sirs, I beg you, one of you fetch a sheet to hide the Admiral from the crew, and above all from the enemy, while you carry the corpse to the cabin. Dr. Click, as you're not a combatant and your place is not here, I order you to remain in the cabin. It will be the same in the future, if a future is reserved for us."

He could not have given me greater pleasure, although I had the apprehension of being cut in two by a cannonball, or simply receiving a bullet, and when I followed the cortege a few seconds later, I found that it was not going fast enough.

"You'd do well, Dr. Click," Harbinger shouted after me into his loudhailer as I was about to be swallowed up by the poop castle, "to put the Admiral's papers in order and deposit them in the drawer in his desk. I'll fetch them after the battle—me or someone else..."

I went in. There too the battle had had its effect. Of four rooms, two were demolished and another breached. Pools of black blood were soiling the parquet, which was smashed in several places. The partition walls were pierced by bullet-holes. Through a hole in the ceiling, blood was pouring like water from a gargoyle. In spite of the broken glass and the gaps opened up by the cannons, there was a sickening warm odor.

From time to time, bullets broke the remaining window panes, or, passing through freely, went to lodge in the woodwork with a splat that caused me to duck. But the battle seemed to be displacing toward the bow; I could hear the cries of the French divisions that were attempting to board, and the explosions of our grenades.

Meanwhile, the two helmsmen had placed the body on the bed. Mr. Squirt was getting ready to examine the wound.

"Sir," I said, making a funnel of my hand next to his ear, "don't forget that I'm attached to His Lordship in the capacity of private physician. It's therefore to me that the sad honor falls of drawing up the death certificate, mentioning all the circumstances of the accident and the anatomical details that..."

"Sir," he replied, ill-humoredly, nevertheless rounding out his phrases with as much affectation as me, "I will not argue with a person under arrest. Since you're holding to your prerogatives, draw up the report yourself and I'll sign it with you, as is appropriate, in any case. The report of the *accident*...well, no, sir" he went on, bitterly, "such a glorious end cannot be called an *accident*. I beg your pardon for the remark..."

I bowed. Having seized a scalpel that he had placed on the table, I cut through the black of the Admiral's frock-coat, having propped him up in a sitting position, and put on a show of examining the wounds while palpating the dorsal region.

"The bullet," I said," after a few moments, "has pierced the left shoulder, penetrated via the sub-clavicular fossa, traversed the lung obliquely in a downward direction from front to back and touched one of the

207

large vessels of the heart, if not the heart itself. Finally, breaking the third lumbar vertebra, it has emerged three inches from the rectum. That's a diagnosis of probability. If the projectile had not touched the heart or one of the vessels, it would have been followed by an immediate paralysis of the lower limbs. I strongly doubt, however, that our art would have prolonged the life of the wounded man beyond fifty minutes, because of the internal hemorrhage."

"That reservation is arguable, sir," said the surgeon. "In any case, it's futile. As I have no objection to your deductions, which appear to me to be evident, I beg you to draw up the death certificate, which I need to sign with you. Duty calls me elsewhere, and there's nothing further to be done here."

I started writing, therefore, and reached for my watch in order to record the exact time. I found nothing but debris; a bullet, striking sideways, had carried away half the case, along with the face. Mr. Squirt nodded his head, and reached for his watch in his turn.

"It's quarter past one," he said.

Then he countersigned the certificate and left, along with the chaplain, who had been reading prayers the entire time. They barely saluted me. Two infantry soldiers replaced the helmsman and kept vigil over the body, leaning on their bayonets, exhausted by fatigue and bandaged around the head.

I put the papers in order and placed them in an envelope in the drawer. Having nothing further to do, I went to throw myself on the bed in the little cupboard that served as my bedroom. There too the disorder was extreme. My mattress was upholstered with bullets. I played with a few of them while waiting to receive one in the body.

The combat lasted another two hours, during which we remained locked with our adversary. Their broadsides, fired at point-blank range, smashed the ship to the point of causing her to list, and I feared that at any moment it might open up beneath our feet. The attempts at boarding continued violently.

Finally, after a volley of grapeshot from the *Audacious*, which came to our aid, the enemy lowered the flag, to cries of victory from our crew. The Mallard song rose up once again.

United by their fallen masts, pushed by the swell and the wind, the three ships drifted toward the rearguard. Through windows and openings I was able to see, on one side, the smashed and dangling poop of the *Formidable*, and on the other, the continuing battle, with its conflagrations and the explosions of powder-stores.

Most of the time, I kept my eyes shut, trying to fix my mind on the formless images of my future happiness. The certainty of perishing harassed the sketch of those dreams as the wind deforms the clouds, and bore my gaze involuntarily toward the horrible reality.

XVI

I did not leave my cabin in the poop for two weeks, during which the carpenters repaired the vessel, to the extent that it could stay afloat until Portsmouth. The pumps were working incessantly to begin with, and then for several hours a day.

On the second day, after having endured an attack by a few French vessels that came audaciously to try to steal our prizes—as if all those burnt-out hulks were worth the life of a single man—I heard Vice-Admiral Hillockwood, Captain Harbinger and a number of officers on the other side of the partition, discussing whether to throw the Admiral's body into the sea, according to naval custom, or conserve it until we reached port. Hillockwood's voice recalled that the Admiral always voyaged with a coffin of which he had made him a present, which was carved from the mainmast of the *Levant*, a French ship that had blown up during the Battle of the Nile. That macabre trophy ought to be in the stores.

It was agreed, out of deference and in order that Westminster Abbey should be a sepulcher worthy of his victory, that he would be put in a barrel of rum that evening, and before any other ceremony, some having objected that he already had a bad smell. If he had been a saint of the Catholic Church, they would have affirmed that he expanded an agreeable odor of myrrh, roses or frankincense, but as the celebrated Ninon said, very nearly, about the great Condé, such is not the privilege of victorious captains.[31] I valued my recovered liberty too much to go against their hallucination, so I kept quiet, and was, in any case, obeying the order not to show myself.

Having not received a visit from Captain Harbinger or Mr. Squirt, I thought that those gentlemen, after a conference, would henceforth consider me to be an inoffensive madman, a despicable landlubber who had lost his head in battle. That, at least, appeared to be the opinion of Allen. He served me in silence and showed me an expression of base commiseration.

When the hero of Barajar had been put in alcohol, I noticed that Allen became more crimson from day to day, and as he gave off a powerful exhalation, especially in the morning, I thought that he had stowed away a respectable provision of his preferred beverage. In my judgment, he must have been drinking at night with the men on guard. I heard them all laughing, and raising their voices close to my ears, That troubled my repose, with the result that I was constrained to knock on the wall to make them shut up. When the relief came, it was necessary to do it again.

It was during one of those sleepless nights that the memory returned to me of the frightful gypsy. "*But what do I see? What mystery? Death striking you twice, and bathing you twice in a barrel of rum.*" I also remem-

---

[31] The famous courtesan Ninon de Lenclos (1620-1705), whose lovers included the great Condé, was packed off to a convent by Louis XIV's mother; although rapidly released, she took out her resentment on those whom she blamed for her maltreatment by writing a book, *La Coquette vengée* [The Flirt Avenged] (1659), in which she passed unkind judgment on many of her acquaintances.

bered that when I had offered her a coin she had uttered a loud scream and hidden her eyes with her hands. Then again, there was the evening when my father had spoken to me for such a long time about the Cretan android, that of Archytas of Tarentum, and Descartes' Francine: that evening when my candle had gone out without any apparent cause and I had fallen on the staircase while going to bed.

That accurate prediction, the gypsy's terror, the ominous presage of the candle and the fall, inevitably made me anxious, casting a shadow over the dreams to which I delivered myself every day during my interminable detention. The Savage King, too, completed my memories and confounded me in his general malediction. The more I pushed away those baneful recollections, the more frequently they returned to my mind, especially as I approached the end of the journey.

I reached it one fine morning, without having yet received a visit from anyone or being summoned by the Captain. In any case, no one was any longer paying attention to anything but the mooring maneuvers, within sight of the jetties where an enthusiastic crowd had gathered.

The forts and ships saluted us with their cannons, and we responded with ours. Already, innumerable flag-decked launches were beginning to circle around us. But I shall not linger over the description of a spectacle that was no longer new to me and which I would not see again in future.

The thing that preoccupied me far more was the placement on a bier of which mention had been made, and to which I lent an ear avidly whenever I heard anyone discussing it. So far as I was able to judge from the voices, those present were Captain Harbinger, Reverend Curton, Mr. Squirt, some sailors and an officer.

"No rum's coming out," someone said—the carpenter, no doubt—after striking a few blows to break the seal. "Perhaps the body has absorbed it?"

Afterwards, I heard the sound of the mallet against the chisel. I was familiar with the operation and I lived a singularly tragic hour.

"Present arms!" said the officer.

"No, there's no rum," said Harbinger, after a few moments. "Take out the body, you sailors—gently, gently...and put it in the coffin. Wait, before placing the lid, for me to cut a lock of hair for Lady... Go!"

Reverend Curton's voice rose up in a prayer, which was followed by a great silence. Then the rifle-butts fell, and I heard nails being driven in, which relieved me of a great weight.

"It isn't possible," said Mr. Squirt, then, "that the body has absorbed so much rum." After a pause: "The barrel is riddled with little holes blocked with black wax, like cartridge-wax. From middle, longitudinally, they're disposed in accordance with the progressive diminution of the level, all the way to the bottom. Not a drop has been wasted!"

"It's those damned dogs of the infantry!" Harbinger exclaimed. "A mariner would never..."

"Might I be permitted," said the bland voice of Reverend Curton, "to advise an enquiry, in order not to accuse anyone wrongly of such a profanation."

"An enquiry! But there were no sailors available!" Harbinger went on, at the peak of anger. "We'd lost seven hundred crewmen, so I ordered good-for-nothing soldiers to be put here. I'll have them hanged, by God! Lieutenant, you take responsibility for finding the names

213

of all those who were on guard until last night. We'll hang fifteen of them, drawn by lot, to serve as an example. And hang them right away, without interrogation or supplementary enquiry, right? Go!"

Before midday, as I had heard the bell summoning everyone on deck, I hazarded timidly to show myself, in the hope that there would perhaps be a landing and that I might be able to slip into a launch. I arrived to see fifteen red uniforms at the ends of the yard-arms, blessing the assembled crew with their heels, on the shoulders of whom fifteen able seamen were weighing all of their bodies.

An officer was concluding the reading of the sentence, of which I only heard the final words: "Great Admiral...Barajar...rum...sacrilege...Westminster Abbey..." After which the fifes and drums made a tour of the deck. The coffin covered with a flag and a white-tailed pennon was resting on the poop. Nearby stood Captain Harbinger. Allen, nonchalantly leaning on the bulwark, sent a long jet of brown saliva over the side.

"In reply to this exemplary punishment," Harbinger shouted into his loudhailer, "arrests and punishments are lifted!" I therefore thought myself authorized to approach him when he came down, almost immediately.

"Mr. Physician-Secretary," he said to me, with an affability that I was far from expecting, even though it was feigned, and before I had opened my mouth, "I hope that those two weeks in your cabin have calmed your emotions and fatigues. So, I can't detain you and don't have the right. If you desire to leave us definitively before the customary ceremonies, receptions and maneuvers, you can climb into the first launch put in the water. Your servant, sir..."

I bowed, and replied with the same expression, judging it as prudent as it was futile to add anything further. A few minutes later, without even taking the trouble to collect my petty luggage, I climbed into a launch carrying several men who were going to pick up supplies, and landed, lightly, without taking any notice of the time of the return journey of which a petty officer informed me.

I was impatient to reach London, where it seemed to me that I would have a keener sentiment of my liberty. There, I told myself, I would occupy myself with the voyage to Bombay about which I had been thinking so much for two weeks. In libraries I would consult documents regarding India; I would make more suitable arrangements regarding my house in Danish Camp, to which I would only return in order to sell it.

After having made a few necessary purchases, therefore, I hired a post chaise for myself, and sat back therein with an indescribable satisfaction. I seemed to be such a new individual that I was astonished. Then I amused myself with fantasies to which my mind gave birth, and which my fortune would permit me to realize. Having drunk a little wine when I departed, I fell asleep, lulled by the rocking of the carriage.

Alas, that slumber was the cause of my misfortune! The demon that has persecuted me since childhood sent me a dream in which I saw myself summoned by King George, who wanted an explanation of my speaking machine and such a perfect automaton. The King, enthused, ordered several thousand androids from me, and I directed their fabrication in the national workshops. His plan was to employ them for war, while the men rendered disposable would cultivate the nourishing soil in the shade of the Pear-Tree of Peace. I was paid in pears, which, at length, did not fail to cause me great embarrassment.

When I woke up, that dream, stripped of its extravagance, seemed to me to contain a realizable idea, and I formed the project of presenting it to the King, supported by my recent experience. I would doubtless not have latched on to it had I not witnessed the Battle of Barajar. The horror that I had conceived therein, and my humanitarian sentiments, therefore reinforced that nascent project, which occupied me all the way to London and which then took on all the importance of an obsession.

In spite of all the objects to which I had given and abandoned myself for a fortnight, I could not get rid of that obsession. The terms that I ought to use in order to present it to my Prince came to my mind of their own accord without my having to search for them, with the result that I soon knew by heart the petition that I had not yet written, and which I can say that I had not meditated in any precise fashion.

Finally, one day, unable to hold back any longer, I bought some beautiful folio Holland paper, and, having retired to the room I had rented in a lodging-house, sitting between two silver candlesticks and dressed for the occasion in a ceremonial costume, I wrote in a single draft, but in a shapely handwriting, the following letter:

Sire,
Will Your Majesty, who will have the benevolence to pardon me for writing to Him, recall that Lord Horatio Gunson took me aboard his ship in the capacity of physician and secretary, and that I had the honor of visiting Him, in the company of the hero of Barajar and the officers of his general staff? It would be very presumptuous on my part to adopt that weak hypothesis as the

foundation for success of my approach, for Your Majesty has received subjects of a much more striking merit than mine—by which I mean men preceded by a universal renown, and who, by the services they have rendered, would not perish entirely in the memory of a Prince.

May it be permitted to me, Sire, to explain briefly to your Majesty what the works and perhaps the merits are that impel me to solicit Him to serve Him in my turn, now that I am placed under the aegis of a great name, that of the Lord Admiral, and may I remind Your Majesty that I have scarcely emerged from the smoke and lightning of Glory.

Born of an artisan father, whose genius for the mechanical sciences extended as far as the functions of regulator at Norwich Observatory, and would have made him famous if Fortune had been less belated, I had the advantage, since my earliest childhood, of being initiated into those professions, or, rather, familiarizing myself with them. Pursuing my studies with the sole aim of realizing when my father had only attempted, I was able, thanks to my masters and sustained by filial love, to acquire the diplomas of an engineer and a doctor of medicine, as well as various titles the merely serve to testify that the ornaments of the mind have caused the aridity of the sciences to flourish.

Heir to a patrimony in which my father had scarcely shared, God having offered him a better one in Heaven, I undertook, on the completion of my studies to construct an android into which I counted on introducing a speaking machine of my invention. I shall not describe either of them to Your Majesty, but I have made scrupulous plans so that I can make Him a gift of them if He designs to express the desire to know them in order to make use of them for the benefit of the Throne and the State.

It is at present, Sire, that it costs me to reveal the truth to Your Majesty. It costs me because that truth is incredible and the consequences that follow from it will appear to be nothing less than chimerical and blasphemous. I mean that they would appear to the world under that aspect if I had not reserved my secret entirely to Your Majesty.

Sire, the android that I constructed, You have seen. You have heard it speak. You have replied to it. You have extended Your august hand to it, the Scots Guards have presented arms to it and the artillery has fired salvos in its honor. What am I saying? Your Majesty even offered it a pear, and Your Majesty sent it overseas to bring back a victory that is considered to be the most brilliant since that of Actium. It was, in fact, that great captain, Sire, that illustrious immortal buried under the paving-stones of Westminster Abbey, that Lord Horatio Gunson whose name served as my introduction. Yes, I only employed it to begin with in order that I might be read and, at the same time, to prepare a surprise for Your Majesty.

I beg Your pardon very humbly. But Sire, will it be said that I cannot present myself smiling before my Prince, I who have given Him Victory and am proposing to give Him others without bloodshed? And may I not, as well, Sire confess that, having been the cause of the involuntary death of Horatio Gunson a few days before the visit that his mechanical double made to You, I thought that I ought to conserve for Your Majesty and the Empire a blade that is nonetheless remarkable. Today, I prostrate myself at Your Majesty's feet in order to be absolved of a homicide by which the destiny of His Arms has not been changed.

Sire, the great captains and the majority of great Statesmen are often no more than representative individuals, in whom a Nation loves to recognize itself, whom it endows with its own virtues and by means of whom it leads itself, while feigning to allow itself to be led. Can they not better be compared to banners, to labarums, which, inert as they are, foment a mystical faith and draw peoples behind them for designs that they have chosen themselves, but whose success is often declare miraculous?

Skillful politics also allowed the belief that neither Charlemagne nor Barbarossa was dead, and one Emperor of China still passed for living ten years after his entombment. Their will, their genius, still commanded— or, rather, was only the will, the obscure genius, of their subjects. Those examples, Sire—which I could multiply if I were not addressing myself to the most learned Monarch in the world in the knowledge of History—and my recent experience lead me to submit to Your Majesty the project of constructing, on the plans of my model, captains, magistrates, and even armies, and, I dare say, Princes and Princesses.

Perfecting my invention and, furthermore, aided by the national resources, I will be able to guide them and move them, those Princes, those armies and those captains, by means of a fluid that I will succeed in transmitting at a distance, and on the subject of which, two centuries ago, Gilbert of Gloucester,[32] in his book *De Magnete*, assembled facts unknown to the ancients. The name of Mesmer, today decried by the vulgar, would

---

[32] In fact, William Gilbert, author of *De Magnete* (1600), who might have coined the term "electricity," came from Colchester, not Gloucester.

doubtless not be a serious support for me if Your Majesty were not incredulous with regard to the fables that Ignorance is pleased to propagate.

Sire, now that Your Majesty is informed regarding my military android, I shall take the liberty to explain the hypothesis of an android magistrate, for it is of scant importance that a machine devoid of conscience and sentiment should render the decrees of the Law, just as it is of scant importance that the Law should be just. What is important, in truth, is that the Law functions, in order that it is known to exist and that its existence should cause criminal desires to hesitate. Whether it condemns Innocence is also unimportant: It is there; It strikes, and the people tremble.

My magistrate, Sire, would only have the word *death* in its mouth for the crimes that demand it; for the rest, fines or imprisonment. Permit me to suggest, Sire, that almost nothing would change within the State, except that Judges would be devoid of complaisance and perhaps less fecund in errors—I mean those to which Reason gives rise, although, once again, that is unimportant. But Your Majesty, for whom Bounty is the supreme virtue, would ensure, ultimately, that the worst sentences are not carried out, and that the guilty parties would be exiled secretly, or sent to work in the mines, where they would never see the light of day again. Is it not the crime and not the criminal, that is hateful?

I can already hear, Sire, the response that I have provoked by saying that almost nothing will change in the State: either my artifice is unnecessary, because men can fulfill these same functions. It is true, but how many years and how much money is wasted in training a jurist who, having only to apply codified laws, nevertheless sees himself constrained to go back to the Digest, the

Institutes and other compilations of a Justinian, who lived in the sixth century, not to mention a host of legislators who are neither of our times or our mores!

Where nothing ought to be manifest but common sense and logic, what developments of needless pedantries to punish the theft of a basket of beets or convict of adultery the wife of a brewer caught in a lover's arms!

Should it not rather be feared that, instead of being imposed by science that discovers its source in the earliest ages of societies, the Law might be confessing its human uncertainty, or appear to be casting the responsibility for its sentences on obscure ancestors? And that young men are preparing by debts, debauchery and the hideous infirmities that accompany it, for a profession that is said to be a sacerdocy, but in which neither need, nor passion, nor anything that belongs to the Human is necessary?

I will not say as much, Sire, of the military estate that traces its science back to Caesar, who knew nothing of muskets, cannons or ships of the line with three rows of gun-ports, and whose greatest campaigns were undertaken against semi-naked barbarians, poor savages who straightened under their feet the bronze or the soft iron of their weapons. That famous science no longer counts for anything on a battlefield, where the most expert is the one who strikes the hardest.

But the experience I have, Sire, permits me not to go on any longer and not to abuse Your Majesty's very precious time. I shall merely remark that in other circumstances, in which I had been protected by my Prince, it would have been possible for me to repair my hero, to conserve him for the enthusiasm as well as the security of his Fatherland; that, finally, if our century cannot yet deprive itself of the spectacle of wars for the glory and the amusement of women and children, one could maintain that amusement by means of an army of automatic soldiers.

They would be neither more nor less than men, charging at the double, marching in step, running with bayonets at the end of their rifles, crying "hurrah for the King of England," and falling like dominos. If conflagrations were necessary, to which one could invite the enemy in a village in Ireland, there are crude huts there of thatch, mud and sticks, which, I think, would blaze without overmuch damage, and for the extermination of the vermin—with all the respect due to Your Majesty.

As for the Princes of which I spoke, they would serve for the most tedious burdens of Power. I mean ceremonies. Thus, Your Majesty, instead of undertaking the review at Spithead, for example, might be tending to his orchard, picking excess strawberries from branches heavy with them, planting out lettuces or contemplating the promise of His pears.

Above all, I could see without dread another Margaret Nicholson striking him with her dagger.[33] Your Majesty would only appear in public in the guise of a machine, instead of exposing His very precious Life to the blows of lunatics and scoundrels.

---

[33] Margaret Nicholson (1750-1828) attacked King George, ineffectually and rather half-heartedly, with a dessert-knife, in 1786. The King reportedly told the soldiers who seized her not to hurt her, because she was obviously mad—as indeed, the letters she had previously sent to the king claiming to be the rightful heir to the English throne (a claim only slightly less implausible than that of the House of Hanover)—seemed to confirm. Apparently, she had been driven to delusion by depression following the desertion of a lover; she spent the rest of her life in Bedlam.

Need I add, Sire, that like Charlemagne, the Enchanter Merlin, Frederick Barbarossa and the Emperor of China, Your Majesty would still be able to collect, under the animated features of his image, the flattering incense of the Glory of which he has rendered himself so well worthy during the overly short seasons that the Creator has measured for him?

Might I, Sire, soon be heard by Your Majesty, for his own safeguard and in the interest of the Nation? It is in that hope, Sire, that I declare myself to be Your Majesty's most humble, most grateful and most faithful servant.

XVII

I sent that letter by express, recommending it to be handed to the chamberlain, as indicated by the address. For a week I waited for a response with such great impatience that I could not remain outside for a few hours without returning to my lodgings to ask whether anything had been left for me—which must, at length, have made me seem like a maniac.

In the end, increasingly agitated, I set off for Danish Camp, which I had feared that I would never see again, and which I saw without enthusiasm. Immediately, it seemed to me that I could not live over a cadaver. As I had left my addressed at the lodging-house in London, however, and as I was still hoping for a reply from Westminster, I stayed at the inn where, if you remember, I had spent an evening drinking and playing cards while awaiting Horatio's arrival.

I saw my childhood comrades there again, but I drew away from them, in spite of the amenity and deference that they showed me to begin with, which hid the secret desire to provoke confidences, an account of the campaign, things that had not been publicly reported in the papers. Then I sensed that my slightest movements were being watched, with an anxiety mingled with hostility. I always found one of them in my path, whether I went to spend long hours beside the sea or on the bank of the little coastal stream where we had played as children, or I went to my house to sit down in the garden, completely invaded by wild plants.

Before the glaucous sea, the desolate beach of my cold homeland, or my garden rotten with damp, I dreamed in spite of myself of the little island of the Savage King, and the eternal serenity of its climate. But it seemed impossible to me that it was only a dream, and I fell back, bewildered, into the reality that was present to me. Then, the frightful spectacle of the Battle of Barajar imposed itself upon me, and I was obliged to flee in order not to see it with my bodily eyes.

On other occasions, I went as far as the Priory of the late Reverend Edmund Gunson, or even the school of Mr. W. Spool, who was also no longer in this world. There, I saw and I heard almost the same things as before, but the young guttersnipes brought less fire and conviction to it than under Horatio's authority.

I abandoned that objective of my strolls for a motive that was rather futile in appearance. One day, talking to a few children over the little wall of the courtyard, I exhorted them not to pay any longer at war, inasmuch as one of them, who was presumably playing the role of a prisoner, had a wound on his forehead and was seeing under his comrades' blows.

My intervention seemed to them so out of place that they burst out laughing. Even the victim shouted, angrily: "It's the madman again!" and they turned their backs on me, their shoulders shaking with an excess of gaiety, which they wanted to hide from me in the name of Christian charity. They turned round from time to time to look furtively at such an exceptional being, whom they apparently considered to be out of his mind.

Those children, I told myself, had not thought of that by themselves, for my moderate advice had nothing suggestive of delirium. It was their parents, some of whom had once thought me a ventriloquist, who were convinced of my extravagance. A man who lives alone, who persists in remaining alone, and who talks to himself on the roads or beside the sea, does not inspire a good idea of his mental equilibrium, and perhaps not of his heart or his mores.

I promised myself that I would renounce going out. In any case, I needed to review my plan and my memory, in order to be ready of the King deigned to express the curiosity of making its acquaintance. The hope that I still nourished enabled me to endure the monotony of the wait and the malevolence of petty individuals.

I therefore brought my work to the inn and spend my days rereading and neatly annotating in the margins the passages that seemed to me to be in need of clarification.

Once, after dinner, as I went back to my room, I found the valet, who was employing is idleness in examining it all, picking his nose and scratching his head. With his free hand he was rolling up the corners of the pages. What displeased me most was the gurgle of hilarity that the bumpkin addressed to me when he saw me. Then I seized my cane from a corner and beat him hard over the head and shoulders. He let himself fall out of the chair in which he was comfortably seated, uttering horrible screams that certainly surpassed his pain.

The landlord did not take long to come up, followed by the cook and a scullion, who were the wife and the sun of the boor. There was a fine exchange of insults. The landlord tried to intervene, almost conceding my entitlement, but the three fanatics were talking about complaining to the mayor[34] and having me locked up,

---

[34] This would not happen in England, of course, because English mayors do not have the same authoritarian functions as French Maires, but as there is no readily-available parallel, I have simply translated the French word.

arguing that madmen as dangerous as me were not to be left at liberty, and that it should have been done long before. Everyone knew what I was...

On hearing that, the landlord made them surreptitious signals to be quiet, and addressed obsequious reverences to me, as if he feared a great scandal on my part. His staff ended up retiring, swearing that it was not the end of the matter. Nevertheless, the innkeeper offered his apologies and wanted to constrain me to drink a tisane made with Melissa balm, which he instructed his wife to bring up.

The rascal patted me on the back saying, "There, there, sir, gently, gently!" I could not restrain myself from boxing their ears and ordering them to get out immediately, with which they complied—but they returned immediately with a numerous company. Before I could seize my weapons to hold them at bay I was lifted from the ground, knocked down and tied up. The landlord, seeing that I was incapable of defending myself, started kicking me, with the men accompanying him stopped him.

"Jim," said one of them, "if you promise to be good I'll untie you until the mayor arrives; someone's gone to fetch him. A man like you, a scholar like you, doesn't get into such a state over trifles. Mere trifles, Jim!" Sitting astride a chair, backwards he added: "Tell me, Jim, do you remember your old friend? It's me who used to give you the waxed thread for the rigging and the copper nails for the hulls. I stole them from my father the harness-maker. Tee hee! You remember? You weren't malign in those days—on the contrary, as gentle as a girl. Damned Jim, the great hero Horatio used to say, all the same. Now, it seems, you're throwing punches. How come?"

"Leave me alone!" I shouted. "I no longer even know your name. In any case, I've always thought you were an idiot. Go weave your bridles for donkeys, with your waxed thread that makes you stink like an ape!"

"Well, let's leave him," he said, "since he doesn't want to hear anything, in spite of our kindness."

Drawing away from me, they went to the window, turning their backs on me. Although they were taking in low voices, I could catch scraps of their conversation. I learned thus that I had been watches since my departure from London, that the mayor was informed of what I had done, but without my guardians having any idea of it; that he had put off the interview that he was supposed to have with me because it did not appear to him to be within his functions. I also heard that they felt sorry for me, the son of a worthy man and a friend of the great Admiral!

I took advantage of that to ask them to remove my bonds, which were hurting me.

"No, now that I'm no longer sure of you," replied the harness-maker's son. "But here's the mayor, with someone else who will doubtless return you to reason.

The mayor came in almost immediately, accompanied by Dr. Vilkind, the innkeeper and his wife, the cook, the valet and the scullion.

Dr. Vilkind, whom I only knew by sight, was initially embarrassed—or so it seemed to me—to have to intervene with regard to a colleague. He began leafing through my treatise with a great deal of interest. I glimpsed my salvation in that curiosity, which would reveal to him the nature of my ordinary occupations and demonstrate to him, at the first glance, that I was in full possession of my faculties.

"Doctor," I said, ignoring the mayor, whom everyone was surrounding with an interrogatory silence, "I put myself in your hands, although I do not have the honor of knowing you, not playing much part in local society, always absorbed in my own endeavors, those which you have in your hand. Since a simple glance will inform you, and I take you to be the only intelligent and educated person here to whom I can explain myself, I beg you to send these dimwits away and talk to me like an honest man, freeing me from these bonds.

"As for you, sir," I added, addressing the mayor, who appeared to me to be in great perplexity, "you should have given that order first, seeing me in this ignominious state in which I was put for two cuffs and five or six well-deserved blows of a cane. This is not the way to treat a respectable subject of His Majesty, who has paid homage to him with his late nights and his inventions, and who incessantly awaits from Him the great privilege of his interest."

"My dear colleague," replied Dr. Vilkind, "permit me to tell you that you're wrong to give such little credit to the mayor, who is fully informed in your regard and full of respect for the scholar that you are, for His Majesty himself has made enquiries of him. But as he is not sufficiently competent to inform Him fully, he has asked me to examine your treatise and to reply on his behalf."

"In the meantime," I replied, ill-humoredly, "I'm still on the floor, trussed up like a sausage."

So saying, I thought about the Savage King—without, nevertheless, expecting his destiny.

"That's to spare you the humiliation, almost as great as the insult," Dr. Vilkind went on, "if being untied in front of everyone. Go, my friends! It's appropriate now, in order to repair our error, that it should be the mayor and myself who restore liberty of movement to the honorable Dr. Click."

Everyone obeyed the doctor and the gesture from the mayor that accompanied those generous words. The scullion went out last, not so much, doubtless, to observe precedence as to have the leisure to thumb his nose and stick out his tongue at me.

"So, my dear colleague," Dr. Vilkind continued, apparently having a greater facility of elocution that the principal municipal officer, "we have not come to punish you and examine the gravity of the contusions of the valet that you thrashed so well, but to get you out of difficulty, to offer you aid and protection. I'll explain: as you cannot remain here after such an incident, and the solitude of your house seems to be odious to you, I offer to lodge you in my house for as long as you please, and to give you the cares that I am sure are merited by such a hard campaign and the upheavals that the Battle of Barajar must have produced in your organism. It's necessary to be a military man to sustain such shocks without them showing."

At the same time, the doctor untied the ropes that were surrounding me.

I accepted his invitation until His Majesty replied to me, after my protector had familiarized himself with my treatise and made a favorable report of it. Dr. Vilkind took charge of my voluminous folio dossier, and we went downstairs arm in arm, on the heels of the village magistrate.

Alas, I must admit that I had allowed myself to be taken in like a child! For several months I thought my host was interested in the summary of my work, since he examined it and discussed it with me. He also seemed to be very affectionately interested in my state of health, since I received the most attentive care from him. By the nature of his care, though, the emergence of rudeness that followed the bait of gentleness, the willful delay that the doctor brought to the drafting of his report and the interminable wait for a response from His Majesty when the report was finally sent, I understood that I was nothing but a lunatic hospitalized by order of the mayor, or someone more qualified.

I protested vigorously, and then disputed it by means of the medical arguments of which I disposed, but I only aggravated Dr. Vilkind's certainty and attracted a more rigorous regime. The feigned amity has now been banished. There remains, however, one other deception, which is that I am treated as mad when I am, in fact, a prisoner. If I rebel, I am knocked down and put in a straitjacket. If I isolate myself in the park a guard escorted by a mastiff brings me back to the limits of my promenade. By night, my door and windows are locked. By day, I do not have the right to talk to anyone, for fear that I might deliver my secret and it leaks outside.

Today, when I am concluding the writing of these memoirs, I think bitterly that I have employed my life badly, on the one hand wasting my youth and maturity in a blind and ridiculous admiration that caused me to construct a machine in which the sciences scarcely found any advancement, and on the other, spoiling my decline and old age is attempting to perfect as aspect of society and give lessons to my King. I am the victim of two opposed and successive sentiments, and I have sinned by delivering myself too entirely to both.

What should the errors, prejudices and inherent evils of the species have mattered to me? Why could I not support them with a smile? Does a wise man become indignant at the flooding of a river or the rigor of the seasons? He thinks freely, that is sufficient for him. If he imparts his thoughts, that is gratuitous play, not a precept or a doctrine. He does not bend down to lift the mask by which we differ from the animals, and which civilization applies narrowly to our faces. For, if we did not dissimulate our instincts beneath conventions, we could not look at one another without fighting. It is already the case that we sometimes battle ourselves!

What more can be expected of humans, whom Nature makes imperfect, but a few degrees of politeness and necessary hypocrisy? Condemned to nourish themselves on the cadavers of the animals they oppress they ornament it and accommodate it in a thousand ways in order to disguise from themselves a gluttony, a brutality and a perfidy that render them imperfectible, and they wear trousers lees to protect them from the cold than to hide reciprocally the issue of their intestines. How, with a hole in the backside, and in spite of all our affectations, can we approach divine Beauty, which we have nevertheless conceived and which gives us an example; or, more simply, how can we take it seriously? Live, with your defects, therefore, for fear of giving yourself worse and unveiling the first.

Why did I not keep silent about Horatio's true nature after the bullet had struck him? Free, I could have enjoyed my fortune, not in my little house in Danish Camp, which would always have represented the sterility of my labor, but where my uncle lived, in the land of supreme Wisdom, Blue Sky and Poetry!

This, I say, is where the thoughts of a sleepless night have led me, when I have put down a pen that I have only held in order to distract myself from a frightful solitude and in order not to suffer too much from the most humiliating of destinies. Now, there only remains to me, in order to escape it, the kind of end praised by Seneca and Cato, and which they gave themselves.

Perhaps I shall find my father again, busy exalting, on the viola da gamba, a real God in whom he did not believe, and perhaps also the incorrigible Horatio, commanding the angels thunderously :

"Unplug your cannons...first and second batteries, fire!"

Epilogue

I finished reading the manuscript late into the night. From time to time I had a desire to get up and knock on the door of Dr. Vilkind's apartment in order to ask him for more ample information about the author, and also to tell him that I believed in the reality of his adventure. But I feared disturbing the savant at work and attracting his sarcasm.

I could not encounter him the next morning, or in the afternoon; I was obliged to wait until the evening in order to find myself with him at the table that he had the kindness to allow me to share. Thus, I had all the time necessary to calm down and put my arguments in order. I thought that I had a way to prove the truth of the matter, but would I be permitted to attempt it? Not wanting to bring too much trouble and curiosity into my manner and my words, I waited with a secret impatience for my host to take the trouble to enquire about my reading. I had placed the manuscript in a pocket, leaving it to protrude, in such a way that it might attract his gaze and provoke the question.

For his part, Dr. Vilkind seemed to put a good deal of coquetry and reserve into broaching the subject dear to my heart. I saw him, however, darting a furtive glance at the manuscript, but he immediately reverted his gaze to his plate, allowing a slight irony to pass over his lips. Finally, when we reached the dessert, he tilted back his chair and burst out laughing.

"It's not to return that work to me that you've brought it, my dear chap, but to discuss it. Except that, as you dare not enter into conflict with an alienist, and

234

do so from the first word, you're waiting for my questions. I won't ask you any. On the contrary, I affirm that you're think that everything therein is the pure and simple truth, and that we've kept a man here who was in a perfect state of sanity. Well, my friend, I must tell you that Dr. Click died mad and that he committed suicide. He was found with his throat cut, bathing in his blood. I was out that morning. It was two years ago."

"What instrument did he use to cut his throat, if you please? A razor, wasn't it?"

"No, a pair of scissors. One doesn't allow the insane to have a weapon as tempting, as facile and as rapid as a razor."

"Why let them have scissors?"

"Because that one was quite tranquil. And he often needed scissors for his manuscripts. He was allowed to have them. It was a mistake, I agree. But I repeat to you, nothing in his words or his appearance permitted the supposition... If there was some insinuation in your question, my dear sir, it would not be tolerable..."

"None," I said, ashamed to have made the deduction. "But after all," I went on, "It would be easy to determine whether or not the body is in the barrel of rum. Dr. Click's house is doubtless sequestered. If it had passed to others, the body would have been found..."

"Supposing it was there, naturally! If all your arguments are as forcible as that, it would be better to talk about something else. Well, yes, the house is sequestered. Do you think that seals can be broken to satisfy a vain curiosity, even though the custodian of the sequestration is a friend of mine? He lives in Danish Camp, not far from here."

"Doctor," I said, "it's not a matter of satisfying my curiosity! There is something more serious at stake."

After a pause, I went on: "This Jim Click, was he mad all the time? Did he really embark? Was he the friend, the secretary, the physician and the schoolfellow of Admiral Gunson?"

"He was the secretary, the physician, the friend and schoolfellow of Admiral Gunson, and he did embark with him under those various titles. I don't see that your questions are embarrassing."

"Sufficiently, though! If he really did embark as a private physician, he wasn't yet mad?"

"No, but very eccentric, at least. For a long time I'd seen him with an eremitic beard and dressed very raggedly. He remained shut up in his house for years. When he went out to get provisions, he no longer took the trouble to open his mouth, but pointed at the goods with his finger. We never greeted one another, although I expected a fraternal salute from a man younger than me, whose father I had known—another bizarre individual."

"And who, if you please, had him locked up here?"

"Who? Who? What if I could reply to you on that point, which might be a professional matter?"

"Then my conviction would be profound. But I'll tell you myself: the famous letter to the King was no doubtless not uninvolved in the unfortunate's internment. Do you recall: 'hospitalized by order of the mayor, or someone more qualified.'"

"I assure you that it's impossible for me to reply to you." He stood up. "However, there are too many disobliging things in your words. I'll try to give you a striking proof of the weakness of your mind. Afterwards, I see that I shall be obliged to care for you more seriously. Let's go see Mr. Clark, the Custodian. He'll do it for me. I only need your word that there will be no consequences. In fact, if I don't give you this proof, your brain will

236

work in a direction injurious to the equilibrium of your reason. Petty obsessions have been known to turn into veritable madness. So, I already excuse our insistence, and your foolish presumptions. They're those of a romantic mind, which is not very stable, like all romantic minds, your Campanellas, your Mores and all their like, who pretend to be philosophers. There's also a little Radcliffe in your case."[35]

We went out. Night had fallen completely. The rumor of the sea was perceptible in the distance, and I recalled what Doctor Click said about it when he heard it through the study window. Was I going to find the body of his schoolfellow, Admiral Horatio Gunson, in that barrel of rum? I dared not talk about it again to my host, for fear of annoying him irredeemably and causing him to go back on his resolution.

"In truth," he said, "the sequestration is a mere formality. Dr. Click has no known relatives. It was at my request that the seals were applied, for it might be the case, strictly speaking, that a mistress or an unsuspected natural son might have come to claim their share with a piece of paper in hand. Above all, it appeared inconceivable to me that a man departing for a campaign full of exceptional dangers would not have deposited a legal testament somewhere and instituted a universal legatee. In any case, the seals won't take long to be lifted, and they ought to be. I don't know, in fact, who told you about the sequestration..."

---

[35] The reference is to Ann Radcliffe (1764-1823), the archetypal writer of Gothic romances—a genre in which false imprisonment in lunatic asylums for nefarious reasons became a standard plot device,

"Me neither," I said. "Perhaps an intuition. After all, it's quite normal."

After twenty minutes of walking, we arrived at Mr. Clark's house. We were shown into a little drawing room, but the doctor requested a private conversation and left me alone for some time. When he came back, in the company of his friend, I saw from their expressions that they were in accord and that the matter would not be subjected to any difficulty.

"The seals," said Mr. Clark, who had a benevolent and jovial face, were due to be lifted last week, but as the property is reverting to the State, there was no urgency. I would not have believed, my dear sir, that a reason as futile and romantic as Dr. Vilkind says could have made me contravene this evening all the customary ceremonial for the lifting of seals."

We stayed there for a good hour talking about Dr. Click and his work, and I believe that Mr. Clark was in no hurry to undertake the expedition. I mean that he did not want to be seen. Even so, we took a lantern, which Mr. Clark swung lightly while making jokes with Dr. Vilkind about the dementia of Dr. Click and my naivety in assigning credence to his crack-brained nonsense.

"Besides which," said Dr. Vilkind, "I don't understand why you've paused for so long on a subject that calls into question the honor the institutions of your country. What we're going to do is in their name, in order that one day, I suppose, you can create a legend that will strike the feeble minds that are called strong minds."

"Here it is," confided Mr. Clark, in front of a small house of which only the roof could be seen above a wall.

He employed a key, which turned with difficulty, and we went into a garden completely invaded by young shoots and weeds. Trees raised up their black and hostile masses over a lawn, seeming to entertain sinister confidences. In the center of the lawn, a small basin full of black water, which scarcely reflected the light, was spying on us, like a sly and resentful eye. But neither Dr. Vilkind not Mr. Clark paused at those evil impressions of a feeble mind that did not consider itself at all to be a strong one. The second of those gentlemen lifted the lantern to the height of the seals and detached the wax respectfully instead of breaking it by opening the door. After that meticulous operation, he deigned to let us in.

We saw nothing in particular, except the famous Jack Tar clock; the water, long dried up, had been replaced by dust. Then, under a globe, there was the little ship made by Admiral Gunson, and finally, the portrait of Mrs. Click, the viola da gamba and the Indian panoply, with the hatchet that Dr. Click claimed to have used to break his automaton. I pointed out all these things to my companions.

"But what does that prove?" they said, in chorus.

"Thus far, a meticulous concern for the truth."

"It's not the first time," said Dr. Vilkind, that a romancer has drawn upon the objects surrounding him."

"Pardon me," I aid, swiftly, "but one of the drawers in that chest might furnish another indication."

I opened the drawer myself and took out an arm, before the astonished eyes of the gentlemen.

"This," I said, with a strong desire to take the manuscript from my pocket, where it still was, "is the arm that Dr. Click amputated when he wanted, after the accident, to make the automaton resemble his friend identically."

We examined the arm; on the section blackened by a liquid analogous to clotted blood, we saw several metallic points shining. The sleeve to the arm lay to one side, not bearing any stripes, and also the sleeve of the shirt.

"Well," murmured Dr. Vilkind, in a slightly constrained voice, "let's go down to the cellar without further delay. It's evident that the madman had constructed an automaton, or procured one. But I refuse to believe..."

"Absolutely stupid!" retorted Mr. Clark.

We found the door to the basement and went down, not into a cellar as such but an underground passage that looked out on the garden though low windows. At the far end, barrels were standing on their brackets.

Pull me a pint, Jim! I thought.

My two companions struck the barrels with folded index fingers. They rendered a hollow sound. But the last, covered with sackcloth like a cannon by a tarpaulin, rendered a full sound. A strong odor of rum filtered therefrom.

"This," I said, "is the famous barrel."

Mr. Clark put his lantern on the floor. The three of us moved the backwards and forwards in order to hear the splash of the liquid. Although the barrel was very heavy, we did not hear the sound we were waiting for— but something solid moved inside. On examination, we perceived that the hoops of the barrel showed traces of blows of a chisel and mallet, as if a hasty hand had redone the original work of the hooper.

We looked at one another without saying a word. I, who, had insisted so much on provoking this experiment, would have liked very much to be somewhere else. My companions thought likewise, to judge by their silence and the anxiety of their features.

"Let's stave it in," I said. "All the necessary tools are there, in a basket. They're the ones he must have used..."

As those gentlemen, overwhelmed, did not move, I picked up the tools and made the basement resound with the noise of the hammer—a noise so light in the depths of the cellar but which, in the circumstances, evoked a funereal operation. Mr. Clark hastened to go and close the garden door, which he had opened in order to drive away the musty odor. He seemed to fear that the sonorous reverberation of the implement might be heard like a tocsin all over England, all the way to the Orkney Islands. Dr. Vilkind had place the lantern on a barrel. Sitting on unoccupied brackets, they remained plunged in black meditation.

Finally, the staves gave way, and I removed one of the ends. The rum had been absorbed; it did not flow. Dr. Vilkind brought the light closer.

"My friends," he said, putting the lantern down on the floor, "there really is a human body in there. What am I saying? I recognize the features of Admiral Gunson, whom I treated in his youth for a purulent otitis. That really is his long German hair, and the right sleeve of his coat is empty...

"Now, my friends, the moment is solemn. Let is remove our hats and swear never to breathe a word of this to anyone, for it is the honor of the English fatherland that is at stake. I shall not indulge in any other commentaries or considerations."

He extended his hand over the barrel. We did the same. Both of them closed their eyes in order to concentrate their minds. A penchant for solemnity prevented me from laughing.

"Only one thing remains for us to do," Dr. Vilkind went on, after a pause that indicated a difficulty in swallowing, "and that is to bury the remains in the lawn. Here's a pick and a spade, Mr. Robertson. You, who are young and, after all, have brought us here, pick up the body and bring it from where it is, as you can and must."

"Doctor," I replied, "I don't feel either the desire or the courage. Help me, both of you, if you will, to roll the barrel with its contents as far as the lawn, lifting it up a little in order to get over the step."

We put a good deal of time and—out of deference—precaution into that task. The barrel having been rolled on to the grass near the basin, under a small cherry-tree, we took the pick and spade and took turns hollowing out a profound ditch. After wards, I succeeded in grabbing the body and laying it down in the fresh earth.

I was about to commence covering it when Mr. Clark began to utter loud screams, which Dr. Vilkind immediately imitated, tearing at the long white hair the curled to either side of his head. Then the former took flight, clutching his temples, and the second followed him, both howling and sobbing.

I attempted to follow them, but those two old men were galloping with a rapidity that I did not have, in spite of my youth. They were, as I say, galloping and bounding like gazelles, on the toes of their patent leather shoes. It was thus that they disappeared through the garden gate and along the alleyway, deaf to my calming words.

Then I returned to the body in order to cover it with earth and cause the disappearance of an item of evidence frightful for my country—a fact of which I finally took full account. Wanting to contemplate the visage of the great man, however, I moved the lantern nearer, which had remained on the edge of the ditch, and I remarked with amazement that the body was not a human body.

I removed the shreds of flesh, which were not flesh: a substance in superimposed layers that the rum had attacked, swollen and stretched. After a long examination I realized that I had before my eyes Dr. Click's automaton, and I wondered whether I might not be on the brink of being afflicted by dementia, in the image of my two companions. I palpated myself and pinched myself to make sure that I was really in a waking state. Unsatisfied, I burned a finger in the flame of the lantern.

After remaining dumbfounded for a long time, as much by my discovery as the odor of rum that as making my head spin, I buried the body. I did so mechanically, but with the greatest care. I even flattened the ground with the back of my spade, not without having disposed clods of turf thereon. Perhaps I thought that it was necessary not to cause trouble for Mr. Clark, since it was not worth the trouble, and perhaps I also thought of meriting his gratitude by my application. Then I retraced the route by which we had come, and I extinguished the lantern, as the moon was shining splendidly.

The walk helped to restore the stability of my mind, as did the sea wind that had risen and was blowing over my sweating body.

That Dr. Click, I said to myself, *was well and truly mad, as Dr. Vilkind sustained. What must have happened is this: having introduced the automaton into the presence of Admiral Gunson, the latter knocked it down with a blow of his fist, and in consequence of the mutual excess of drink. Dr. Click mistook the one for the other, and went to bathe in rum what he believed to be the body of his friend. Madness succeeding drunkenness, he remained the victim of his confusion.*

However, I continued, *within myself, what does that change? That madman has conceived a satire that contains elements of truth and reason, against an individual who never ceased to appear to him to be an automaton*

243

from the first day he thought it until that of his death. Had not the idea that his friend was only an acting and talking machine engendered that of constructing a machine in his image?

That, I went on, *is a thought that is occurring to me a trifle belatedly, but which I shall submit to Dr. Vilkind, who is skilled in disentangling the origins of dementia, and observing the secret development of obsession all the way to the deadly blossoming.*

But perhaps I would have returned to the doctor, without making a copy, the manuscript that I was palpating in my pocket, if an extraordinary incident that happened at that very moment in my reflections had not rendered me the proprietor of that work and free to dispose of it at my whim.

After a few minutes when I was walking with my eyes raised to the heavens, it seemed to me that a growing light was invading a part of the expanse. Smoke brightened by flames and spitting out sparks soon rose up impetuously and was followed by a confused rumor, like that of pebbles that the sea is throwing against one another. I hastened my steps, for I had an intuition that Dr. Vilkind's house had just fallen prey to the conflagration, and that its vast roof, the most considerable in Danish Camp, had collapsed.

Another surprise awaited me on my route. A few paces from Mr. Clark's cottage, I perceived a form swinging from a lantern fixed at a right angle to the wall. I recognized Mr. Clark himself, first by his white kerseymere trousers and his long frock-coat, creased in the tails. His head was inclined over his breast; his little wig had fallen over his eyes and his tongue was protruding over his chin.

I saw that he had hanged himself with his cravat, twisted several times. A mounting-block situated directly under the lantern had permitted him to hoist himself up without effort as far as the iron gibbet. Poor Mr. Clark must have been in a great hurry, for he was at his door! His hands were cold; the pulse was no longer beating. Then I rang with all my strength and agitated the knocker.

A hirsute head passed through a bull's-eye window and asked whether "Sir" had forgotten his keys.

"Go to the devil, you stupid idiot!" I cried. "Or, rather, get down here quickly. Mr. Clark has hanged himself from the lantern, and I fear that Dr. Vilkind's house is in the process of burning down."

"Go to the devil yourself," was the reply, "if you don't want me to crush your damned potato nose!"

The bull's-eye closed again violently.

Popular wisdom says that it is unnecessary to take down a hanged man when he us no longer alive, and besides which, it serves no purpose. I therefore refrained from taking Mr. Clark down. I limited myself to placing the lantern at his feet, which I was no longer using, and I resumed my course in the direction of the fire. Unable to do anything for Mr. Clark, I thought of making myself useful at the scene of the disaster—especially, I say without hypocrisy, useful to myself, by saving my effects, if it was not too late.

While running, I did not take long to encounter other people running. Some of them shouted to one another: "It's Doctor Vilkind's house!" I found others who were forming a chain and passing buckets, which were splashing their feet. I was soon required, like everyone else, to collaborate in the extinction of the flames and not to exempt myself unworthily from the respiratory distress.

From where I was I could take account of the fact that it was no more use than taking Mr. Clark down from his lantern; nothing any longer remained of the habitation than a heap of ruins, from which flames and smoke were still emerging. I also saw a few furious lunatics who were being forcibly restrained. They were uttering screams whose tone reminded me of those that Dr. Vilkind and Mr. Clark had uttered.

Finally, making use of my capacity as a guest and friend, I was allowed to approach more closely, inasmuch as I had satisfied the civic abnegation and spoiled my satin-finish trousers forever. I made enquiries of a man who seemed to be directing the action, and showing a great deal of importance, regarding the state of the doctor and the part of the crowd that I had been able to join.

"He's in there!" was the reply.

There was the half-collapsed walls, whose demolition the fire was completing.

I collected more ample details from various places, and succeeded in finding out from the domestics that their master had set fire to the house himself, and that they had seen him climbing on to the roof as the flames reached it. Those people immediately thought, from his gesticulations and his hurrahs in honor of old England, that he had gone mad. All efforts to save him had been thwarted by his malice in closing and barricading the doors that gave access to where he was. The people in question also thought that the violence and rapidity of the blaze was due to chemical compounds of which the doctor possessed the manipulation and the secret, and which he had spread from the cellar to the loft.

They were also mourning the deaths of several people, including two or three inmates, who had thrown themselves into the flames with cries of joy. As for me, whom no one interrogated, I assumed that I had not been seen going out in company with the doctor, and I refrained from saying where we had gone. Nor did I say any more about Mr. Clark and his lantern.

A few days later, having returned to London, I read an account of the fire and the two suicides in a newspaper. Thanks to the gentlemen's hats, which had remained on the lawn, a close relationship had been discovered between their stroll and their end. It was thought that the two men had had the idea of going to visit Dr. Click's house, of which the sequestration should have been lifted some time before. There, they had drunk an excess of rum, as the barrel left on the grass demonstrated, and in the excess of their drunkenness, had committed suicide. All that seemed quite natural to the reporter. Perhaps he put a little humor into it, however, to cheer up the material. There was no mention of the freshly-dug earth. I would not have believed myself such a good gravedigger.

In publishing a manuscript that, I repeat, seems curious to me, I ought to render homage to the memory of Dr. Vilkind, whom I had unjustly suspected, and above all to the great patriotism that made him prefer death and the annihilation of his house to the triumph of the utopias against which he fought. I ought to say, too, how much I regret his death for the understanding of this work, because the savant alienist might perhaps have been to cast some light for me on the case of Dr. Click. At least, he could have furnished me with numerous details about his tenebrous career, and I would have been able to extract information from the conversations they had had.

J. H. D. Robertson

SF & FANTASY

Adolphe Alhaiza. *Cybele*

Alphonse Allais. *The Adventures of Captain Cap*

Henri Allorge. *The Great Cataclysm*

Guy d'Armen. *Doc Ardan: The City of Gold and Lepers*

G.-J. Arnaud. *The Ice Company*

André Arnyvelde. *The Ark; The Mutilated Bacchus*

Charles Asselineau. *The Double Life*

Henri Austruy. *The Eupantophone; The Olotelepan; The Petitpaon Era*

Barillet-Lagargousse. *The Final War*

Cyprien Bérard. *The Vampire Lord Ruthwen*

S. Henry Berthoud. *Martyrs of Science*

Aloysius Bertrand. *Gaspard de la Nuit*

Richard Bessière. *The Gardens of the Apocalypse; The Masters of Silence*

Albert Bleunard. *Ever Smaller*

Félix Bodin. *The Novel of the Future*

Louis Boussenard. *Monsieur Synthesis*

Alphonse Brown. *City of Glass; The Conquest of the Air*

Émile Calvet. *In a Thousand Years*

André Caroff. *The Terror of Madame Atomos; Miss Atomos; The Return of Madame Atomos; The Mistake of Madame Atomos; The Monsters of Madame Atomos; The Revenge of Madame Atomos; The Resurrection of Madame Atomos; The Mark of Madame Atomos; The Spheres of Madame Atomos; The Wrath of Madame Atomos* (w/M. & Sylvie Stéphan)

Félicien Champsaur. *The Human Arrow; Ouha, King of the Apes; Pharaoh's Wife; Homo-Deus; Nora, The Ape-Woman*

Didier de Chousy. *Ignis*

Jules Clarétie. *Obsession*

Michel Corday. *The Eternal Flame*

André Couvreur. *The Necessary Evil*; *Caresco, Superman; The Exploits of Professor Tornada* (3 vols.)

Camille Debans. *The Misfortunes of John Bull*

Captain Danrit. *Undersea Odyssey*

C. I. Defontenay. *Star (Psi Cassiopeia)*

Charles Derennes. *The People of the Pole*

Chevalier de Béthune. *The World of Mercury*

Georges Dodds (anthologist). *The Missing Link*
Charles Dodeman. *The Silent Bomb*
Harry Dickson. *The Heir of Dracula; Harry Dickson vs. The Spider*
Jules Dornay. *Lord Ruthven Begins*
Alfred Driou. *The Adventures of a Parisian Aeronaut*
Sâr Dubnotal *vs. Jack the Ripper*
Odette Dulac. *The War of the Sexes*
Alexandre Dumas. *The Return of Lord Ruthven*
Renée Dunan. *Baal; The Ultimate Pleasure*
J.-C. Dunyach. *The Night Orchid; The Thieves of Silence*
Henri Duvernois. *The Man Who Found Himself*
Achille Eyraud. *Voyage to Venus*
Henri Falk. *The Age of Lead*
Paul Féval. *Anne of the Isles; Knightshade; Revenants; Vampire City; The Vampire Countess; The Wandering Jew's Daughter*
Paul Féval, *fils. Felifax, the Tiger-Man*
Charles de Fieux. *Lamékis*
Louis Forest. *Someone is Stealing Children in Paris*
Arnould Galopin. *Doctor Omega; Doctor Omega and the Shadowmen* (anthology)
Judith Gautier. *Isoline and the Serpent-Flower*
H. Gayar. *The Marvelous Adventures of Serge Myrandhal on Mars*
G.L. Gick. *Harry Dickson and the Werewolf of Rutherford Grange*
Delphine de Girardin. *Balzac's Cane*
Léon Gozlan. *The Vampire of the Val-de-Grâce*
Jules Gros. *The Fossil Man*
Edmond Haraucourt. *Illusions of Immortality; Daah, the First Human*
Nathalie Henneberg. *The Green Gods*
Eugène Hennebert. *The Enchanted City*
Jules Hoche. *The Maker of Men and His Formula*
V. Hugo, P. Foucher & P. Meurice. *The Hunchback of Notre-Dame*
Romain d'Huissier. *Hexagon: Dark Matter*
Jules Janin. *The Magnetized Corpse*
Michel Jeury. *Chronolysis*
Gustave Kahn. *The Tale of Gold and Silence*
Gérard Klein. *The Mote in Time's Eye*
Fernand Kolney. *Love in 5000 Years*
Paul Lacroix. *Danse Macabre*
Louis-Guillaume de La Follie. *The Unpretentious Philosopher*

Jean de La Hire. *Enter the Nyctalope; The Nyctalope on Mars; The Nyctalope vs. Lucifer; The Nyctalope Steps In; Night of the Nyctalope; Return of the Nyctalope; The Fiery Wheel*
Etienne-Léon de Lamothe-Langon. *The Virgin Vampire*
André Laurie. *Spiridon*
Gabriel de Lautrec. *The Vengeance of the Oval Portrait*
Alain le Drimeur. *The Future City*
Georges Le Faure & Henri de Graffigny. *The Extraordinary Adventures of a Russian Scientist Across the Solar System* (2 vols.)
Gustave Le Rouge. *The Mysterious Doctor Cornelius* (3 vols.); *The Vampires of Mars; The Dominion of the World* (w/Gustave Guitton) (4 vols.)
Jules Lermina. *Mysteryville; Panic in Paris; To-Ho and the Gold Destroyers; The Secret of Zippelius; The Battle of Strasbourg*
André Lichtenberger. *The Centaurs; The Children of the Crab*
Maurice Limat. *Mephista*
Listonai. *The Philosophical Voyager*
Jean-Marc & Randy Lofficier. *Edgar Allan Poe on Mars; The Katrina Protocol; Pacifica; Robonocchio; Return of the Nyctalope;* (anthologists) *Tales of the Shadowmen 1-11; The Vampire Almanac* (2 vols.)
Xavier Mauméjean. *The League of Heroes*
Joseph Méry. *The Tower of Destiny*
Hippolyte Mettais. *The Year 5865; Paris Before the Deluge*
Louise Michel. *The Human Microbes; The New World*
Tony Moilin. *Paris in the Year 2000*
José Moselli. *Illa's End*
John-Antoine Nau. *Enemy Force*
Marie Nizet. *Captain Vampire*
C. Nodier, A. Beraud & Toussaint-Merle. *Frankenstein*
Henri de Parville. *An Inhabitant of the Planet Mars*
Gaston de Pawlowski. *Journey to the Land of the 4th Dimension*
Georges Pellerin. *The World in 2000 Years*
Ernest Pérochon. *The Frenetic People*
Pierre Pelot. *The Child Who Walked on the Sky*
J. Polidori, C. Nodier, E. Scribe. *Lord Ruthven the Vampire*
P.-A. Ponson du Terrail. *The Vampire and the Devil's Son; The Immortal Woman*
Georges Price. *The Missing Men of the Sirius*
Edgar Quinet. *Ahasuerus; The Enchanter Merlin*
Henri de Régnier. *A Surfeit of Mirrors*

Maurice Renard. *The Blue Peril; Doctor Lerne; The Doctored Man; A Man Among the Microbes; The Master of Light*

Jean Richepin. *The Wing; The Crazy Corner*

Albert Robida. *The Adventures of Saturnin Farandoul; The Clock of the Centuries; Chalet in the Sky; The Electric Life; The Engineer Von Satanas*

J.-H. Rosny Aîné. *Helgvor of the Blue River; The Givreuse Enigma; The Mysterious Force; The Navigators of Space; Vamireh; The World of the Variants; The Young Vampire*

Marcel Rouff. *Journey to the Inverted World*

Léonie Rouzade. *The World Turned Upside Down*

Han Ryner. *The Superhumans; The Human Ant*

Pierre de Selenes: *An Unknown World*

Angelo de Sorr. *The Vampires of London*

Brian Stableford. *The New Faust at the Tragicomique;The Empire of the Necromancers (The Shadow of Frankenstein; Frankenstein and the Vampire Countess; Frankenstein in London); Sherlock Holmes & The Vampires of Eternity; The Stones of Camelot; The Wayward Muse.* (anthologist) *News from the Moon; The Germans on Venus; The Supreme Progress; The World Above the World; Nemoville; Investigations of the Future; The Conqueror of Death; The Revolt of the Machines; The Man With the Blue Face*

Jacques Spitz. *The Eye of Purgatory*

Kurt Steiner. *Ortog*

Eugène Thébault. *Radio-Terror*

C.-F. Tiphaigne de La Roche. *Amilec*

Simon Tyssot de Patot. *The Strange Voyages of Jacques Massé and Pierre de Mésange*

Louis Ulbach. *Prince Bonifacio*

Théo Varlet. *The Golden Rock. The Xenobiotic Invasion; The Castaways of Eros; Timeslip Troopers* (w/André Blandin); *The Martian Epic* (w/Octave Joncquel)

Pierre Véron. *The Merchants of Health*

Paul Vibert. *The Mysterious Fluid*

Villiers de l'Isle-Adam. *The Scaffold; The Vampire Soul*

Gaston de Wailly. *The Murderer of the World*

Philippe Ward. *Artahe ; The Song of Montségur* (w/Sylvie Miller) *Manhattan Ghost* (w/Mickael Laguerre)

Victor Margueritte. *The Bacheloress; The Companion; The Couple*

MYSTERIES & THRILLERS

M. Allain & P. Souvestre. *The Daughter of Fantômas*

A. Anicet-Bourgeois, Lucien Dabril. *Rocambole*

A. Bernède. *Belphegor*; *Judex* (w/Louis Feuillade); *The Return of Judex* (w/Louis Feuillade); *The Shadow of Judex*

A. Bisson & G. Livet. *Nick Carter vs. Fantômas*

V. Darlay & H. de Gorsse. *Arsène Lupin vs. Sherlock Holmes: The Stage Play*

Séamas Duffy. *Sherlock Holmes in Paris*

Paul Féval. *Gentlemen of the Night; John Devil; The Black Coats ('Salem Street; The Invisible Weapon; The Parisian Jungle; The Companions of the Treasure; Heart of Steel; The Cadet Gang; The Sword-Swallower)*

Émile Gaboriau. *Monsieur Lecoq*

Goron & Émile Gautier. *Spawn of the Penitentiary*

Paul d'Ivoi. *Around the World on Five Sous* (w/Henri Chabrillat)

Rick Lai. *Shadows of the Opera: Retribution in Blood; Sisters of the Shadows: The Curse of Cagliostro*

Steve Leadley. *Sherlock Holmes: The Circle of Blood*

Maurice Leblanc. *Arsène Lupin vs. Countess Cagliostro; Arsène Lupin vs. Sherlock Holmes (The Blonde Phantom; The Hollow Needle); The Many Faces of Arsène Lupin; The Island of the Thirty Coffin; 813*

Gaston Leroux. *Chéri-Bibi; The Phantom of the Opera; Rouletabille & the Mystery of the Yellow Room; Rouletabille at Krupp's*

Richard Marsh. *The Complete Adventures of Judith Lee*

William Patrick Maynard. *The Terror of Fu Manchu; The Destiny of Fu Manchu*

Frank J. Morlok. *Sherlock Holmes: The Grand Horizontals; Sherlock Holmes vs Jack the Ripper*

Jean Petithuguenin. *The Adventures of Ethel King*

Antonin Reschal. *The Adventures of Miss Boston*

Frank Schildiner. *The Quest of Frankenstein*

P. de Wattyne & Y. Walter. *Sherlock Holmes vs. Fantômas*

David White. *Fantômas in America*

Pierre Yrondy. *The Adventures of Thérèse Arnaud*

SCREENPLAYS

Mike Baron. *The Iron Triangle*
Emma Bull & Will Shetterly. *Nightspeeder; War for the Oaks*
Gerry Conway & Roy Thomas. *Doc Dynamo*
Steve Englehart. *Majorca*
James Hudnall. *The Devastator*
Jean-Marc & Randy Lofficier. *Royal Flush*
J.-M. & R. Lofficier & Marc Agapit. *Despair*
J.-M. & R. Lofficier & Joël Houssin. *City*
Andrew Paquette. *Peripheral Vision*
Robert L. Robinson, Jr. *Judex*
R. Thomas, J. Hendler & L. Sprague de Camp. *Rivers of Time*

NON-FICTION

Stephen R. Bissette. *Blur 1-5. Green Mountain Cinema 1; Teen Angels*
Win Scott Eckert. *Crossovers* (2 vols.)
Jean-Marc & Randy Lofficier. *Shadowmen* (2 vols.)
Randy Lofficier. *Over Here*

ART BOOKS

Jean-Pierre Normand. *Science Fiction Illustrations*
Raven Okeefe. *Raven's L'il Critters; Rave's Faves*
Randy Lofficier & Raven Okeefe. *If Your Possum Go Daylight...*
Daniele Serra. *Illusions*
Randy Lofficier. *Over Here*